ELLIE'S
ALBATROSS

A NOVEL

ELLIE'S
ALBATROSS

A NOVEL

RON PRASAD

ELLIE'S ALBATROSS
A NOVEL

Copyright © 2022 Ron Prasad.

All rights reserved. No part of this book may be used or reproduced by any means, graphic, electronic, or mechanical, including photocopying, recording, taping or by any information storage retrieval system without the written permission of the author except in the case of brief quotations embodied in critical articles and reviews.

This is a work of fiction. All of the characters, names, incidents, organizations, and dialogue in this novel are either the products of the author's imagination or are used fictitiously.

iUniverse books may be ordered through booksellers or by contacting:

iUniverse
1663 Liberty Drive
Bloomington, IN 47403
www.iuniverse.com
844-349-9409

Because of the dynamic nature of the Internet, any web addresses or links contained in this book may have changed since publication and may no longer be valid. The views expressed in this work are solely those of the author and do not necessarily reflect the views of the publisher, and the publisher hereby disclaims any responsibility for them.

Any people depicted in stock imagery provided by Getty Images are models, and such images are being used for illustrative purposes only.
Certain stock imagery © Getty Images.

ISBN: 978-1-6632-4561-8 (sc)
ISBN: 978-1-6632-4570-0 (hc)
ISBN: 978-1-6632-4560-1 (e)

Print information available on the last page.

iUniverse rev. date: 09/23/2022

For my wife

Part I
Affliction

I will love the light for it shows me the way;
yet I will endure the darkness for it shows me the stars.

– Og Mandino

Chapter One

Ellie Price knelt on the kitchen floor, too exhausted to cry anymore. She looked down at her trembling hands. In her left, a tuft of her own crimson hair. In the other, a large serrated chef's knife— the same one she used to cut fruit for breakfast each morning.

She leaned her head back against the lower kitchen cabinet in utter defeat, glanced at heaven above, and begged for some sense of guidance.

Each cell in her body buzzed at an immeasurable vibrational frequency.

Through her right eye, a miniscule, but nagging blind spot obscured her vision, while deafening tinnitus rang through her head: daily reminders of the burden she carried.

In that moment, Ellie missed her mother; like she always did when the pain was this bad.

The depth of her loss was profound. Her sense of self was long gone, like her mother. Only an infinite chasm remained; and Ellie's heart ached, more than even her ribs.

Ellie swallowed watery saliva, and grit her teeth, trying to suppress the dizzying nausea from enveloping her brain. But it was unrelenting.

She swallowed again.

She wished things hadn't changed, and yearned for who she used to be: a loving wife, a successful career woman, a marathon runner— a human being, who desired a future. At thirty-six years old, she'd been robbed of so much already. She ached for a life with some joy; she'd take any little moment. Ellie wanted her job back. Friends. She had wanted children once, and to hear their laughter throughout their home. She wanted to run again, even just a single mile.

These days, Ellie was but an apparition of herself, hovering in a constant realm of pain, dizziness, and insomnia.

That's who she was now: a ghost in shackles, bound to her home.

The sounds of the rain outside fused together with her vertigo, conjuring a tempest storm inside her every cell. Her muscles buzzed in agony. She gnashed her teeth, until her jaw muscles began to seize.

Ellie pushed up and got to her feet, using the white quartz countertop as a balance. Still feeling light-headed, she made her way down the hall towards the room where her husband and dogs slept, kitchen knife still quivering in her right hand. She held the wall as she walked, to keep the world from collapsing unto itself.

When she walked past the glass French doors to her husband's office, she stopped to examine her reflection. Standing at five-foot-five, her height was the only thing about her appearance that hadn't changed in the last few years. Aside from that, she could barely recognize her own face. Her once vibrant and lustrous red hair had diminished into a wispy, dull veil; thinning by the day. Her face was gaunt and colorless, making her green eyes fade into her skull. They had once stood out, gleaming with vitality—but not anymore, and she struggled to remember when they weren't so pale, and so void of life. The curves and muscle tone she'd developed as a runner, had all but wasted away. Thin limbs were all that remained. She tried to mask her figure in the oversized T-shirt and sweatpants she wore around the house, but it only made it worse. Her heart sunk. Ellie no longer felt like a woman. Like a human being. She wondered if her husband was still attracted to her.

She turned away.

Shuffling, Ellie finally reached the doorway of the master bedroom. She steadied herself against the frame. From behind her, weak ambient light poured into the dark room. Ellie looked down at her left fist. Then, to the knife clutched in her right hand.

She stared, using the dim light to make out a faint pulse in her wrist; beating blood to her veins, pumping life to her vital organs. Ellie looked into the bedroom, and gazed at her little family in sorrow, listening to their steady breathing.

Was it like this for mom? she thought to herself.

In a pass between the waves of vertigo, she was instantly overwhelmed with guilt and remorse. Anxiety flared like a strobe light in her chest.

There's no way.

No way I could do this to them.

Ellie hung her head down, and backed away.

She slunk back into the kitchen and opened the dishwasher, slipping the blade on the top rack. She discarded the loose hair from her hand into the garbage can, and covered it with some crumpled paper towels. She stuffed it lower and added more paper towels; hoping her husband wouldn't see the mass of ruby strands, as he made his breakfast in the morning. He would know exactly what had gone on the night before.

Ellie glanced at the microwave clock.

4:34 am.

She turned off the lights, and stumbled into the bedroom— this time with no knife. On her way, Ellie stopped to steady herself against the vertigo.

There was utter stillness in the house; too early for even the morning birds outside. She wished she still had the resolve to pray, but any shred of faith had left her long ago. She had never felt so alone. So angry.

Ellie looked past the dark hallway, towards the front entry. She gazed at the stars through the transom window above the entry door. She adjusted her footing so that she could make out the moon beaming in the night sky. Her lips pursed. Through that window, and still steadied against the wall, she whispered to God directly. "I wished You *did* exist, just so I could hate You."

Instantly, her heart panged. She unfurled her balled fists, and hung her head low, trying to regulate her breathing. Remorsefully, Ellie took the thought back.

"I'm sorry," she whispered into the darkness.

Ellie crawled silently into bed next to her sleeping husband, laid her head on the pillow, and stared up at the ceiling.

Please take this pain away, Ellie begged.

She listened in silence for the voice of God, hoping for a response.

But nothing came.

Chapter Two

A loud gust of screeching wind awakened Bishop Price before his alarm did. He snapped up in bed, confused. He could feel the mid-February cold penetrating through the windows, even behind the blackout drapes. He shuddered.

Hesitantly, Bishop arose and peered through the blinds. Frigid darkness consumed any sign of early light that the universe could muster. During an average West Coast winter, the world wasn't lit until after eight in the morning, and darkness could set in as early as three-o-clock in the afternoon. This year, the city seemed to have skipped the fall season entirely, and leapt from the warmth of late summer, to the bleakness of winter without a moment's hesitation.

"Fuck you," Bishop whispered to the rain outside. His words created a mini-explosion of condensation on the cold window.

He got back into bed, and pondered taking a sick day; although he knew he was kidding himself. Bishop never took sick days.

He squinted in the darkness, rubbed his dry eyes, and made sure his wife Ellie was still sleeping to the right of him. Although not entirely certain it was her, the form of her body shaped underneath the white duvet cover. He wondered if she was awake.

"Ellie?" he whispered.

No response.

Bishop hadn't experienced a restful sleep in months, but not like her. He wouldn't dare complain about not sleeping. She was a bona fide insomniac.

When he did sleep, it was fragmented, and it never took much to heave him back into the waking world.

When he woke, it was always as if he was suddenly plummeting from the sky.

Bishop massaged his temples with firm pressure, and moved onto the base of his skull. As he did so, he regretfully glanced down at the shape of his sleep apnea machine near the foot of the bed, unplugged and tucked neatly away.

A winter gale shrieked angrily from outside their dark bedroom window, begging for the warmth inside. Bishop lay on his back; an unnatural sleeping position for him, and listened to the wind, dreading its bitter coldness. "Fuck you," he repeated.

He closed his eyes, and desperately willed the energy to face the day. Already, Bishop's muscles and joints ached. His neck and back were tightened steel ligaments. He opened and closed his hands several times, trying to stretch the muscles before he cracked his knuckles.

He pushed on the back of his neck again. Bishop could feel tension crawling towards his ocular muscles, like a cluster of spiders. Bishop closed his eyes again, to mask the dim light illuminating from the clock on his smartphone.

In that moment, he wondered if he had inherited rheumatoid arthritis from his mother.

He took care to recall the words of Ruth Bernthal, their family counselor and psychologist: "Try and consciously awaken each day," she had said. "And center yourself through concentrated, willful breath and purpose."

A better idea than spiraling into a default state of brooding anxiety about the coming day, he supposed.

Knowing this, he found it a difficult exercise to undertake, nevertheless.

Bishop opened his eyes in the dark room, letting his retinas make sense of the familiar shapes. As would often occur against his will, the rhythm of his lungs turned from his forced and consciously peaceful breath, to one of short, rapid, and panicked gasps. He wasn't surprised.

This occurred the moment he thought about his day. Every day.

He turned his focus instead to try and imagine the apprehension leaving his body through the rapid exhalations, and use it to his advantage.

Bishop inhaled and counted to four: *Energy in, through my nose.* He took a breath out, slowly counting to five and remembering Ruth's words: *Panic out, through your mouth.*

Slowly, he could feel his diaphragm beginning to open.

Although he tried to focus on his own body, Bishop could feel the weight of the others sleeping next to him. His wife Ellie on the right side of the bed, and their two dogs, sharing the middle space. Bishop remained on his designated left side.

He closed his eyes, and continued practicing his meditation. He held the precious air in his chest for a few moments with intent, before letting it pour out of his lungs, determined to start the day under his own control. Four long seconds in, and five long seconds out. He repeated, trying not to think about the time nagging at his brain.

Izzy, their rescued Bichon Frise, shuffled her legs and pushed closer to him, exhaling deeply, as if to mirror her Dad's morning routine. Bishop tilted his neck and glanced at Winston, their Miniature Schnauzer, who was snoring at the foot of the bed. Bishop shaped a tired smile in the darkness, momentarily forgetting his anxiety.

He lay for a few moments longer, before shifting his weight into a seated position on the side of the bed. Bishop planted his feet flat on the floor, placed his palms on the mattress next to his hips, and stretched his weary back.

Another deep breath in.

This time, with his breath, he imagined his unfocussed energy as a black, viscous fluid that flowed from his head, through his neck, first down his spine, then his legs, and finally out through his feet. He let it branch out like roots and merge with the ground beneath him; connecting through the floor, and through the Earth, where he imagined it being reabsorbed.

Not bad energy, but *unused* energy.

He was sending it back to the *Source*, to make room for more light. Of course, another suggestion from Ruth Bernthal— their *spiritual gangster*.

His wife's voice whispered through the silence. "What time is it?"

He half-turned, not surprised to hear her up. Bishop whispered back. "It's five-thirteen."

"Are you working from home today?"

"I have to go in, Ellie," he said. "I've got a few big meetings today, remember?"

Ellie offered no response. After a short silence, Bishop asked what he already knew. "You haven't slept, have you, Ellie?"

"No."

He could tell, she was a million miles away.

Bishop unplugged his cellphone and proactively turned off the alarm, which was set to go off at 5:30am. He shuffled around the bed and scratched Izzy's soft pink belly. She rolled on her back in response, eyes still closed, and let herself be vulnerable. Paws praying to the sky and mouth open in a smile, she stretched. Even beneath her body, she wagged her tail, her curly white fur visible in the darkness. In an instant, from sleep to consciousness, Izzy's default was always *happy*.

Bishop tried to let himself be inspired by her outlook.

As he passed Winston, he softly rubbed behind his stubborn Schnauzer's ears. Still sleeping, but aware he was safe, Winston snorted in elation and yawned lazily.

Bishop rounded to Ellie's side, sat on the edge of the bed, and gently put his hand on her temple. He tucked Ellie's cinnamon hair behind her ears and gave her a soft kiss on the forehead. A glint of light caught her face. He could see a trail of tears faintly shimmering at the corners of her open eyes. Discreetly, he felt the dampness on her pillow, instinctively gauging how many hours she'd been up crying.

He swallowed through the lump in his throat. "You okay, my love?"

"Uh-huh," she lied.

He took a deep breath in. "It's my day to go in, I've got a few presentations today that I can't get out of."

"I know," Ellie said, pausing. "Am I ever going to get better?"

"How about we start with *good morning*?"

She offered him silence, and in the darkness, he found it impossible to assess the precise actuality of her mood. He could take a guess though. Bishop had long held a strong belief in waking up and going to bed without the mention of negativity. Why bookend each day with anxiety?

Bishop subdued his nagging frustration at the way she had chosen to start both of their days. He tried not to let it put him in a sour mood.

Good morning was such an easy thing to say. Why couldn't she say it? He tried to ignore it. He tried instead to be sensitive in that moment. To be understanding. To be a good man, and a good husband. She had asked him to try and be more gentle, and he'd been trying. Bishop could get angry quickly. And she was right, he needed to be softer, more caring.

It didn't matter how long she'd been sick. That wasn't her fault. He'd asked her to try and not fall into her default negative space each day, and she was trying. He could see that. And it couldn't happen overnight.

He formulated his next sentence carefully, trying not to sound as if he was giving her a lesson of some sort. She hated that. "You can't start your day like that," he sighed. "Your words have impact."

Again, the silent treatment.

Damn, he thought. *Was that condescending?*

"What can I do?" he asked helplessly.

"Nothing," she finally said.

His heart sank. "You gonna be okay?"

"I don't know, Bishop."

"Can I warm up your heating bag?"

"No, it's okay."

"Water? I have time to make you tea. Anything?" he offered.

"No."

Bishop slid his hand from her shoulder down her arm, and clasped her hand. He pulled the covers over her chest, and tucked her in, giving her another kiss on the forehead. He could sense her throat trembling, and knew instinctively that she was holding back more tears. He tried gently to massage the lymph down the sides of her throat. She didn't move or react.

Feeling powerless, Bishop lumbered into the bathroom and closed the door. He placed his large hands on the countertop, and stared back at his tired face.

A problem-solver by nature, Bishop's job as a project manager afforded him the luxury of working from home most days. With Ellie being sick, it helped them make the balance.

He'd had to ensure that he went into the office a few days a week to connect in person with the small team of managers reporting to him. It was important to him that he maintained strong relationships with his team. That was something that couldn't be done exclusively from home. More, the majority of the budget requirements he asked of his superiors could not be requested remotely; it just wouldn't look good. So, he chose his in-office days wisely, to coincide with how Ellie might be feeling that particular day. On other days, he didn't have the choice: it was his workload that made the determination.

He gazed in the mirror, pondering the protuberant bags under his eyes, and dark follicles covering his face and neck. With the recent move and the endless repairs around the new house, Bishop barely found a single minute to even shave. Under normal circumstances, he kept himself relatively well-groomed: clean-shaven, and in relatively decent physical shape; for a man in his mid-forties, anyway. This had recently and suddenly, given way to tired eyes and puffy cheeks. He pulled down on the bags on his face with both hands and examined his eyes. Bishop tilted his head and ran a few fingers through his dark black hair, counting the greys like weeds. He made a mental note to make an appointment for a hair-cut. A trim, but he couldn't go too short. The gap was already closing from the inevitable male pattern baldness coming his way.

Shirtless, he pinched a mass of ever-increasing fat that had begun to congregate around his mid-section. He hadn't exercised in the months leading up to their move. Now, in this new city, he still hadn't been able to muster the time or energy for a single run. Luckily, his Polynesian athletic ancestry kept his metabolism burning at an acceptable rate; for now.

But he could feel the specter of time catching up.

His eyes focused on the gray hairs sprouting in his beard. Bishop normally took pride in his appearance, but lately he'd been too exhausted. He should have been clean shaven and his dress shirt should have been better ironed. Despite this, he put himself together as best as he could. It only ever took him fifteen minutes to get ready, and even less so now.

He placed his laptop bag on the floor and sat on the bed next to his wife, the room still concealed in darkness. He could see that she had finally let go and fallen asleep. His wife's deteriorating state of health swirled in his thoughts. Bishop told himself that their move to the city was part of the plan. That they were there for a reason.

Innately, Bishop had always, and somehow, managed to find his way— to remain optimistic. His life hadn't been easy, and wasn't getting any easier. He was losing sight of his lighthouse. Yet, he wouldn't fail her; and she couldn't know he'd been struggling.

Bishop had always consciously aimed for the peak of the proverbial mountaintop, although he felt, his beacon hid behind a never-ending obscurity of impenetrable mist.

Still, he forced himself to constantly look up: through his own sheer will.

He'd always imagined what a clear view from the top would look like. If nothing else, God-given optimism drove him forward. It needed to be a way of life for him. It was his means of survival.

Bishop had fallen many times— but he had tended to his wounds, and conjured up the resolve to progress forward, time and time again. Bishop *had* to climb; it was simply in his nature. Content in his solitude, he trudged along, until one day, he found a remarkable flower growing on his rocky path.

This flower was her: his Ellie.

He'd never met someone like her.

Her light, complimented his own.

In her reflection, he felt his own connectedness. It didn't take him long to realize she was going to be his wife, and that he'd continue his ascent with her by his side.

The ticking of their bedroom clock brought Bishop back to the ground. He tried to breathe, collectedly, through his diaphragm. His thoughts spiraled in a repeating cyclone. Bishop tried to daydream, but struggled to float his way back out of the moment. He tried to stop himself from worrying, but his apprehension grew with each passing minute.

Words matter, he told himself.

Thoughts matter.

Energy matters.

His heart drummed like a tribal ritual, increasing in intensity— beat by beat.

Suddenly, a sharp pain pierced through his chest. In the split second that he clutched the ribs on his left side, the pain had subsided.

Bishop sat stunned and motionless, reeling from the pain. He tried to catch his breath. He willed his heartrate to slow down.

"It's okay," he whispered to himself. "Indigestion. You're okay."

The sudden pain in his chest had left him shaken, and an inexplicable doom began to radiate from his sternum. He tried to ignore the fear.

Here it comes, he thought. *Right on time.*

He focused his every ounce of energy into suppressing it as far down as it could go. Overcome, Bishop finally gave in. He let the doom sink in; basking in the acceptance of it, and hoping it would soon pass. It was the only way.

He thought about the move to the new city.

He panicked over their finances.

He worried about Ellie.

He feared failing at his job.

"I think I made a huge fucking mistake," he finally lamented out loud. Bishop glanced at Ellie, praying to God she hadn't heard. She didn't move. He pulled up covers to her chin. "Bye baby," he whispered, careful to not wake her. "Love you."

Chapter Three

"How are you adjusting to the new city?" Ruth asked. "You haven't said much."

"I haven't been out, to be honest," Ellie said.

Ellie sat on her bed cross-legged, and gazed at Ruth through the video chat on her laptop. Izzy lay next to Ellie, eyes half shut, with her white fluffy tail wagging optimistically for no particular reason. Winston the Mini Schnauzer, antisocial as always, slept a short distance away in the living room. Close enough to listen, but far enough away not to care.

Although not much in the mood to talk, Ellie had reached out to their therapist for an emergency session after Bishop had left for work. That's what he would want her to do. It was the right thing to do; considering the incident from the night before.

The handful of hair.

The sobbing.

The…*knife*.

Ruth had made the time for a virtual meeting, as she often did when Ellie was in crisis. She smiled and waited for Ellie to speak. Ellie fidgeted with her fingers, trying to think of anything to say, and made a point to continue— since she was paying Ruth by the hour, after all.

"We're still unpacking," Ellie mustered awkwardly. "Working on the house. Will be a while still. Maybe years until we've got everything done to our liking."

Ruth leaned in. "I can barely see you, sweetheart."

"I'm sorry, I need to keep it dark," Ellie said, hearing the rain outside. "My senses are overloaded today."

"Do what you need to do, dear. I can still hear you fine."

Ellie adjusted the brightness on the laptop camera, even though the truth was, she hated the way she looked. She was too thin, even for her. Her eyes were sunken in, and her skin was pale. Not to mention, the thinning hair. "Better?" she asked.

"That's better," Ruth smiled. "Tell me, what are you feeling today?"

Ellie hated listing off her symptoms. Despised it. It was usually everyone's queue to start rolling their eyes. They'd ask how she was doing, and then checked out when she actually told them. A fake interest in her actual well-being. She'd seen it a million times before. She hesitated, but Ruth urged her on. Ruth was different.

"The blind spot in my eye is still there, and my entire body is aching," Ellie began. "But the worst of it, is my ribcage. There is such a deep level of pain, I can barely describe it, Ruth. It hurts to breathe. I feel like I want to reach inside and pull out each rib, one by one."

"How many total symptoms are you at now?"

Ellie hesitated, her tone deadpan. "Upwards of ninety."

Ellie rested an elbow on her knee, propped her cheek in her palm, and nervously adjusted her hair. She could hear heavy rain pelting against the dormant grass outside.

Ellie peered at the laptop screen.

On the other end of the connection, she could see the sky through Ruth's open office window. In her neck of the woods, the clouds were starting to break. As they parted, bright sunlight began transferring through the window. It illuminated Ruth's whitish-blonde hair from behind.

Ellie pined for her small suburban beach community on Vancouver Island. She missed it so much that it made her heart ache. It was only a few hundred miles and a ferry ride away, from where she and Bishop now lived. Maybe a five-hour round trip. They had hesitantly traded their beloved nature oasis for the busy city, towards a single purpose: better access to medical care. Once Bishop had been successful on the new job posting, the deal was sealed. They had sacrificed everything for a shot at healing.

Ruth still lived in Parksville, and so did everyone else they knew. It had utterly broken Ellie's heart to leave her family behind. And she hated seeing Ruth through a computer. She didn't realize losing that human contact would affect her so much.

Ellie stared, contemplating Ruth's likeness to her own beloved mother, Catherine. The resemblance carried beyond just their similarity in age. Ellie fought back her tears. Her utter weariness was indescribable.

"Ellie?" Ruth asked.

Ellie bowed her head, and continued the exhausting task of listing off her day's symptoms, which seemed to change each time the Earth took another revolution around the sun. "My muscles are buzzing," she said solemnly. "As if every cell is vibrating."

"Any luck with the specialists there? Are they any further towards a diagnosis?"

"It doesn't matter, Ruth. No one knows what's going on. They just call it *Fibromyalgia*," Ellie sighed. "It's easier for them."

"A generalized term to encompass what they don't know."

Ellie nodded. "It's what they told my mother at first too."

"Did you go to your recent appointment?"

"I've been to so many; they don't know what to do with me anymore. My general practitioner Dr. Jones has been extremely kind and helpful—but I can tell, he's giving up."

"Has he said that?"

Ellie slumped her shoulders. "No."

"That's your perception."

"Regardless," Ellie said. "It's been nine years now. There's no hope."

"There's hope, dear," Ruth smiled. "Always."

Ellie averted her eyes. She suppressed more tears. Subconsciously, she pet Izzy's soft back with her left hand. "Last week, I experienced one of the worst headaches of my life. I sincerely thought I was having an aneurism. We waited in the emergency room for twelve hours. *Twelve hours*," Ellie exclaimed. "After the ER doctor finally saw me, he handed me mental health pamphlets. They can never find anything. They all think I'm crazy. It's all in my head. Like I have nothing better to do. They think I'm making this up. I feel Bishop thinks so too."

Ruth glanced at Ellie guessingly. "Has he said that?"

"No."

Ruth paused for another brief moment. "Again, your perception," she said. "Did Bishop wait with you for the twelve hours in the hospital?"

"Yes."

"Was that his first time, waiting with you?"

"No, he's always there with me."

"In all your years together, how many times has he waited with you? How many times has he sat in a waiting room, or napped in the car while you were being tested?"

"I don't know. Hundreds, maybe."

"That should tell you all you need to know," Ruth said.

"I can tell," Ellie snapped back. "He doesn't want to be there."

"He's there. Maybe he's tired, maybe he can be short, maybe a lot of things…but he's there."

Ellie's throat clenched, and she tried to smile to signal the acknowledgment, but couldn't. Tears welled in her eyes. Ruth let the moment exist, careful not to push. After a few moments, Ellie finally conceded. "I know," she said.

"Bishop is your *Orpheus*," Ruth smiled.

Ellie furrowed her brow. "He's *what*?"

"Whatever Bishop and I talk about in his own sessions, is confidential to us, although I'm sure both of you share certain things," Ruth said. "However, one thing I can tell you, is that he cares about you deeply and would go to the ends of the Earth for you. But he is not a perfect person, and so he needs to learn in his own way how to navigate those waters."

"I don't always feel that."

"I know dear, that's marriage. For everyone. There are ebbs and flows, and you know that. Marriage is difficult under normal circumstances. I can't imagine the pressure you two are feeling. These days, many couples couldn't endure what you are having to go through."

"What's an *Orpheus*?" Ellie asked.

"He's a character in Greek mythology. An artist, a musician. Orpheus refused to accept the death of his wife, Eurydice. He travelled through the abyss to reclaim her from the God of the Underworld."

"How does that relate to us?"

Ruth smiled again. "Because that's what Bishop would do for you."

Ellie contemplated Ruth's words, letting the tears come through; letting herself release.

"And, because he knows you'd do the same for him," Ruth said.

Abruptly, pain swelled in acute agony around Ellie's ribcage. She was left breathless. She winced in pain, and tightly clamped her side.

Concerned, Ruth moved closer to the screen. "Do I need to call someone?"

Ellie exhaled deeply, trying to control her breathing. She clutched her ribs even harder, hating herself. "There's no one to call," she gasped through her nostrils. "It'll pass."

Ellie heard the sound of Winston's paws on the hardwood floors, approaching the bedroom. She had left the door slightly ajar. He had developed the habit of head-butting the door to push it open, and curiously poked his head in. From behind, ambient light illuminated his wizardly Schnauzer beard. Ellie moved her gaze from the laptop screen, to Winston. Slowly, she watched him walk across the room. He used the bench at the foot of the bed as a step, and jumped on the mattress. He planted himself next to her, and pawed her knee. Ellie scratched behind his ear.

"Looks like you've got a friend," Ruth said.

Ellie looked down at his thoughtful, deep brown eyes. Winston was stoic by nature, true to his breed, and rarely impressed by anything. Unlike his adopted sister, Izzy, who presented affection every chance she had.

Ellie and Bishop often quipped that if lucky, they could bear witness to Winston's elusive tail wag, which happened perhaps only several times a year. Despite this, and even as a puppy— Winston had exhibited great empathy towards Ellie. He somehow sensed and comforted her when she was in pain, simply by being close and offering tender compassion; a trait that was not lost on her. A trait that made Winston so special to the both of them.

Winston had helped her get through many bedridden days, in a way that humans couldn't. Without judgment, and on days when she felt most alone. Not even Bishop could do that. Petting him, she was reminded it had been nine years since she had first met Bishop. Around the same time her first symptom appeared. Almost a decade of being sick. Of life, stolen from her.

Ellie took a slow exhalation and moved her hand off her side.

Ruth moved onto addressing the elephant in the room. "Do you feel like talking about last night?"

Ellie averted her eyes, but continued on. "This last bout of pain has felt endless," she said. "It's been a few weeks without a break, at least. I can barely function. My hair started falling out again."

"How long has that been going on?"

Ellie sighed. She tilted her head, and exposed the sides of her head to Ruth, letting the camera focus. There were small, but noticeable patches of hair missing. "It's coming out in tufts now, getting worse over the past few months."

Ruth shot Ellie a sympathetic look, genuine in her concern. "Can be the stress."

More tears rolled down Ellie's cheek. She wiped them away. Her paper towel was thoroughly drenched, and nearly in shreds. "I know," she said.

"It's not your fault," Ruth offered.

"I feel so ugly."

"If you had a child, you would never speak to her that way. Remember the little girl inside you, Ellie. She can't be spoken to that way either."

The idea of a child going through this, caused Ellie's diaphragm to tremble, and she tried to gather herself. "Bishop had gone to bed and I couldn't sleep, like usual," she recalled. "I was just sitting on the couch, trying to will my pain away. It was unbearable. My brain felt like it was sizzling. I was trying to massage my head, and a large clump of hair came out in my hands. I didn't know what to do."

"Were you feeling detached from your body, like before?"

"Yes. The pain is there, that's all I feel— but the rest of me is disconnected from who I am," Ellie said. "I'm lost. I have no spirit left."

"Depersonalization is common with chronic pain. It's a natural coping mechanism. It's important to understand that, dear. Your body is in defense mode. It can be a symptom of depression, and prolonged stress and anxiety. People don't often remember their past trauma; depersonalization is partly the reason why. You're living it in real-time."

"Doesn't make it easier. Even now, I don't feel like I'm here." Ellie looked away. "I feel distant. Like I'm slipping."

Ruth leaned back in her chair. She gazed into Ellie's eyes, wishing she could hold her hand. "You're not lost, love, you're here."

"I found myself on the kitchen floor, with a knife in my hand," Ellie recounted.

"What was your intent?"

These past few years, Ellie's mind had become consumed with finding ways to end the pain. With ways to stop the hurt.

Permanently.

Although she couldn't tell that to Ruth. She wouldn't.

"I don't know," she weakly offered instead.

The night before, in her desperation, Ellie had instinctively clutched the blade, not knowing what to do with it. She had been afraid, and her mind had begun to check out.

But she needed *relief.* Of any kind.

It was a manic action. She was like a rabid wolverine. She needed to somehow, mitigate the agony. In suppressing the need to scream, the energy had manifested physically, launching her with purpose towards the knife block. And she didn't resist, as if outstretching her arms and letting the river's current take her. She simply grabbed hold of the knife without any thought. If they had owned a gun, this would have all been over long ago.

This hadn't been the first time Ellie had resorted to this.

A month ago, her headaches had become so unbearable, that she began hammering her fist against her temple in frustration, in an effort to drive out the pain— to mercilessly beat the demons that had gripped her cortex into submission.

It was to no end.

Bishop had walked into the room and found her thrashing in agony. He ran to Ellie and physically restrained her, something that was so completely unsettling to him. It made him feel nauseous, having to impose total control over a woman's body in that way. Putting his hands on a female was against his personal code of ethics. Having been witness to the physical abuse of his mother growing up, he despised the violence of it all, but he'd had no choice.

Her wrists in his hand, they melted onto the floor, sobbing together. He had felt so utterly helpless in trying to take her hurt away. She begged him to end the pain.

He knew what she meant. And had refused.

"Dear?" Ruth said, regaining Ellie's focus. "I'd like us to try something."

Ellie wiped away more tears, and turned her attention back to the computer screen. "Okay," she sniffled.

"You must remember that your body is yours, it's sacred. It has not failed you," Ruth said. "It wants to get better, and it will get better. You mustn't forget that."

Ellie closed her eyes, suppressing her overwhelming fear.

"We have a lot of work to do, and I think you know that," Ruth reassured Ellie. "You and Bishop will continue to pursue what ails you physically. But there is a contributing factor here. One that plays a large part in all of this: *your past trauma*."

"I know," Ellie agreed. "Sorry."

"We'll get to that," said Ruth, adjusting her position. "No need to apologize. You have a right to be here, to take up space in this world. You didn't cause any of this. It's not by choice, and therefore, there is no need to say sorry."

Ruth smiled tenderly. "Understand?"

Ellie nodded.

"Let's get you comfortable," Ruth said. "I want you to lie on your back. No need to see me on the screen— you can simply focus on the sound of my voice."

Reluctantly, Ellie moved into position.

Ruth moved closer to the camera. "Exactly."

Ellie closed her eyes.

"We are going to start a new regiment; which I am hoping you can take forth with you to practice on your own," Ruth said. "I will guide you into a state of consciousness, somewhere between sleep and wakefulness."

Ellie placed her hands on her chest, trying to keep her frustration at bay. Even after several months working with Ruth, she still wasn't sure. Candles, essential oils, and crystals: it didn't make any sense to her. It seemed preposterous that one could meditate away illness.

Ellie tried to relax.

She tried to ignore the searing pain.

"This happens in several different stages," Ruth continued. "Intentional breath work, awareness of your body, and awakening of your consciousness.

This will help you accept, cope, and progress as you heal, if that makes sense. Okay?"

"Uh-huh."

Ruth walked Ellie through the breath work, making her aware of her natural inhalations and exhalations, step by step. Ellie tried her best to focus. It was new to her. She felt a sense of coolness as she inhaled, and warmth when she exhaled. But her mind wasn't in it. Every sound around the house seemed distracting.

"Allow your breath to become deeper," Ruth said. "Be aware of how distinct each one is."

Ellie had done these exercises before. But as hard as she tried, her mind would often revert to her innate skepticism. She had long ago given up on praying. Instead, she focused on an intention, hoping for another way. She was willing to try anything. Ellie tried to plant a seed in her own mind, but she struggled.

Heal, she desperately thought.

End this pain.

Let me come back to who I was.

Ellie fought back more tears. Fought the buzzing in her ribs. Ruth walked Ellie through each part of her body, naming each one. She took her time. "Be conscious of what you feel," she said. "Each cell."

Ellie focused intently on Ruth's guiding principles.

Connect to yourself, even if in pain.

Imagine weightlessness.

Imagine calm.

Visualize yourself in a state of bathing light.

Your Source is always with you.

"We are never disconnected, my dear," Ruth said. "You have to allow yourself to be in the sunlight, because that is your right."

Tears rolled down Ellie's eyes. She couldn't hold them back. Her throat quivered. Still, she maintained her steady breathing, mustering up any remaining resolve.

Her grocery list popped into her mind. She shooed it away. Even breathing was distracting.

Winston lifted his head momentarily to check on her, then laid back down.

"Breathe," Ruth said, almost knowingly. "Your body is not an imposter; it's trying. Get out of your own way."

As hard as Ellie tried, her panic returned. Her pain never wavered. She fought back the gasps. She tried to cage the animal inside, but it was stronger than her.

Ruth noticed Ellie's labored breathing. Since their first session together, her spiritual healing had, although slow, progressed gradually. *Healing happens at a pace beyond our experiential space and time,* Ruth had always repeated. It took work and confidence; the latter, something Ellie had always struggled with.

Ruth always guided Ellie to the base of the mountain, but the climb was hers to undertake. Ellie would only understand the progress she made when looking back, but Ruth already knew this, of course.

Minutes passed in silence.

And a few more.

Finally, Ellie's breathing began to return to a slow, structured pace.

Another few minutes passed.

"I want you to continue," Ruth said, confident that Ellie had returned to a safe place. "Remain, for as long as you need."

Ellie focused. She kept her eyes closed. Yet, she struggled to hold the emphasis on her breath.

Silence enveloped the room, save for Winston's steady snoring. Ellie tried to remember her session. She started again, fighting through the brain fog, recalling her body parts.

She started at her fingertips and worked her way through.

She acknowledged both the pain, and the strength— the way Ruth had outlined. *Meditative homework*, as Bishop liked to call it.

Ellie's cell phone rang. It shattered her concentration immediately.

When she opened her eyes in annoyance at the phone, she quickly realized that Ruth had discreetly disconnected their video session, leaving her to the silent meditation. Ellie was unsure how much time had passed. She may have even fallen asleep. She tried to shake the cobwebs from her brain.

Ellie glanced over to see the display reading *Private Number*. She reached for the phone, and decided not to answer. A telemarketing phone scam for sure. But with each ring, she felt a pull. Hesitantly, she pressed the *decline* button and threw the phone on the bed.

Thirty seconds later, it rang again. Same Private Number. This time, she let it ring until the voicemail picked it up.

Ellie sunk her head down, knowing the moment had passed. It would be an impossibility to return to a meditative state. That ship had sailed. She pinched the bridge of her nose, and felt her stomach rumble. The dogs tilted their heads.

"Breakfast?" she asked. Without hesitation, the dogs jumped off the bed and darted down the hall.

Suddenly, the doorbell rang.

Izzy and Winston launched into a fury of barking, running from one corner of the house to the next, trying to locate the source of the omnipresent sound. Once they noticed Ellie walking towards the door, they quickly followed suit. She tried to quiet them as she went along. "I'm coming!" she called out.

Finally reaching the door, Ellie peered through the peephole, not recognizing the visitor. She hushed the dogs to silence, unchained the door, and let it open only a few inches— using her foot for a wedge. "Yes?"

A man stood in the doorway, awkwardly balancing from one foot to the other in his worn Adidas sneakers, presumably to try and stay warm. He held a clipboard in one hand, and a bouquet of white and pink roses in the other. His long dirty-blonde hair was tied in a loose, disheveled ponytail, a few strands covering his eyes and cascading onto his homemade plaid scarf, and red winter jacket. The glass on his round rimmed frames had fogged up in the short walk between the sidewalk and his still running, early-model silver Toyota Tercel. Ellie pondered the resemblance. He looked like a less-handsome John Lennon.

The windshield wipers made a squishing sound behind him in the quiet winter streets. "I'm looking for Eloise Price?" the man asked.

"That's me," Ellie replied.

The man extended the bouquet and smiled nervously. "These are for you."

Ellie reached for the flowers, and immediately searched for the card. Finding the little mini envelope, she tore it open.

Wish I could be there today, & wish I wasn't stuck at work. Hope you are feeling better. XOXO. Love Bishop.

Ellie's eyes welled up. "When did he send these?" she asked.

The man looked at his clipboard, and used his index finger to follow the lines down. "Uh, looks like he ordered these last night, around eight. Order came through online, and we assembled it this morning. He paid for rush delivery— so here I am."

Ellie smiled at the man. He smiled back. "Just after Christmas, it gets a bit slow again," he said. "So we were happy to get these to you."

"What's your name?"

"Ted."

"Thank you, Ted."

He smiled again. "Take care."

Ellie took the flowers into the kitchen and began to unwrap them. They were healthy and vibrant, surprising for this time of the year. As she was filling up the vase with water, the doorbell rang again.

This time, the dogs didn't bark.

Ellie approached the door without looking through the peephole, assuming the delivery driver had forgotten something. Perhaps another card, or a ribbon? Maybe some chocolates. She could use something sweet.

Ellie opened the door quickly, expecting the Beatle lookalike. She was jostled at the sight of someone else instead, but this time, recognized him immediately.

"Mrs. Price?" he asked.

It was one of Bishop's direct reports from the office. His protégé, and friend. Ellie nervously adjusted her copper hair behind her ear. "Khalil?"

She opened the door all the way, and gazed down the street on both sides. No sound. No cars. Just silently falling snow. He didn't look good. Something was off.

"You remembered," he said.

"Of course," Ellie said. "I don't think I've seen you since last year's office Christmas party." Ellie tried to mask her anxiety. She hadn't noticed until now, how flush his face had become.

"I'm sorry to just arrive like this," he said. "I tried calling a few times."

That's who it was.

Subconsciously, Ellie grasped the back of her neck, feeling her heartrate quicken. Khalil held his jacket closed with one hand and covered his head with the other. Beneath his arm, she noticed at once that his eyes were red and swollen. Her own eyes searched manically, trying to process. She tried to breath. "Please," she said, feigning control. "C-c-come in."

She hated herself for stuttering.

Wordlessly, he stomped the snow off his boots and stepped past Ellie into the entryway. The dogs ran to greet him. Khalil bent over and gently pet each dog behind the ears.

All the while, her pulse thundered through every vein. Her lungs were hungry for air, but she couldn't seem to get enough of it. "What is it?" she finally said.

Khalil stood and looked Ellie in the eyes. He placed a soft hand on her shoulder, and his lips began to quiver. Tears began streaming down his face. He gritted his teeth.

Ellie struggled to force out a single word. She took a long, deep breath in.

Fog enveloped her brain like a dark, unknown entity. A vacuum emptied her chest. Somehow, she already knew. She could see it in his eyes. She could sense it. Her hands began to tremble. She tried desperately to stop her knees from buckling. She held herself against the door frame. In the few seconds she stared at Khalil, she prayed to God for everything to be alright.

Then, she cursed Him— because she knew in her heart it wasn't.

"I'm so sorry Mrs. Price," Khalil said quietly. "I don't know how to say this."

Ellie held her palm tightly against her throat, almost choking, trying to calm her pulse. It was impossible. Suddenly, as if God had answered her plea; Ellie understood what Khalil's message would be, even before he said it. Her anxiety imploded into an inexplicable calm, that passed over her soul like a summer breeze. "It's okay," she said, staring blankly into Khalil's eyes.

Khalil stopped for a moment, and began to weep. "Bishop's dead," he said.

Those were the last two words that Ellie heard before the world turned black.

Part II
Abyss

No one ever told me that grief felt so like fear.

– C.S Lewis

Chapter Four

Ellie lay sprawled on her bed; in a daze, and eyes barely open. Not quite sleeping, and not quite awake: wading in a muddy labyrinth, somewhere in between. Even the scorching sun outside couldn't penetrate the darkness looming around her.

Her own little slice of purgatory.

Early-June, and the city had already started breaking all-time heat records.

The fortified bedroom windows shunned the light like a cosmic vacuum. She had kept the blackout blinds permanently extended for so long that they seemed to meld with the window sill. That wasn't enough to drown out the outside world, so she had been keeping the drapes fully drawn over top of the blinds. Initially, she and Bishop had installed the specialty blinds and curtain rod with custom drapes so that both of them could try to get better sleep. He, for work. And her, to heal.

Now, the drapes acted as a welcomed shroud around her home.

The tip of Ellie's nose burned in the frigid air. She picked up the air conditioning remote to ensure it was still on high. Bishop had always used his South Pacific ancestry as the reason he never liked it too cold inside the house. *It was his tropical blood*, he always reminder her. And he always smiled when he said it.

They would have spats over the house temperature on occasion, like many couples do. Ellie needed it freezing cold throughout the year, because the heat exacerbated her symptoms. Bishop conceded for her, and constantly lived his domestic existence in a hooded sweatshirt, even in the midst of summer.

Since he was only a ghost in their home now, it didn't matter.

With little light and cold recirculated air, the inside of their home remained in a state of eternal, punishing winter.

Like a tomb.

Ellie lay on her stomach, and nervously fiddled with the wedding ring on her finger. She knew she'd better get up; her Dad would be back with the dogs soon. But mostly, she didn't care. Every day was exactly the same, anyway. Despite her instinct begging her not to, Ellie forced herself to slowly sit upright: a grueling feat for every muscle in her diseased body. She let out a deep yawn, and immediately began to feel vertigo setting in. Ellie held herself steady, as if trying to stop a canoe from rocking.

She glanced down at the handful of loose hair that had collected on her wrinkled sheets. There were dozens of red strands that had fallen out over the past few weeks, snaking in every direction. She quickly brushed them aside, under the duvet and out of vision in the unmade bed, feeling guilty. The need to hide the reminder of her imminent balding, overpowered her innate sense of cleanliness and associated OCD.

She straightened out the opposite side of the bed. For reasons that were inexplicable, even to her, she had begun the odd habit of only making Bishop's side. Sometimes she did it subconsciously, walking by and seeing his side made-up, and not remembering having done it.

Today, it was a natural process to cover up her sickness, and trick her own mind into thinking everything was okay: that her hair wasn't falling out, and that Bishop was still alive.

Ellie pushed her palm against the right side of her ribcage and took a few short, controlled gasps. Her spine felt as if it were trying to lurch out of her body. The aching suddenly jolted her more awake.

The breeze from the wall mounted air conditioner came down in gusts. The artificial wind enveloped the room, and left a chilly coating over every surface in the room.

Ellie averted her eyes to a flapping sound on the bedside table.

On its top, beating like a heart, was a letter.

Bishop's letter.

A message he had thought to leave her from beyond the grave.

He had left it in their fireproof safe, tucked away in his office closet. Ellie had no idea the letter was there, until she frantically stumbled on it looking for his passwords and life insurance policies. Handling the household finances was something that he did. The realization of her status as now being a widow came quickly, when the bills started piling up. It didn't take long for collectors to start calling after Bishop died.

"Fucking vultures," she muttered to herself, recalling the thought.

Ellie had paused her grief to anxiously search for his passwords, trusting that Bishop always had a *Plan B*. And she was right. He had left her everything she needed neatly organized, and in sequential order.

Leave it to him.

Despite the situation, she had smiled when she found the envelope, remembering his nature in that brief moment. Enclosed with their financial overview, was a typed letter addressed to her.

Now, the letter found a permanent home in her bedroom, and always within reach.

The incessant wind from the air conditioner always blew it off the table. Days earlier, sick of picking up the paper from the floor, she had finally conceded to using a black *Apache Tear healing crystal* some friend of Bishop's had mailed to her as a gift, a few months prior.

Someone named Hannah.

They'd met at a party years ago, and hadn't spoken since, but Hannah had sent the rock in a small box with a note of condolence. Ellie couldn't exactly remember the connection between her and Bishop. The greeting card was warm and the concern seemed genuine. Hannah's handwriting was impeccable, but it was an odd gift, Ellie had thought. And out of the blue. It had arrived months after he had passed. The description card for the rock said it was supposed to absorb grief, dissipate trauma, lift depression, and restore energy.

It did no such thing.

Ellie had finally found use for it as a paper weight. That's all it was worth to her. Just a goddamned stone.

Sometimes, weeks went by where she couldn't stand the sight of the letter. And other days, she read it over and over. The letter danced with the wind from the air conditioner. She watched the beating paper, eyes barely open. With each flutter, she could make out the first few words.

My Ellie...

The letter flapped. A few more words bared themselves.

... I suppose if you are...

Ellie wiped her eyes with the back of her hand. She swallowed. She couldn't help herself any longer. Her heart swelled. She reached for the tear-stained letter:

... reading this, it can mean only one thing: something has gone wrong.

None of us want to bring any attention from Death, himself, but I needed to write this for you. Morbid, I know, but I couldn't leave you with nothing...

She stopped reading. She couldn't do it. Not today.
Ellie looked down, and suddenly realized she had inadvertently crumpled the letter. She eased her grip, and unclenched her fist. Frantically, she used both hands to try and iron out the wrinkles in her only copy of the letter. Ellie couldn't stop the deluge of tears, and sobbed so hard, she cajoled herself to the edge of hyperventilation. The letter absorbed a few more fresh water stains.
She used her breathing technique to calm herself, and took in a chest full of air. Four seconds in, and five seconds out.
Again.
It was like pushing a grand piano with no wheels. Heavy, awkward, yet requiring delicate care.
After several repetitions, her vision started to refocus.
The words on the page beckoned to be read. The love of her life, called out to her, and still— she couldn't bring herself to do it.
Ellie held a hand to her forehead and felt the heat emanating from her skin. It burned beneath her palm. She steadied herself on the bed and

swallowed the anxiety. Her eyes averted the letter, but she had to. It was the only connection to Bishop she had left.

Ellie held the letter in front of her in the near-dark, trying to catch what little light she could. She focused on the words, blinking rapidly through the liquid induced blurs in her vision. She bit her quivering lip, until she tasted coppery blood. Although at this point, she could've recounted the letter from memory. She read each and every word:

My Ellie,

I suppose if you are reading this, it can mean only one thing: something has gone wrong.

None of us want to bring any attention from Death, himself, but I needed to write this for you. Morbid, I know, but I couldn't leave you with nothing...

I have tried my best to be the best person I could be, and I hope you know that. I cannot bear the thought of leaving you without letting you know what you mean to me.

My ambition never let me be utterly satisfied with anything, and each goal that I set out to fulfil, would only be replaced by some other objective. Living by this discipline however, made it difficult for me to find true happiness. And I'm sorry that you had to deal with that. My unhappiness, was never your fault. And my happiness, was never your burden.

It isn't a tragic thing. Because in those exceptionally rare moments of happiness, I was fully aware. When they did happen, I absorbed them, even though maybe it didn't always feel that way.

Remember the first concert we saw together? I dragged you along to see my favorite band, that you hadn't heard of. But you went, to make me happy, even though I knew it wasn't your thing. The universe was in alignment that night. The musicianship, the performance, the art, the energy, the love, us- I can't explain it. I could feel the force in the stadium coursing through my veins. During one particular song, together, thousands of us spontaneously, and simultaneously, synced our vibrational frequency in a single moment. Even you. I saw it. You let go. We all met each other on the same plain of consciousness. We levitated. I felt connected and normal, for once. It was a once in a lifetime thing, maybe, and I've always been grateful to have experienced even that. It was perfect. It was magic. And I've been afraid ever since, that I would never experience that perfect alchemy again.

On the day I married you, I did. The same connectedness. And I knew.

I've walked a long way to leave behind the place where I came from. I walked to get to you. We made it through, even if it was painful sometimes. This illness, doesn't define you. I hope you don't forget that there is perfect magic still out there somewhere. Please don't forget to smile, and you should let people help you when you need it. It's a good thing.

Know that I have never met another human being with as much light as you, and know that I love you. More than anything. And I'm proud of you.

- Bishop

P.S. I left you a tactical document in the yellow Manila envelope, so that you aren't lost in handling our affairs. It has info for our accounts, bills, insurance, and the location on my drive for my passwords document. There is both mortgage and life insurance. No need to worry about money anymore. You know I wouldn't leave you hanging ;)

From the bedroom, she heard the front door lock disengage. Quickly, her shaking hands returned the letter to the table top, and she placed the black Apache stone on top.

Suddenly, Ellie felt consuming guilt.

She shouldn't be reading the letter, because Bishop shouldn't be dead. She should have done more.

I caused him the stress. It's my fault.

The front door opened.

Ellie squinted at the flood of light suddenly illuminating the hallway.

She could hear the sounds of heavy footsteps crossing the threshold, tiny chains jingling, the delicate sound of scampering canine paws, followed by thirsty panting.

Quickly, she folded the letter and tucked it into the top drawer of the bedside table. She didn't want her Dad to see it. She sniffled, as his voice called out.

"Ellie?"

Ellie looked around, and conceded to using the bottom of her shirt to wipe away her tears. "I'm here Dad, just a second."

She straightened her clothes as best as she could, and quickly pulled back her thin hair into a bun. She peered her head through the doorway. Her heart raced for no good reason. She watched as her Dad lazily crossed into the kitchen, Izzy and Winston following along. Ellie heard the water running and slunk down the hallway. She cursed the walking cane that hung balanced on the hallway closet doorknob when she passed, refusing to use it.

She would have rather crawled, than use that wretched cane again.

As she passed into the kitchen, she noticed that the blankets were neatly folded in a stack on the couch, and her Dad's belongings were missing. He must've been getting ready to leave and already loaded his truck while she slept.

Her Dad filled up the dog bowls with water. "Morning," he said, not turning around. Winston and Izzy didn't hesitate, loudly lapping up the cool refreshment. The tap was still running. Ellie tried to suppress her neuroticism as she watched him carelessly spill droplets onto the hardwood floor. He washed and dried his hands and uncapped a large plastic jar filled with teabags, taking a deep sniff. "You want some?"

"Shoes, Dad."

"Shit," he said, scampering to the front entry like an inept cat burglar. He kicked off his shoes onto the mat, and tiptoed back. "Sorry, I forgot. Was chit-chatting with the neighbor kid when I was outside; lost my train of thought."

"Roland."

"Who?" her father asked.

"Roland," Ellie repeated. "The kid outside."

"Oh. Yeah," her Dad said, holding up a teabag. "So, do you want some?"

"No, thanks," Ellie said, taking a seat at the island. The dogs approached her and sniffed her calves, returning to see what grandpa was up to, hoping for a treat.

He offered her the jar, shaking the contents. "I'm making us some tea."

"I don't feel like any."

He placed a tea bag in two cups, and started filling up the kettle. "It's good for you. I'll make you some."

"Whatever."

Her Dad opened the blinds above the sink. Ellie covered her eyes and recoiled. "I need it dark in here."

He ignored her, and started advancing towards the dining room windows. "You can't stay in the dark all day," he said. "It's gorgeous outside. You need to get out."

"It's too bright."

He ignored her, and started raising the rest of the blinds.

Ellie shielded her eyes. "Dad," she raised her voice. "It makes my headaches worse."

He solemnly looked to the floor, and released the string of the blinds. He lowered them again. "Oh, sorry," he said. "I forgot."

"Yeah."

The electric kettle whistled for a moment, and turned itself off. Her father wordlessly poured the boiling water and slid her over a cup. He took a seat next to her, when the doorbell rang. Instantly, the dogs began barking. Ellie walked to the door, making a futile attempt at quietening them down. She opened the door a crack, and the brightness of the sun made her eyes burn. She squinted. The dogs tried to push their way into view. Finally, she let Izzy and Winston peek their snouts outside. They leaned forward, tails wagging, trying to catch the scent of the knockers.

Ellie smiled faintly, and opened the door; once her eyes adjusted. "Hey, you guys."

"Hi Ellie," the man said. The young boy he was with simply waved at her.

Ellie called out to her Dad, who came walking over. "Dad, this is Sean," she said pointing to the man. "And this is his son, Roland."

Her Dad reached forward and shook hands with Sean. "I'm Charlie."

"Nice to meet you," he responded, placing a soft hand on his chest. "I'm Sean."

Her father turned and high-fived Roland. "We've met," he smiled, pointing at Roland. "One hell of a soccer player. This kid's going places."

Roland laughed. Ellie noticed that Sean was dressed impeccably, especially considering that it was only ten-o-clock, on a Sunday morning. She might've asked her neighbor where he was going, dressed so dapper— but she knew him all too well. Sean wasn't going to church, nor did he just finish an important meeting. It was simply his style and sense of self.

Every day.

Sean was wearing gray wool slacks, and a fitted shawl-collar cardigan. Brown belt, and brown shoes. The oatmeal-colored sweater highlighted his crisp white collared shirt. Sean's tall limbs carried him around the world like a graceful peacock. His blonde hair was perfectly set, and she could gauge his vibrant health, simply from the way his masculine bone structure protruded through his toned face. His husband Elias, who dressed less formally, was more of a T-shirt and denim kind of guy. But you could tell, those jeans and V-necks were high-end. Commonly wearing only comfortable basics, Elias still managed to somehow look like a distinguished actor.

Sean grinned as he handed over a small cardboard box. His kindness always brought a smile to her face.

"What's this?" Ellie asked, feeling the weight of the box.

"We made you some soup," Sean said. "Coconut cream base, celery, kale, ginger, garlic. There is a container with chick peas you can top it off with, and some fresh sourdough."

"It's vegan," Roland said. "I helped."

Ellie heart dropped, overwhelmed at their gesture. She handed the box to her Dad, who took it into the kitchen. "You guys, this is so nice of you." Her eyes started to water. "I don't know what to say."

"No need," Sean said, hugging her tight. "Anything you need Ellie, we're right next door."

"Thank you," Ellie sniffled.

"We've gotta run, get him to the field. But you call, anytime. Okay?"

Ellie held his hand for a moment and nodded, unable to verbalize her gratitude. She admired Sean as he walked across the lawn with his son. He was the archetype on how a man should look in his fifties. She thought of Bishop, and ached that he didn't live to see that age.

Ellie met her father in the kitchen. She studied him as he stared down at the white quartz countertop and nervously ran his fingers through his thinning white hair; before massaging his neck, through his thick beard. She looked over him as he sniffed his Earl Grey tea. His skin looked thin. His face was gaunt. Her Dad's blue T-shirt draped over his torso, and his tan cargo shorts seemed oversized. The short sleeves of his T-shirt nearly reached his elbows. She noticed his bare feet. Ellie had always remembered him as a towering figure, but now, was but a skeletal apparition of his former self. The only thing that seemed the same, were his large hands and thick fingers. Years of manual labor.

"You've lost weight, Dad."

"A bit," he said, staring into the depths of his tea. "You too."

Ellie ignored his latter statement. She pulled out two small prescription bottles from a drawer. "You're starting to look like a really skinny Tommy Chong," she said over her shoulder.

"Tommy Chong's already skinny."

"Exactly."

He chuckled and took a sip of his tea, retreating from the burn. "Forget about me," her father said, unfolding his reading glasses. He punched the security code on his cell phone, and opened a crossword app, still trying to maintain the conversation. "How are you doing?"

She peered at him. "I'm still struggling, Dad. Bishop's gone. I have no career, no friends. Everything's gone."

"You have me," he said. "And the dogs."

Ellie filled up a glass of water, and took a pill from each bottle. "Yeah," she said.

Her Dad tried to distract himself with the crossword. He couldn't seem to focus on the screen. "Strong stuff you're taking there?"

"Yes," she confirmed, placing both hands on the countertop for balance.

"Should I be concerned?" he said.

"It's supposed to help. One's an anti-depressant. The other is for neuropathy pain."

Her father pushed the side button and locked his phone, placing it back into his pocket. He refolded his glasses. They both were quiet for some time. He broke the silence with a gentle question. "Is it helping?"

"No," Ellie curtly responded.

Her father nervously twitched his fingers. "Well, maybe not *yet?*"

"Don't know Dad. The doctor said that if we see any improvement at all, it's a win."

"Is it from the chemtrails?"

Ellie rolled her eyes. "The *what?*"

"Not the depression. The pain that you have. Is it from the chemtrails?" he asked sincerely. "I've been watching a lot about it on YouTube. The government is spraying chemicals into the atmosphere. With the toxins they're spraying, we should all be detoxifying."

"Why?"

Her Dad turned his seat and made enthusiastic eye contact. "No one knows yet," he said. "When I was a boy, we had blue skies. I mean, dark blue skies. You don't see that anymore. Well, you might for a bit in the early morning but before long, you'll see jets flying, covering the sky in systematic cross hatching patterns. Normal aircraft have water vapor, that quickly dissipate after a few minutes. Those are called *contrails*. Normal. But…there are those vapor trails that don't go away, they remain."

He slowly sounded out the next word, nodding with conspiracy: "*Chemtrails.*"

When Ellie didn't respond, he carried on. "By suppertime, they fade into a thin white, wispy haze. Then, no more blue sky."

"You mean clouds, Dad," she said. "Those are called clouds."

"No, I do not," he snapped back. "No, I do not," he repeated. "Clouds are fluffy, and natural. These are not the clouds we remember. It's the biggest global atrocity ever perpetrated against the citizens of planet Earth."

Ellie massaged her temples. She tried to stop listening. She carried on sipping the water, wishing he would just go away. She loved him, but just couldn't. Not right now.

Undeterred, her Dad pressed on. "Every government does it. How can we all be so blind as to not see it above us every day? When something slowly changes over a long period of time, we cease to see it. Even if it's as common as the everlasting sky to every human on the planet. I wonder how much money they spend in fuel alone, with their *training exercises*. It's making us sick. It's what's making you sick Ellie."

Ellie slammed her palm on the countertop. "Enough!"

Her Dad jumped back, and quickly wiped away the spilled tea, when her sudden reaction had startled him. Unblinking, he nervously swiped the crumpled paper towel back and forth.

"Sorry Dad," she lowered her voice. "I didn't mean that. I'm not myself."

"I'm sorry," he said solemnly, keeping his eyes affixed to the counter. His hands were shaking. He pursed his lips. "I shouldn't have brought it up."

"It's me," she apologized. "I have a short fuse these days."

Ellie clenched her jaw in pulses, the way Bishop used to. "There's a lot making me sick. But I highly doubt your theory of chemtrails is one of them."

"I don't understand, what made you so sick."

"Why don't you ever talk about mom?" she accused.

He froze in place, as if he had been bitten by a rattlesnake. "I do talk about your mother. What does that have to do with anything?"

Ellie placed both hands on the counter and bent her elbows. Her stomach churned with fluttering hornets. The sudden anger had come from nowhere. "You don't, Dad. Not only do you not speak of her, you don't acknowledge her existence at all, or how her loss affects me every day."

Her father scratched his white beard, blinking nervously. "That's not fair."

"Mother's Day was less than a month ago. You could have called. That's a hard day for me, Dad. It's always been, and not just because Bishop's gone now too. It's hard every year."

He rubbed his forehead. "I didn't think of it."

"You could have called," Ellie sniffled. "You make it a point to never call on that day."

"That's not true."

"It is true. It didn't matter, because Bishop always helped me get through those days. But he's dead, Dad. He's been dead for months. And it would've been nice to hear from you, that's all."

"I'm here now, I'm trying to help," he said. "Forgive me. I made a mistake."

In that moment, Winston headed for the bedroom. He'd had a habit of leaving the room at the first sign of conflict, and had been doing it since he was a puppy. Even if Ellie and Bishop were speaking excitedly about something, Winston always ran for the hills; not knowing the difference. She'd often find him in the bedroom obsessively licking his paws. His way of self-soothing.

One day, after an intense argument with Bishop— Ellie had found Winston lying with his head under the bed. It had broken her spirit, and she and Bishop had vowed to try and control themselves better after that.

When she saw his little body darting off, her heart sunk, remembering the effect it had on him. It reminded her to reset.

Ellie lowered her voice. "Dad, I know. I'm sorry I brought it up."

He nodded. "I picked you up some groceries this morning," he said. "The usual. Everything's in the fridge. I left the receipt on the table."

She discretely shook her head in disappointment. Ellie hadn't been surprised in the least that he had so quickly glazed over the subject. She simply just accepted it. It's what he always did.

"Thanks Dad," she whispered, inconspicuously wiping tears from her cheeks. "I'll transfer the money later."

"I'll finish my tea and head out to catch the ferry back. Truck's packed. Anything need fixing?"

"No Dad."

"Let me know. I can make a list and bring my tools next time."

Ellie reached for his hand. "Look Dad, I appreciate you coming. You've been a big help. You've been coming nearly every week since…well, you know. The dogs love seeing you, and so do I. But I know it's hard on you. Taking the long trip. The ferry's expensive. You're sleeping on the couch. I know it's hard on your back. Take a break. You can wait a while before coming back."

He squeezed her hand. "It's okay."

"You come here, help with the dogs, pick up groceries, fix things, grab me food. I appreciate it. But I'm worried about you too. It's affecting you. I can see. I'll be okay."

"Bishop was a good man. And he'd want me to help."

"I know Dad," she sniffled. "I know. He loved you."

His eyes were welling up. He fought back tears, and spoke through quivering lips. She'd seen her Dad cry less than half a dozen times in her entire life. "I've been thinking," he said. "You should take a trip. Get away. You're here too much, it's stifling. It would be good for you."

"By myself?"

"Yeah," he smiled. I could stay here and take care of the house and dogs." He reached down and patted Winston on the head. "It'll be fun."

"I'm not in the right space," Ellie said. "I'm too sick."

"Think about it."

"I will."

He gave his daughter a hug. "I'd better go."

"Call me when you get home, please."

"No problem."

Abruptly, Ellie's head throbbed sharply. It was like a powerful robotic arm was suddenly squeezing on her brain. She gasped at the pain and squeezed her temples. "I want to die," she whispered to herself.

Her father was taken aback. He searched for something apt to say, but found himself at a loss for words. His heart sunk. Finally, he choked out what he could. "It will pass."

Ellie reached for his hand, and looked him in the eyes. "I mean it," she said. "I want to die. And I need your help. I can't do this anymore."

His eyes watered, but he fought back the tears, like he always did. Her Dad squeezed her hand. "It will be okay," he whispered. "I promise."

"It won't."

Ellie released his hand and slumped against the wall, without another word. She stared blankly at floor. He called to her, but received no response.

Again. "Ellie?"

Silence.

"Ellie, I'm staying," he said. "I can't leave you like this."

Her focus returned, and she blinked. "I didn't mean it Dad," she finally said. "I'm sorry."

"You sure?" he asked hesitantly.

Ellie nodded her head.

She wasn't serious, he thought. *But what if she was? What are you supposed to do?*

Now, he was leaving on a ferry.

"If something happened," he said. "I'd never forgive myself."

"It's okay Dad, I promise."

"Will you make an appointment with your therapist?"

She hugged him as hard as she could. "I will Dad."

Her father forced his emotions down as deep as he could, and hugged her back. He backed out of the driveway, temples pulsating and hands trembling. He worried for his little girl, but she was tough. That much he did know. She just needed time.

Ellie watched his truck disappear down the street and into the early afternoon like an ancient, forgotten memory. She locked the front door and walked into the kitchen, knowing his drive to the ferry terminal would be nearly an hour.

Ellie contemplated both prescriptions on the countertop for a moment, before emptying the entire bottle of pain meds down her throat with a bottle of Bishop's leftover tequila. She sat cross-legged on the kitchen floor, and texted her father with surprisingly steady hands.

> Dad. By the time you get to the ferry and see this, it will be too late. Don't blame yourself. It's not your fault. But please, come back for the dogs. I love you.

Ellie lay on her stomach and relaxed her muscles, setting the phone on the floor next to her resting head; her crimson hair sprawled across the hardwood planks. The agonizing loneliness would only plague her for a little while longer. One final time. She counted backwards from one-hundred, while she waited for the release of death; and for the first time in a long while, she didn't feel the need to cry.

By the time she reached thirty-four in her countdown, the world started fading to black.

Chapter Five

Bishop had packed a bottle of carbonated mineral water and a bag of mixed, raw nuts for Ellie in the console of their car. That day, he had opted for a cup of herbal tea, rather than the black, double Americano he usually took with him. Ellie had been giving him gentle reminders that he needed to cut down on the caffeine, trying to maintain the fine line between *caring* and *nagging*. She remembered feeling glad that he'd surrendered to the herbal tea, without much debate.

Even from her current vantage point on the kitchen floor, straddling the space between the living and the dead, Ellie recalled this vivid memory from the deepest caverns of her mind. She stared unfocused through glassy, hazy eyes. As she thought back, Ellie could almost smell the aroma of mango and hibiscus emanating from her husband's tea, and she basked in the recollection.

It won't be long now, she thought. *I'll be sleeping soon. Focus on that memory.*

The car had cruised down the highway in the mid-afternoon traffic, light for that time of day. Ellie was sat in the passenger seat in a waterproof coat and a black New York Yankees baseball cap; with her red pony tail protruding from the back.

Over that past year, she had rarely left the house without a hat of some sort. A sporty look to those looking in from the outside, but in truth— it was her best attempt at masking her thinning hair.

Ellie leaned against the headrest in silence and peered through the window, not focusing on anything in particular. Bishop moved his hand from the gear shift to hers, squeezing it for reassurance. "You okay?" he had asked.

She'd nodded in response, lying to both him and herself. She kept her gaze on the passing streetscape, while she spoke to him, deciding just to tell the truth of how she'd been feeling. "Am I *ever* going to be okay?"

Bishop took an intense breath, and glanced at the speedometer. She'd noticed he'd started to drive faster in the last few moments. He tapped the brakes a few times. "Ellie, you wear this disease around your neck like an albatross. It's your burden, right now. But it's dead weight. This…thing. It doesn't define you," he had said. "Those of us in your life, have hope for you, and you have to have it too."

"Nothing ever changes, Bishop."

"I don't want to be the one to tell you, but there's also the reality that you may suffer with this for the rest of your life. What if we never find out what's wrong? You have to find a way to come to terms with that, and find a way at still finding meaning in life. You could still be bearing that cross."

"I won't do it."

She remembered him reaching for her hand; the warmth of it. "You may not have a choice."

"I do."

"The choice you have now, is to cut it loose… this weight. It is not your life's *curse*; it doesn't have to be. What if it's your life's *purpose*?"

Silence.

Ellie's heart had sunk, thinking of that possibility: pain, as her life's purpose.

She turned towards him, wiping away tears. "Everyone wants me to *Eat, Pray, and Love* my way out of this, and that won't help. I'm sick Bishop, and I don't know what's wrong with me. Meditation isn't going to help. Everyone's telling me to stay positive."

She noticed him sulk. "I get it."

"How can I possibly heal myself?" she had demanded.

"As if you feeling sick wasn't enough, nothing is going right," he had said. "You miss your family, I get it. Money is a concern, I get it. These sellers left us a damaged house, and there's a lot to fix. I get it."

Ellie had shouted, not meaning to. "They breached everything on the fucking contract, and destroyed the house before they left!"

"I know hon, I know. The realtor is checking into our legal options. If I could, I'd wring that asshole's neck myself. But, we're getting there."

"We have so much left to do."

"Look how much is already done. I'm busting my ass every day after work, and so are you. Every day, we get a little closer. Every day, we take another step away from that experience. You have to see that."

"It'll be at least two years until everything is done," Ellie sniffled. "We have to save and fix things as we can."

"I know," Bishop agreed.

"I need a stable place to heal," Ellie said. "I can't even unpack until some of this stuff is done. I'm not grounded. I'm floating."

"We're always going to find ourselves with situations we need to deal with, right? You are strong, and always have been. Look what you went through with your mom."

Outside, rain had begun pelting the windshield. Bishop slowed the car, and engaged his windshield wipers, reminding himself to focus on the road. "Both of us are out of energy," he'd said. "There's nothing left in the vessel. That's why mundane issues are so compounded. If you spill some water, it's not the end of the world. Just clean it up. I'll help. If something is broken, we fix it. Everything takes time. There is always going to be something. You can't keep overwhelming yourself. It's going to make us both even sicker."

Ellie slumped in her chair. "Life is passing us by. We're handcuffed."

"That's your current perception."

"I feel like I'm dying every day. I can't take you with me. I can't do this to you."

"You're not dying," Bishop shook his head. "And I made my choice to be with you."

"We're running out of money, it's all going to private doctors and naturopaths. And we haven't even started any kind of proper diagnosis and protocols. How are we going to pay our bills? How are we going to pay for treatment?"

"We'll find a way."

"Bullshit," Ellie turned. "It's what you always say."

"Exactly," he'd said. "That's the point, isn't it? I always say that, and we always find a way. Imagine if I told myself there's no hope? It's self-defeating. That's all I'm asking from you."

Bishop clasped her hand and kissed the back of it. She'd tried to pull it away, but he had held it steady. "I told you when we were dating and nothing has changed," he said. "I only need one thing from you: for you to stay positive. I don't give a shit if you get fat, and I certainly don't care if your hair is thinning. But I can't have you giving up. It affects the both of us."

Ellie gave in. "I'll try."

"Thank you," he smiled.

Bishop started to slow the vehicle and eased into a handicapped parking spot. Out of habit, Ellie pulled the blue decal from her purse, and attached it to the rear-view mirror.

"That's all I can ask," he'd said. "I'm proud of you."

Ellie sulked. "Proud of what?"

"For fighting through this."

"Doesn't feel that way."

Bishop grinned. "That's what the enemy wants to hear. This…thing, in your body. It wants you to give up. It's trying to break you down. But we're soldiers. Samurai. Shaolin monks."

Ellie smiled back, something she hadn't done in a while. He kissed her hand once more, and nodded through the windshield. "Look."

Ellie hadn't noticed him pull up to the rocky beach. She peered through the glass to find an endless ocean in front of them, fading into the consuming horizon.

"How did you find this place?"

"I found it by accident, on the way to a meeting at a customer site."

They had pulled along an embankment that overlooked the water. A small parking area held room for only four vehicles, all of which were empty. Around them, the street was spotted with multi-million dollar private homes, complete with spectacular views of the waves. By nature,

Bishop and Ellie avoided crowds, and to find a beachfront in Vancouver that wasn't teeming with people was a rarity, even in the gloomy winter weather. There were always joggers and dog walkers, wherever you went.

Getting lost one day, had afforded Bishop the luck to come upon this unique spot along this unknown stretch of beach, known only to the affluent families that lived in the neighborhood.

Ellie had slowly exited the SUV, careful of her throbbing muscles. She took a deep breath, and inhaled the brisk, salty air. Most of the sky was blanketed in dark grey clouds, and the rain fell harder.

She raised the hood on her jacket.

Through the downpour, and far in the distance, a minuscule sliver of sun peaked through a break in the clouds, like a hovering UFO. Despite the ocean drifts and rain, Ellie tried to focus on trying to feel the bit of warmth that could be emanating from that little piece of sun.

She felt only cold. Her muscles ached beneath her winter coat.

She could hear Bishop messing about in the back, and felt the hatch close with a thud. He emerged from around the vehicle with a bouquet of white roses, loosely wrapped in plastic. "It's been a while," he'd said. "Thought we'd say hi."

Instantly, she knew what he meant.

Bishop held Ellie's hand in his, and led her down a gravel embankment. He slowed his pace, and firmed his grip to help her maintain her balance. She wished she could move faster, and felt flush with embarrassment in front of her husband.

Ellie subconsciously tried to push forward beyond her means, but he held her steady with his grip. "Careful!" he'd shouted. When he bellowed, his voice was carried off hungrily with the wind. Bishop had later told her, that he could feel her excitement to connect with the Earth. That he was happy for her, and could sense her exhilaration.

Ellie thrived in expressing herself physically, and felt alive in all forms of movement. This was in stark contrast to Bishop, to whom although fitness was a lifestyle— felt more at home in the arts. In another life, she'd ran marathons, hiked, and had pursued dance; while he preferred to write creatively or to take photographs of still landscapes in solitude.

While he only needed to find the time, the illness had robbed her of even the slightest possibility of expressing her energy in the way she wanted. She had dreamed of one day being able to pulverize a heavy bag again, or to challenge her muscles in the tranquility of a yoga class.

But for her, those days were gone.

When they'd had the chance to be in nature, he'd always tried his best to allow her the freedom to enjoy the moment. They'd argue about the impending pain he knew she would endure if she pushed too hard. Sometimes, she'd struggle to get one foot in front of the other. And yet, he couldn't take that away from her. He'd always kept a spare cane in the back of the car, in case. But she refused to use it in public.

They stopped to look ahead.

A large black rock formation protruded from the dark water. Bishop headed in that direction, with his wife in tow. Waves crashed violently against the stone stage, erupting into infinite molecules of mist. Dozens of seagulls reveled in the commotion of the elements; the dissonance, a symphony to them. The acrobatic birds mewed loudly as their wings cut through the salty air.

Ellie had followed Bishop towards the water, hand-in-hand, exhilarated by the wild and picturesque seascape. The bitter cold wind drove into her numbing cheeks. She licked her lips, and tasted salt. She was reminded of the adrenaline that coursed through her veins when she'd ran marathons. A mix of pain, inspiration, and drive. The promise of accomplishment— of conquer. The absence of it ached like a voracious hunger. Just being outside, along the rocky beach, was enough; even if it was just a tiny morsel to satisfy her withdrawals.

Carefully, Bishop walked her down the embankment. He helped her navigate the rocky outcrop. The rain intensified. He pressed forward; a bouquet of white roses clutched in one hand, and his wife's fingers in the other. They leapt carefully from rock to rock, nearing the water's edge. Thunderous waves pummeled the moss-covered blackness of the stony earth.

Seawater spewed into the air and doused the approaching figures. They descended, with little care about their drenched clothing, venturing as close to the water as they could. It was a deep intense blue, almost black. So cold, it was nearly viscous.

Bishop had cautiously watched her every step, ready to pull back, should she slip. They reached the closest point to the water as they could, several feet below the jetty. They recoiled with every crash. Without direction, Bishop handed Ellie the bouquet. They crouched and he positioned his hands on her shoulders from behind.

She took the lead, knowing exactly what to do.

Assured of her husband's harnessing support, and confident he wouldn't let her fall into the water— she carefully unwrapped the flowers and handed him the discarded plastic, which he zipped up in his jacket pocket.

Ellie inhaled the fragrance of the flowers. Although not in season, they emanated a strong floral aroma. She recited a silent prayer as she threw each rose into the water, one-by-one, until none were left.

"For you, mama," Ellie had whispered.

The whitecaps swallowed each stem. They disappeared beneath the blue-black water the instant they were thrown in, not a petal to be seen.

A gift received.

They looked to the sky. Rain plummeted from the clouds above.

Ellie was fighting back her body aches, and the cold didn't help. She received a kiss from her husband on the forehead. They stood for a few moments together, admiring the horizon before setting back. Bishop opened the passenger door for Ellie, and had gently helped her in.

As he was adjusting her seatbelt, a voice bellowed from behind the vehicle. "You know, that's a handicapped spot?"

Ellie glanced at the floor in embarrassment.

Without even looking up, Bishop had responded. "I do."

"Should you be parked there?" the voice pressed.

Bishop clicked Ellie's buckle in place, and straightened up, clenching his teeth. Ellie grabbed his arm. "Don't. It's not worth it."

He'd half-turned and smiled at her. "I won't."

Bishop rounded the back of the vehicle, to find a man standing there. Ellie peered through the tinted back window. Bishop stopped, his face hard and unsmiling. The man looked to be in his early-sixties. He wore a tweed coat with elbow patches, an English cap, and a black scarf that danced in the wind. He glanced at Bishop through his rounded foggy spectacles, underneath a white golf umbrella, pointing feebly. "You don't look handicapped."

Bishop scowled at the man, and took a step forward, baring his teeth.

Intuitively, the man stepped back. Ellie could feel her hands starting to shake. Bishop stared squarely into the man's eyes, unblinking. "You see that little blue decal hanging on the rear-view?"

The man moved his umbrella to clear his view. Defeat passed over his face.

"Good enough for you?" Bishop had asked.

Bishop had managed to contain his anger, and peered through the back window at Ellie's silhouette. She faced forward, fidgeting in her seat. She guessed that he could sense her nervousness. She turned again and saw Bishop unclench his fists. He turned back towards the man, glaring. Embarrassed, the man continued walking, wordlessly.

"What did he say?" Ellie had asked, once Bishop started the car.

"Nothing to worry about," he had said. "Just another rich prick thinking it's his job to patrol the neighborhood."

Ellie had kissed him on the cheek. "Thanks for not hitting him."

"Sure," Bishop smirked. As he reversed the vehicle his phone began to ring over and over, unanswered.

She remembered glancing at Bishop, wondering why he wasn't picking up the phone.

Then she realized Bishop wasn't moving.

He was in freeze frame.

She squinted through the glass, and noticed everything had stopped. The waves of the ocean were as still as a photograph, as was the car.

As was the world.

Still, the phone rang, penetrating her eardrums with a shockwave.

Suddenly, Ellie opened her eyes with a jolt. Her cell phone rang loudly and vibrated across the kitchen floor, dancing past her head. Immediately, she was aware of the drool pooling from her open mouth. She tried to move her hand, but was overcome with paralysis. Her eyes scanned the display on the cell phone.

Incoming call: Dr. Grace Green.

As suddenly as it came, the ringing ceased.

Ellie pushed to move her muscles, suddenly overcome with the need to get up— but her body disobeyed. She willed it as hard as she could, but not a single muscle so much as twitched. A bell toned on the phone. She focused on the display of her cell phone. It showed a preview text message for a moment:

> Ellie, this is Dr. Green's office. Confirming the appointment that Bishop had set up for you. Please call...

The screen went black. Ellie could feel her throat constricting. She didn't want to die. Even in that moment, she knew she had to live. Ellie knew that Bishop had sent her a sign, from wherever he was. She ached to see him. To see her mother again. She'd only have to let the blackness take over. But something pulled.

Ellie grit her teeth and pushed as hard as she'd ever done in her life. Her throat clamped then released, and she vomited onto the floor. This was enough to shake her into the present moment, and she clutched at air with her flailing arms. Suddenly, her body came to life. Ellie rolled onto her side and heaved— viscous bile spewing from her mouth, burning her throat with every breath. She fought for her consciousness, and sat up; her body rocking back and forth like a drunk, unable to exude control.

She couldn't hold it any longer, and fell back onto the floor. Winston and Izzy looked on helplessly from a few feet away, pacing. Her heart ached with shame and love simultaneously, while her beloved pets whined worriedly. She tried to tell them she was sorry, and that she'd loved them— but nothing came.

Ellie fell back against the floor, the ceiling spinning uncontrollably.

The room went silent. She could hear her own shallow breathing, and she released once again, knowing it was time. In the distance, the sound of an ambulance cut through the stillness of the world.

Ellie knew it was too late. She knew she didn't have it in her to hold on any longer. The poison was already coursing through her veins.

At least she'd see her husband soon, and her mother too. The pain would be gone, and the hurt would go away. She closed her eyes.

It was time.

Chapter Six

"Same as yesterday Ellie, if I'm going too fast, let me know," the doctor said. "How do you feel today?"

Ellie bit her lip. She spoke slowly. "I feel okay, I guess."

"I'll think you'll be fine to head home soon," he said, glancing down at the chart. "Maybe even tomorrow."

Ellie sat atop the hospital bed, wearing a seafoam-green hospital gown. She could feel the coldness on her open posterior, exposing her gaunt back. She had lost an incredible amount of weight in the three days she'd been in there. Her legs dangling precariously over the edge of the raised bed. The bed squeaked loudly as she nervously adjusted her seating.

She felt like a child.

The doctor continued. "Luckily in your case, everything has come back relatively normal. You're getting back on track," he said. "Blood pressure is fine. ECG, fine. Blood tests, also good. The drug you took, for your nerve pain? It has a long half-life. If we didn't get to you when we did, well…you got lucky."

Ellie nodded her head in shameful agreement. She just wanted out of there. She could smell the dried vomit that still lingered on her skin. Ellie didn't feel like a human being. She felt like a discarded husk.

Ellie glanced at her father, who was sitting silently in the corner of the room. He was looking out of the second story hospital window, trying to give her privacy and acting like he couldn't hear the conversation between her and the doctor.

"Still, I'd like to ask you a few questions, and then I can determine next steps," the doctor said. "Okay?"

Ellie subconsciously ran her thumb over the butterfly needle that penetrated her forearm. "Okay."

The doctor looked boyish for his age, which Ellie guessed was close to her own, but with barely a crease on his face. His distinctive nose and wispy blonde hair made him look a little like Owen Wilson, although oddly enough, his voice sounded like Dustin Hoffman. He had bright green eyes; reminding Ellie of the mid-century modern ceramic tiles she had chosen for their kitchen backsplash.

The doctor wore typical attire: comfortable sneakers, stethoscope dangling around his neck, and a white lab coat covering his jade scrubs, matching his eyes. Ellie couldn't ascertain between the doctor's arrogance or confidence; she was too tired to care.

"Start from the beginning," the doctor said. "Tell me what happened. This is the first time I have the chance to hear it from you."

Ellie averted her eyes. "By now, I'm sure my Dad has told you about what's going on. What happened… with my husband."

"He did," the doctor said.

"I have fibromyalgia. I'm on some medication. For depression and neuropathy. I took that entire bottle, on a whim. Obviously, the anti-depression one isn't working."

"Takes time Ellie, in conjunction with therapy."

The doctor pulled over a chair and took a seat. "Listen Ellie, what happened was serious. You almost didn't make it. Had your Dad not called the ambulance, you wouldn't be alive."

Instantly, Ellie remembered sending her Dad the text. About the dogs. Telling him it wasn't his fault. She was overcome with guilt. She put a hand to her forehead.

"Do you feel nervous now?" the doctor asked.

"Do you mean nervous because you're grilling me, or in general?"

The doctor smirked weakly. "In general."

"Yes. But I'm keeping the panic at bay, if that's what you're asking."

"Do you feel any pain or pressure, discomfort? Be specific," the doctor instructed.

Ellie thought about it for a moment. "You ever eat hot rice too fast?" she said. "You know that feeling when it gets stuck in your esophagus on the way down? That's what my chest feels like. Heavy. It won't go away, even after gulping water."

"It will," the doctor said, jotting down notes. "When you arrived here, your body was failing. You were unconscious. In order for us to remove the drugs from your system, we had to give you hemodialysis. We basically, filtered your blood."

Ellie looked down at her wrist.

"The pain you're feeling in your chest, is likely due to the resuscitation the paramedics administered."

Ellie's face flushed. She wanted to crawl into a hole, and never come out. She'd put her father through so much.

Although the curtains were drawn around the bed to allow for some privacy, Ellie could hear noisy chaos emanating through the open ward. She could hear the clanging of beds being adjusted, the rapid footsteps of children running, and people arguing with triage nurses. And that smell; something Ellie could never get used to. Even after working in hospitals most of her adult life. Some kind of acrid mix of stale whiskey, disinfectant, and wet, moldy clothing. If she were to describe it with a single word, she'd have chosen: *sickness*.

She had spent far too much time in hospitals these last few years, and not because of work. Ellie choked back the nausea. Her feet fidgeted, getting antsier by the minute.

"Shortness of breath? Lightheadedness?" the doctor asked.

"No."

"What do you do for work?" the doctor continued, rapid-fire.

"I'm an X-Ray and MRI tech."

"Oh?"

"Yes," Ellie confirmed. "But I've been on disability for a while now."

"I don't have to ask about stress at home," the doctor said.

Ellie nodded, and tucked her red hair behind her ears. It felt stringy.

The doctor continued to write on his clipboard, never looking up. "You seeing somebody about that? We can provide some resources."

Ellie stared passively through the doorway. Her father made eye contact. "Yes, I have a therapist," she said.

"Okay, Ellie," the doctor said. "I've got most of what I need. Judging by your tests, you've stabilized quite nicely. We'll keep you in for another night to monitor, but you will be discharged in the morning. Any questions?"

"No," Ellie said. "Just, thank you. And I'm sorry."

"Had your Dad not stopped for gas and called nine-one-one after seeing your text, you wouldn't be here."

Ellie glanced at her father. "I know."

The doctor squeezed her hand. "You'll be okay."

He slipped through the curtain and Ellie watched him move onto the next patient. She sat in contemplation on the bed for a few moments The pain in her chest was still there, in addition to a hollow and heavy emptiness, like radioactive sludge.

It was something she felt nearly every single day. Inexplicable, low-grade dread. Humming, just beneath the sternum. At least these days, there was some cause. Some reason. Normally, it popped up without rhyme or reason; as if she was always bracing for an impact that never came. Ellie swallowed, trying to clear the lump in her throat. She understood it better now, than ever before.

Her therapist Ruth, had suggested that her racing mind, lived primarily in both the states of *past*, and the *future*— with little of it in the *present*.

Once Ellie had heard that out loud, the realization dropped like a piano on her head. Living in the future meant she had a stranglehold on her ambitions; that she could focus and drive towards them. It was a gift from God, really. It was what helped her break her family pattern. It was what drove her towards success.

But it was also a curse.

In opposition, future-thinking propelled her into a constant ether of uncertainty. Of wondering what would happen if she suddenly lost her job, or if something happened to the dogs.

What if I never get better?

What if something happens to Bishop?

She'd always struggled to harness her constant anxiety. The incertitude was a caged beast, teeth gnarling and stalking in silent anticipation, poised to strike without a moment's notice.

On the other side of the coin, Ellie unwittingly clutched onto her past like a stack of school books. The loss, kept her numb. Kept her in a state of emotional cold storage. She struggled with forgiveness, both of herself and of others. Their therapist had helped her see that the expectations she kept of her family, may never come.

And that she needed to accept that, in order to find her own freedom to evolve.

Ellie slid off the bed and walked towards her waiting father. When she hugged him, she could feel him trembling. She'd never seen him cry so hard. She'd never felt so much pain all at once. "I'm sorry Dad," she whimpered.

He hugged her closer. "Me too," he said.

Chapter Seven

"How are the dogs, Dad?"

"They're okay," he said, peering through the large glass window of Ellie's hospital room. "They miss you."

"I'm sorry I put you through this," Ellie said.

"Just promise me, you won't do this again. I'm here. I'll stay for a while."

Ellie rubbed his hand, and looked outside. She could only see blue sky. She wanted to get outside, to feel the wind on her skin. And to see her dogs. "I promise," she said.

There was a soft knock on the door, and they looked to see an unfamiliar woman standing at the room's threshold. She held a tray of drinks, and spoke through a friendly, throaty tone. "Ellie?"

"Uh, yes?" Ellie said.

"My name is Hannah," the woman said. "Hannah Nichols."

Ellie rapidly searched her memory banks. "Sorry?"

"Tony is my brother. He was a friend of Bishop's."

Suddenly, it came to her. "You're the one that sent me that *Apache Tear* rock," Ellie said. "The one that was supposed to absorb grief."

"Yes," Hannah exclaimed. Quickly, her tone subdued, as if reminding herself of the current situation. She took a few steps into the room. "I'm sorry, maybe that was a dumb thing to send," she said. "I wanted to let you know I was thinking about you, and I didn't want to overstep. Maybe it was stupid, I don't know." Hannah hesitated for a brief moment. Her manicured eyebrows perked up. "Did it help?" she asked.

Ellie thought about the useless stone she now used to weigh down Bishop's letter from blowing off the table. "Yes," she lied. "It helped."

"I'm glad," Hannah said. "I hope you don't mind I came to see you. I spoke with your father, he said it would be okay to visit."

Ellie locked eyes with her Dad. He stood, and offered his seat to Hannah. "She called on your phone Ellie, I answered it. Though you could use a friend."

Ellie flushed with embarrassment, and wondered if Bishop and Hannah had ever dated. Her father made for the door. "I'll leave you two to talk. I'm gonna go get a cup of tea. Okay?"

Ellie nodded, giving him the go-ahead. She turned to Hannah. "Why are you here?"

"I called to check in. Reach out. Hoping to buy you a cup of coffee. Your Dad told me what happened."

Ellie analyzed Hannah's tone.

Condescending?

Pity?

No, that didn't make sense. Unless she was an ex-girlfriend. Then it would make perfect sense. But what did she want? Maybe she was looking too much into it. Ellie couldn't figure out the angle. Maybe it *was* genuine concern.

"Look," Hannah continued. "I know I may be assuming, but in some strange way I have been in your shoes. I *am* in your shoes, still. I mean about loss. I, well…I, just wanted to reach out, just because. To see if you're okay. To see if you needed anything."

Ellie's heart sunk and she let out a silent breath. Her voice quivered. "Thank you."

Ellie wondered if she would have taken Hannah up on her offer, if she wasn't currently imprisoned in the hospital. She'd been a shut-in. Even before Bishop had died. Her Dad had been trying to encourage her to get out more lately. Maybe she did need it.

Human contact wouldn't have been so bad, she thought. Especially with a woman her own age. Maybe it would be refreshing. Maybe it would have stopped her from trying to kill herself.

Unless it was Bishop's ex.

Ellie was relieved to see at least, Hannah looked like a *regular* woman. She was pretty, but not *too* pretty. She'd had an athletic build, but you could tell she worked hard for it. Her energy somehow conveyed that. She was dressed appropriately for her age: blue jeans and a casual white blouse, with a thin, open weave, oatmeal-colored sweater. Hannah had effervescent, cobalt eyes, and immediately, Ellie somehow found kinship in them.

Still, Ellie's insecurity nagged. Especially since she was laid up in the hospital for an attempted suicide, covered in two-day old vomit. Mostly, she didn't give a shit.

Lack of self-confidence was her default, after all. She wasn't sure where she'd picked it up from. *Nature or nurture?* She was still trying to figure that out, and work through it with Ruth.

Hannah drew closer, and set the drink tray atop the table. "It's nice to meet you."

Ellie reached out her hand, trying to keep some distance— but was pulled unwittingly into a warm hug. Ellie delicately resisted for a split second, but released her muscles and simply fell into the embrace. It felt like a genuine gesture of concern. And love.

It wasn't as if Ellie hated hugging, it was the fact that she was unable to hold it together with a stranger. She discretely wiped away the beginnings of a tear, and had the hug continued for another few seconds, she wouldn't have been able to stop the waterworks at all. "I feel gross," Ellie said. "I'm sorry."

Hannah held Ellie's shoulders with both hands, and gazed into her eyes. "You are beautiful. And I'm glad you're here."

Ellie was taken aback, and she began sobbing when they hugged again.

When she sat, asking about Ellie's late husband was the first thing she'd uttered. Hannah didn't mince her words, nor did she waste much time with surface-level pleasantries. "What exactly happened to Bishop?"

Although it caught her off guard; in some strange way, Ellie appreciated the directedness. She detested small talk, and was long done with superficial conversations and phony Instagram personas. Even more so now.

Ellie looked up from the floor. "Sudden cardiac death."

As Hannah settled into her seat, she handed Ellie a hot cup and a handful of varying sweeteners. "Tea," Hannah said.

Ellie fidgeted with a packet of *Splenda*. Her mind fidgeted as well, wondering pointlessly how on Earth anyone could ingest such foul stuff into their bodies. And yet, she was the one that was sick. Her mind wandered.

The fiddling was simply a distraction from the aching in her knuckles. Keeping her fingers moving at least kept the blood flowing, easing the aching and subduing the Raynaud's syndrome from creeping into her extremities. Depression wasn't the only thing she was worrying about. Her disease, never took a day off.

Hannah was somber. "Is that the same as a heart attack?"

Ellie adjusted the blanket over her lap, taking in a deep breath. It was the first time she'd spoken of her husband in a long while. She'd been avoiding it. Her throat vibrated. "No, that's caused by a blockage," she choked out.

Ellie took a moment to regain herself, and said, "Bishop took care of himself. It's as if the electric motor to his heart had a short circuit. It malfunctions and causes irregular fluttering, stopping blood from getting to the body, to the brain. Arrhythmia. There was a history of heart problems in his family."

"Was there a chance?" Hannah asked. "Could they have done something?"

"No," Ellie averted her eyes. "It was quick. Unexpected. He was at work. There wasn't anything anyone could have done. It was his time."

"I'm sorry," Hannah offered. "That's a hard thing to accept, I'm sure."

Ellie sipped her tea wordlessly, and squinted her eyes, trying to suppress the tears. She glanced at the doorway, hoping for her Dad to return.

Hannah opened her small cross-body bag. She retrieved a black hair tie, and used it to casually tie her hair back in a ponytail. She smiled at Ellie. "My brother Tony says hi."

"Say hi back," Ellie said, spontaneously noticing the lack of a wedding ring on Hannah's hand. "I saw him at the funeral."

"He took Bishop's loss quite hard," Hannah said solemnly. "He doesn't say much, but I can tell because he's my brother. He's deeply hurt. We all are. We grew up with Bishop. I was there too, the funeral. You had a lot on your mind, I don't expect you to remember. I wouldn't have."

Ellie stared out the window, biting her lip, and fidgeting with her cup. "I'm sorry."

"No need," Hannah smiled.

"Is that how you knew Bishop, through Tony?" Ellie asked after a few moments.

"Yes," Hannah said, swinging her bag on the back of the chair. "They've known each other for years. Since school. I'm the younger sister, so I was always floating around in the background. You know their annual guy's fishing trip? Our parent's own the cabin that they all go to."

"I can never keep track of the guys he goes with," Ellie said. "I only met your brother a few times."

"Yeah, they rarely saw each other except for when they got together for their lake trip. There were always five or six of them that went; high school friends. Few days at the cabin. The trout fishing there is incredible."

Ellie closed her eyes, and tried to visualize her husband's face with an ache. "I've been having trouble remembering Bishop," she said. "My mind can't cope. I remember him as a person, but can't remember *us*. Any good times. These last few years have been only struggle, with my health. And everything that came with it. That's all I can remember. I have so much guilt."

"Being sick is not your fault, Ellie. He loved you. He loved his friends. I hadn't spoken to him in years, but I know Bishop. He had no regrets."

Ellie wiped her tears. "He loved that lake," she whispered. "He talked about it a lot. It was a special place for him."

"It's peaceful, serene. We're grateful for it."

From outside the hospital room, a nurse was adjusting a bed in the hallway. The metal side rails made a *clack!* as she slid it back. Ellie recoiled at the sound.

Hannah reached out a hand. "You okay?"

"I'm sorry, my nerves are a bit shot. I must seem like a weirdo," Ellie said embarrassingly. "I have an extremely low tolerance to stimuli. Sounds, people, lights. It's getting worse by the day."

Hannah smiled. "No need to apologize. Everything you've been through, I can't imagine. You're run down."

Ellie averted her gaze. "I'm run down, yes. But I'm also sick. I don't mention it much, not that I talk to many people. But I'm trying to be more honest about that now."

Hannah maintained contact with her crystalline blue eyes. "Talking about it is a good thing."

"Everyone likes to call it Fibromyalgia," Ellie said. "Because they don't know what it is."

"How long have you been suffering?"

"Ten years."

Hannah placed a hand gently onto Ellie's.

Ellie tried to stop her lip from quivering, and her eyes from watering. The pain in her knuckles swelled. She gritted her teeth. "Doesn't make a difference. I'm sorry," Ellie mustered, and began to rise, as if she was going to make a break for it.

Hannah reached out and touched Ellie's shoulder, guiding her back onto the bed. "For what?"

"To drop everything on you like that. We basically just met. And within thirty seconds I'm crying. You must think I'm such a loser."

Hannah smiled. "I don't, absolutely not. It's the opposite," she said, gulping her coffee. "I think you're honest, courageous, and kind. And I think you're a total fucking badass."

Ellie chuckled nervously. She let out a breath and rubbed her forehead, feeling the heat on her skin. She inched out a smile, feeling relieved. "I always thought that I couldn't get better, because we didn't exactly know what I had. I imagined once we knew, we could attack it, together. Bishop and I. Like cutting out cancer. But it's not like that. It's not that simple. I feel as lost as I ever did. We…" she said, stopping to realize her mistake. There was no *we*. Not anymore.

"I," she corrected herself. "Still don't have any direction. All I know now is that, *I* have a long fight ahead of me. I may not ever get better."

"Cancer isn't that simple either."

"Sorry, that's not how I meant it."

"I know," Hannah said. "I know what you mean. Cancer is something at least people can understand. You have it, and you try to attack it. Cut it out. Radiate it. But what you have, is *faceless*, at the cellular level. It's harder for people to understand that."

Ellie sighed. "Because I look fine on the outside."

"Exactly, because you look fine on the outside," Hannah confirmed. "When you lose all of your hair, everyone knows you have cancer."

Ellie subconsciously pulled at her thin copper ponytail. The realization came quickly. She stopped in her tracks. Ellie stared at Hannah's eyes, and she could tell immediately. "Oh Hannah, I'm sorry."

"It's okay," Hannah smiled. "I'm in remission. We caught it early, thank God."

Ellie placed her hand on her chest. "Thank God."

"The cancer's gone, but it took its toll. Funny thing, you find yourself counselling everyone else around you, telling *them* it's going to be okay. Even though you're not sure if it will be. Even funnier, is how life changes afterwards. My husband left me, *after* treatment, and *after* I went into remission. I considered the same as you; I didn't want to be here anymore either."

Ellie couldn't think of anything to say. "I'm so sorry."

"You don't have to be," Hannah said. "I guess it confronted him to know who he really was. When I was diagnosed, and throughout treatment— he was there. Really, I couldn't have asked for anything more. Detached, but he was there. He took care of me, and our little girl. He worked; he took me to treatment. He cooked, he cleaned. He did love me, but at the end, it was too much for him. I could tell he was hurting. He was a good man, but wasn't built for that, plain and simple. It wasn't in his DNA. He started checking out the moment we found out. I think the guilt kept him there, because how would it have looked if he'd walked away when I was sick? It didn't take long after we found out I was clear. We celebrated, and three months later, he left."

"I can't believe what you're telling me," Ellie said. "Are you okay?"

"It's been a process, but I'm coming to terms with it. Understanding it a bit better. Getting over the anger," Hannah replied. "I'm working on it, let's put it that way."

"What's there to understand?" Ellie said. "For better or for worse. In sickness and in health. I'm sorry, but why would he do that?"

"He just told me he wasn't happy. That's all I could get out of him. But I'm starting to understand, that it's just not what he wanted in life. To take care of a sick person, in case it ever came back. To him, I'm a ticking time bomb."

"I can't believe him. Sorry, but he sounds like a bad person."

"It's more complicated than that. It's not just good or bad. He was good, but he wasn't perfect. There was a way he pictured his life, and having a sick wife to take care of, didn't fit into that. Instead of overcoming or changing, he left. That's what was right for him."

"And you forgive him?"

She contemplated for a moment. "I'm trying to. We have a daughter," Hannah beamed. "Her name is Charlotte. She needs us both, so we have to come to some kind of reconciliation. I can't change him, and I stopped trying. It's his life too. It's easier to remove an obstacle entirely, instead of trying to push it in front of you. It's utterly immovable that way. But lift up and out? That turned out to be as light as a feather. To be honest, I can't stand the thought of living with him, if he was miserable. And if I was the reason? And he stayed only out of guilt? Nah. It's not my style. I'm worth more than that."

"I was always worried about Bishop that way. As if he'd leave one day. My fault for being sick."

"Not true. I knew Bishop. He was cut from a different cloth. And that illness? Not your fault."

"Well," Ellie sighed. "I'm sorry your husband left. You seemed to have found a way to stay balanced and find forgiveness for him. You're a stronger woman than most."

"It doesn't come easy," Hannah said. "I'm *living, laughing,* and *loving* like a motherfucker."

Ellie laughed so hard, that she sprayed a slight bit of tea from her mouth. Embarrassed and still dribbling, she quickly reached for a handful of tissue. It made them laugh harder. Ellie felt dizzy from laughing so hard. It had been so long.

Hannah finally caught her breath. Still red-faced from laughing, she asked Ellie a more serious question. "I don't remember Bishop ever mentioning any kids. Do you have any?"

There it was. That searing knife.

God would never let Ellie's happiness last long.

Her smile quickly faded. "No, just two dogs," Ellie said. She tried her hardest not to reveal her sore spot. "We just couldn't, not with my illness. It wouldn't be fair. Bishop and I made the choice not to."

"What are their names?"

Ellie was puzzled. "What?"

"Their names," Hannah repeated. "The dogs."

Ellie took a deep breath and smiled. "Izzy and Winston."

Hannah smiled back. She looked at her watch, still grinning, and finished her drink. She held Ellie's hand in hers. "My mom is looking after my daughter, and I've got a few things to do before heading home, so I'm going to run."

Now, Ellie wished for a longer visit, but nodded along. "No problem."

"Thanks for seeing me," Hannah said. "I know it probably wasn't easy. We don't even know each other."

"We do now," Ellie said.

Hannah gathered up her belongs and gave Ellie a heartfelt, lingering hug. Ellie reciprocated, feeling as if a bit of new life was breathed into her, even if only for a brief moment. She watched Hannah disappear through the door, after promising to keep in touch.

Ellie laid back down.

She looked into her quarter filled cup of cold tea, and swooshed it around aimlessly. Loneliness began to seep in like a heavy mist. She nervously adjusted her gown, and pulled at her ponytail, remembering how horrible she must have looked.

Abruptly, the door was swiftly pulled opened, and Hannah walked back in. "Ellie?" she said.

Ellie turned.

"I have an idea," Hannah smiled. "When you're feeling better, I want you to come somewhere with me. You have my number. Tell me you'll keep in touch?"

"I'll keep in touch," Ellie said. "But I'm in no place to take a trip."

"When you're ready," Hannah said. "I'm here."

"Okay," Ellie surrendered. "When I'm ready."

Chapter Eight

Ellie reluctantly checked the date on her phone.

June 21st. It had only been a few weeks since she'd been discharged from the hospital. Barely two weeks since she'd tried to take her own life.

Ellie had awoken early that morning to find her father muttering to himself as he peered through the blinds in the dark. Even half asleep, and without looking through the window, she knew it must have been coming down. She could hear the soft pitter-patter on the rooftop.

The utter absence of ambient street noise, was something that only rain in summer could suppress; ruining everyone's plans for the day. And… nothing upset her father more than rain pooling on the ground.

"Is it bad?" Ellie asked.

Her Dad jolted, and peered down the dark hallway. "I didn't know you were up."

"I'm guessing it's not good?" Ellie said, making her way into the living room.

"I don't why the hell it's raining in June," her Dad sighed, closing the blinds. He walked into the kitchen, presumably to make some coffee. Through his time there, he had learned not to open the blinds until she was ready to face the day. Ellie listened to her Dad shuffling around in the kitchen. She took a seat on the couch next to her dogs, and rolled over onto her other side, rubbing Izzy's belly, and listening to the water running in the kitchen.

She had barely slept, like usual. Fatigue overpowered her entire being. Ellie habitually swallowed the overpowering nausea arising from her intense muscle pain. She glanced at her phone, and noticed that the phone display indicated an unread email. She unlocked it, hoping Ruth had responded. Although they'd had a session less than a week ago, she desperately needed another.

"How are you feeling?" her Dad asked.

"Not good," she said. "I had a flare up last night. Acute health crisis; whatever you want to call it. I'm exhausted."

"Pain scale?"

"Seven," Ellie said.

Most days, Ellie's symptoms remained at a steady drone, perhaps a 6 on the scale. It was a method of measurement she and Bishop had developed to understand each other. The variety of symptoms tended to circulate and affect different areas of her body, however the intensity generally remained constant; if she was lucky. Level 6 remained her baseline. A few times a month, her symptoms took an acute trajectory. Most times, she knew what would set it off. Sometimes, even something as simple as cleaning bathrooms could cause physical over-exertion. Or, weeks where she suffered increased stress. She and Bishop had learned to avoid these triggers; but mostly, it was random, and with no cause. If the pain level dipped below 5, they'd consider it a win: that much closer to being a *normal* human being. Sometimes they'd celebrate by going for a walk, careful not to go too far, only to flare it up again. Anything above that baseline, was debilitating: usually resulting in bedridden days.

Recently, and to no surprise— it was nearly every day.

Ellie leaned her head back, listening to the rain. "It's taking a toll on my spirit."

"I know," her father said. "Were you able to arrange a meeting with Ruth?"

She nodded.

Ellie lived her life in perpetual mind control over the wraith that had overtaken the cells in her body. In late afternoon, the day before, her nervous system lit up like a Tesla coil. It started with some dizziness, some increased pain, but quickly mutated into a full-blown crisis. It had shot *past* level 10— without warning.

She and her father utilized everything in their arsenal: heating pad, massage, coconut water, stretching, breathing, meditating, pain relieving medication.

Nothing had worked.

Panic set in, and remained for nearly twenty-four hours. Those endless and recurring thoughts that swirled around in Ellie's brain like a blazing house fire, searing fear into her soul, and altering her neuroplasticity with each burn.

This what dying feels like.
I'm going to end up immobile.
In pain.
Like my mother.

After the first eight hours and no relief, her Dad had suggested that she try and reach out to Ruth. There was only one thing to do: brace and suffer through it. Her Dad had used key phrases to signify positivity. He had used words like *endure* and *overcome*; the way Bishop used to.

Ellie, not so much.

She had lain on the sofa in cold chills, sweating through her clothes. It was as if she'd contracted a tropical flu, without the benefit of having at least been on a sandy beach. Her Dad had provided the usual provisions: wet cloth, dry cloth, blanket, a small bucket, a bottle of water, and the only food she could choke down; a handful of gluten-free, vegan-cheese crackers.

At some point, she had emerged from the fog long enough to contact Ruth. Ellie had wanted to respect Ruth's time, as well as her other patients, and had opted to email, rather than call to request an impromptu appointment for the following morning.

Ellie heard the tap shut off in the kitchen.

She turned to her side, and opened the email from Ruth with anxiety, and read a single sentence: *Of course, dear, let's meet at 10am— Ruth.*

She exhaled with relief.

"Any change since last night?" her Dad asked. "You seem a bit better."

"Not much," Ellie said.

"Is it worse? Better?"

"The same," she said.

Ever the optimist, he responded with as much consolation as he could. "At least it's not worse, right?"

Ellie didn't respond, a bit annoyed at her father's sanguinity. It didn't matter, when the pain was always there. It was hard to agree with him, as hard as she tried. He tried to sound cheerful, but not too much. Enough to provide her a life raft.

Something.

Anything.

But she'd have to reach out for it. Not something he could do for her. There was a fine line, and it was a skill he'd had to learn, like her husband had. Enough to buoy her, but not enough to jostle her in an already agitated state. He walked towards the door with a travel mug, the smell of coffee wafting with him. The dogs raised their heads. "Anything you need before I go? I'm running some errands."

"No thanks Dad," she said.

She watched the latch lock shut, left in the partial darkness. Ellie looked around the silent room, feeling the lack of her husband's presence. How empty the house seemed, even with her father staying with her temporarily. She saw the side table, and a memory formed of the tiny little tree Bishop had set up for her. Their last Christmas together, which seemed like a lifetime ago— was only in fact just over six months ago. She wished she'd known. Ellie closed her eyes, and remembered.

It was early still. She watched Bishop through the window taking baby steps through the house; a hot cup in each hand, and trying carefully not to spill a drop. Izzy followed closely behind, peering through her large black eyes, curious to see if he'd had any treats. When he'd reached the front patio door, Bishop used his elbow to engage the doorknob and his backside to push the door open, leaving Izzy inside. Ellie watched him duck through the doorway.

Bishop's face had flushed the minute he crossed the threshold. He was met by bright sun and cold, brisk air. Ellie could see the dryness on his lips. Bishop squinted, left with but a sliver of vision.

Glistening frost had covered the rooftops in their neighborhood, and week-old snow lay in frozen heaps along the street side. It had collected dirt over the course of the week. Bishop stopped for a moment and scowled at the sight of it. Ellie's nose was burning in the subzero temperature, yet she remembered relishing the fresh air. Anything was better than being stuck in the house, she'd recalled. The streets, at least, were relatively quiet. That much she could remember. Enough to hear the creaks and cracks as the bit of sun melted its top layers.

Ellie had already been outside for some time. Her cane was leaned against the house, behind her chair, and hidden from street view.

She hated the sight of it.

Ellie had sat with her arms crossed, gazing into the distance through her dark sunglasses. She was bundled in a thick, black blanket with tassels. When her husband had come through the doorway, Ellie reached out for the steaming cup. "Peppermint tea?" she asked.

Bishop nodded. "I let it sit for ten minutes, like usual."

Ellie spoke through tendrils of steaming breath, which engulfed her red hair. In the winter, the color of her hair stood out against the drab background. She noticed Bishop admiring her. It made her feel self-conscious. When she'd asked him, he'd said he was observing her radiance; that he was remembering the way her crimson hair complimented that green dress on their first date. He grinned when he said it. She recoiled even more, wondering if he was feeding her lies to boost her diminishing confidence. "Thank you," was all she could muster.

Bishop smiled. "Merry Christmas, my love."

She looked up, although she was sure he couldn't make out her eyes through the dark sunglasses. "Same."

Bishop placed a warm hand on her neck. "Not feeling good?"

"It never changes," she said. "It doesn't matter. I'm not going to get better."

He had taken a seat next to her, and furrowed his brow. "It *does* matter." He tilted his head and glanced down both sides of the street. "You find a new chronic pain specialist yet?"

Ellie massaged her own neck muscles. "Not yet."

"I'll do some research today," Bishop said. "See what I can find."

"I know."

Bishop had taken a sip of coffee and looked to the sky, teeth chattering. "Not sure how long I can sit out here," he'd said. "It's freezing."

Ellie's Albatross

"It's not that bad."

He turned to her. "I'm from the South Pacific. It's bad. My people don't do well with snow," Bishop sighed. "I wish we were in Cabo."

When Ellie didn't respond, he paused and continued anyway. "We haven't travelled in so long."

Ellie watched him pause for a moment, as if he was remembering. He exhaled deeply and followed the plumes of mist dissipate. "Wouldn't it be great to go to Mexico for Christmas one year?" he said. "Just leave everything and enjoy the sun for once. Fuck this cold-ass weather."

In that moment, Ellie hadn't responded, and now she wished she had. She wished she had let him live in that dream for a moment.

Bishop had closed his eyes and inhaled the warm, rich smell of his black coffee. She liked watching him do that. She knew he used the aroma to help him visualize enjoying breakfast in a high-end Mexican resort, or so he had told her. It seemed easy for him to imagine the sounds of the crashing sea, and the warmth of the sun on his dark skin; something she struggled with. He had closed his eyes and smiled. She admired his ability to whisk himself away like that.

Now, thinking back; Ellie regretting saying what she said. She had dismantled Bishop's smile, with four simple words. *"We can't afford it."*

She hadn't meant it that way. He had opened his eyes, and peered at Ellie, swallowing through the lump in his throat. She remembered him avoiding eye contact and rapidly clenching his back teeth, like the way his own father used to. "Thanks for reminding me," Bishop said.

"Sorry," Ellie conceded.

"Can you come inside?" Bishop asked. "I want to give you something."

"I have an appointment with Ruth in an hour," she'd said.

Bishop looked confused. "An appointment, on Christmas?"

"She's Jewish, she doesn't celebrate Christmas."

"But you do."

"Barely," Ellie had mumbled.

He had stood and stared at her until she got the point. "Fine," she finally agreed.

Bishop had led Ellie back into the house by her hand, and she could tell: her husband was glad to get out of the cold. He'd held the door for her while she slowly made her way in, encumbered by the cane she used for support. Izzy waited for both of them, tail wagging.

They situated themselves in the living room, next to the Christmas tree.

Winston had momentarily awoken from his nap to see what was going on. Realizing there were no snacks, he resumed his side-sleeping position. The Christmas tree, which stood blinking on a side table, could barely be classified as one. With the move, the recent stress of Ellie's health— they had decided against decorating that year. It had been too much.

Although both Ellie and Bishop were not much into the holidays, eventually, Bishop decided that it may do them some good to try and find some normalcy in the spirit of the season. He had scurried around the crawlspace and found an old mini-tree that his aunt had given him years prior. Bit of a pathetic attempt, he'd recalled to her, but it was *something*. Something to make them feel normal. He'd dusted it off, and had arranged the little tree on the table, set up a few strings of lights, and placed a few little holiday statues around the living room. None of it matched their décor or sense of style. But it was good enough.

As Bishop had taken a seat, his phone buzzed. He glanced at the call display. "It's your Dad," he'd said.

Ellie had sighed.

Bishop answered the phone. She could tell; he was trying to sound cheerful. "Charlie, Merry Christmas."

Ellie could hear her Dad's voice through Bishop's phone. He spoke through a gruff, but friendly voice. "Hey bud, how's it going?"

She pretended not to listen.

"Not bad," Bishop answered. "Having a coffee. About to open some gifts."

Ellie shot a questioning look at Bishop. Her eyes went wide. "I thought we said no gifts?" she whispered.

Bishop had shrugged his shoulders and she'd shaken her head at his extra-toothy smile. "How about you?" Bishop asked into the phone.

"I'm okay. Just got back from a walk. Just wanted to say hi," her Dad said. "I tried calling Ellie's phone, but she's not picking up."

Bishop tapped the speakerphone button, and held up the device. Ellie recoiled. Bishop had inched closer until she was cornered. "Sorry Dad," she finally conceded. "I haven't been feeling good, and I must have left my phone in the room. Haven't felt like talking much. Not doing too great today."

"Oh, okay," her Dad said through speakerphone.

Ellie shot Bishop a disappointed glance. Her Dad tried to carry forth, seemingly ignoring how she felt. He did what he did best, half-stepping around any serious conversation. Friendly, but unplugged.

"You guys doing anything for Christmas," her Dad finally asked. "Dinner? Visiting friends?"

Ellie had blinked soundlessly, and rolled her eyes.

"No, we're keeping it quiet," Bishop finally chimed in. "Just the two of us, and we're cooking a small dinner later, something basic."

"Good. Why don't I let you get back to it?" Dad said. "You can call me later if you want. Say hi to the dogs for me."

Bishop cocked his head back in surprise. "Will do Charlie."

He mimed the words *that was quick,* and signaled to Ellie to say something to drive the conversation forward. He used his hand to gesture the motion of a spinning wheel.

She had stayed silent.

After a few moments of quiet, her father said, "Okay, love you guys. Bye."

Bishop said, "Love you too," and hung up the phone. The screen showed the conversation as having lasted one minute and twelve seconds, before fading to black.

Bishop gazed into the ceiling for a moment.

"That was awkward," he said. "Why didn't you say anything? He knew you were acting weird. He knew you didn't want to talk."

"Maybe if he'd actually ask me how I was doing."

"He did, didn't he?"

Ellie peered at Bishop. "No, he did not. Even after I told him I wasn't feeling well. He just skates over it. It's what he does. I don't remember the last time he did. It's like he doesn't want to hear it. He phones to check it off a list. Did you check the mail? Did he even send us a Christmas card? *Anything?*"

Bishop had stared solemnly at the floor. "No."

"I rest my case."

"He's trying."

"Is he?" she had asked. "Everyone else's parents invite their kids for dinner. Mail them a gift, or a card in the least. Take them on vacation. Nothing from him. He can't even bring himself to ask me how I'm doing. He could have acknowledged how hard this day is without mom."

Bishop could feel his temples pulsating, and his ears getting hot. He reached for her hand. No response. He squeezed it anyway, without reciprocation. "We've been through this; we can't keep reacting in circles. My family's the same. That's just not who they are. And, unless we change the expectations we have, we'll never get out of this pattern. They carry on, and we continue to be affected. It's a radioactive weight we're carrying, and it's affecting our health. Remember what Ruth said."

"So, they get a free pass?"

"We can't change them, only our own reactions. Let it go."

"Let it go? It's easier for you, because you don't care."

"That's part of it, to be honest," Bishop said, taking a sip of his now cold coffee. He made a face, and set it back down. "I don't care," he said. "Not anymore. It's been too long; I refuse to beat myself up for everyone else's shortcomings. I refuse to constantly feel let down. I've accepted it. This is our life. We need to set and enforce some borders."

"Easy for you because you're a man. And besides," she had accused. "You're not very emotional on a good day, are you?"

Bishop scratched his stubble. "It's easier now. But it wasn't always. It's a tough thing to change the relationship dynamics and see them as anything but family. I just accepted it. I stopped trying to help people when they never asked for any. It was eating me up."

Ellie averted her eyes and stared at the black TV. "Well, aren't you a saint."

"That's not at all what I'm saying Ellie," Bishop said.

She had watched him clench his teeth in pulses.

"Your Dad stays emotionally checked out," he continued. "You told me yourself. He worked all the time, was rarely there for you guys because he was trying to hold the family up. And after your mom died, he checked out even more. He's not a bad person. I think he's trying, just not in the way you want. Or need. Remember, it was his wife. And he's lost because of that too. Scarred. He's like everyone else. They feel they can't help you when you're feeling sick. They don't know what to say. Shit, I feel like that sometimes."

"Thanks."

Bishop sighed. "You know what I mean."

Another spell of awkward silence. Ellie had felt sick inside.

Helpless.

Angry.

Ellie had felt like a burden to everyone around her. She hated herself in that moment, as much as now. Even more so. No one knew how to talk to her anymore. Her sickness defined her.

Is that what he was saying?

Izzy jumped on the couch and crawled onto Ellie's lap, making herself a little nesting spot in between Ellie's crossed legs. The peppermint tea that Ellie was balancing almost spilled. Izzy snorted a few times, and dropped heavily onto her back. She canine-smiled up at Ellie, and outstretched her curly white paws: exposing her pink belly. Her subtle way of communicating with her human.

Ellie had remained stoic, still upset with both Bishop and her Dad, suppressing the need to cry. Not in front of Bishop. Not again. And not now. He was sick of it. She knew.

Izzy wagged her tail thunderously against the couch, her tongue still protruding through the rapid panting. The belly rub was just a ruse. Izzy had a sixth sense for tension. For sadness. For pain.

As dogs can do.

It was her instinct to try and break that, by injecting some sunshine. It may have come from her own history of abuse. Now that she had been given a loving home, it was Izzy's way of repaying her rescuers. An environment of sorrow or worry, she would not tolerate.

Finally, Ellie gave in and rubbed Izzy's belly.

Ellie had let herself smile. It was impossible not to.

Bishop beamed. "That's better."

"I'm still upset. I'm still in pain."

"I know."

"I'm trying."

"I know, sweetheart."

Ellie's eyes watered. "I'm sorry."

"No need, my love." Bishop nodded towards the mini-tree. "Why don't you grab that box under the table and open it?"

"We said no gifts, with my treatments we can't afford it."

"Bah! No tree. No decorations. No turkey. *And* no gifts? Ellie, we can't sacrifice everything. Fuck that, I got you something," he smiled. "Deal with it. And I expect something back in return. Something grand and elegant."

She chuckled. He was glad to see. Bishop loved making Ellie laugh. It was the greatest compliment a husband could receive.

Ellie reached for the box and shook it against her ear, pantomiming an eager child on Christmas morning. The box was heavy and in actuality, it made her shoulders throb. She didn't let him notice.

It wasn't wrapped very well, paper over-folded and uneven, and a few small makeshift patches. Typical for a man, she supposed, but appreciated his effort nevertheless.

"I tried," Bishop said, reading her mind.

Ellie smirked. "I know." She carefully tore the paper, removing it in neat ribbons.

"Tear it!" he shouted. "Rip it! Shred it!"

Ellie let out an inadvertent laugh and pulled at the remaining paper, letting it fall to the ground. Bishop had giggled with her. She could still remember the sound of his laughter.

She had opened the box to find several smaller gold-colored boxes inside, all labeled with the word *Nikon* in bold, black print. She looked at him with scolding astonishment. "What did you do?"

"I got you a camera."

Ellie made a face and slumped her shoulders. "It's too much."

"No, you deserve it, be happy," Bishop urged. "But don't worry, it wasn't over-the-top expensive. I went with a more entry-level one; I hope that's okay. It's similar to mine. It comes with a bag, and an 18-55 kit lens."

Ellie said, "I don't know what that is."

He carried on. "But…I also got you your own zoom lens, and we can share my wide-angle."

"Why did you do this?"

"We haven't done much lately, and I figured this was a good way for us to get out together."

Ellie wiped away a tear. "I love it."

"You already know the basics from your X-ray days," Bishop said. "*Aperture, shutter, ISO.* I can teach you the rest. We can drive out and find some cool landscapes. Give us a reason to walk. We don't have to go far."

Bishop paused eagerly. "Well...what do you think?"

Ellie was taken aback. She opened the camera box. "I love it Bishop, it's so thoughtful. Thank you."

"You're welcome, my love."

"Your turn."

Bishop shook his head and straighten his expression. "We said no gifts."

Ellie laughed. "Yeah, that always works. It's in that closet," she motioned.

Bishop returned, dragging in a large and heavy rectangular box. He had smiled wide, as he pulled it along the floor. The dogs looked up curiously.

It was expertly wrapped with blue and white paper, depicting children throwing snowballs. He set it on the floor and knelt next to it, looking to her. "What the hell is this?" he exclaimed excitedly.

"Open it."

Without hesitation, Bishop unfurled the box with barely two swift movements. Inside, it wasn't a box at all, but rather, a thick plastic black case. Along its length, brass lunchbox-style latches. Slowly, he unlatched each one. He looked up at Ellie, brows furrowed, and opened the case.

Ellie waited in anticipation, and sipped her tea with both hands. It reminded her of the scene in *Pulp Fiction* when John Travolta first opened the mysterious briefcase. She smiled as she watched, hoping for a bright, translucent glow to illuminate his face. Bishop had stared inside the case, silently and with no discernable expression.

Ellie waited.

Bishop said nothing.

Finally, she broke the silence. "I've been saving for this for over a year. It's used though, it's all I could afford. But it's in mint condition."

Still, nothing from Bishop.

"The guy barely played it," Ellie said eventually. "Or so he tells me. I wrote it down on my phone, hang on. Here…it's an *ESP EC-1000, LTD deluxe.*"

Silence.

"Bishop? You're not saying anything. Is it wrong? Do you hate it?"

Inside the case, was the most beautiful electric guitar that Bishop had ever seen. Single cutaway-style body, mirroring the iconic Gibson Les Paul model, a shape that was instantly recognizable to most music lovers. Its sleek and glossy black paint complimented the gold hardware, and handcrafted abalone inlay around the body and frets. It was absolute perfection.

He'd ran his fingers gently along it's precious curves. Although he told her later that his heart was fluttering; he did not pick it up.

It was to him: a masterpiece, and yet, he couldn't bring himself to say a word.

Instead, he ran his palm along the neck, and closed the case without another word.

Ellie opened her eyes, back to the reality of an empty house. She sobbed into a pillow until she fell asleep.

Chapter Nine

The session wasn't helping at all. Ellie tried not to let Ruth see her anger. By the time they had met, Ellie's pain had at least started to subside. In its wake, it had left numbness. Confusion. Brain fog. She peered into her laptop screen through undead, swollen eyes.

They had started by enacting their usual breathing ritual together, trying to calm the mind.

Then the body.

Next, Ruth had moved onto the spirit. But Ellie hadn't been in the mood. She just wanted the pain to go away. She couldn't commit to the required focus, and that only frustrated her more.

Eat, pray, love.

Fuck off.

It wasn't helping today. It could have been the weather. The progress wasn't fast enough. Or maybe the burden on her father. Maye he was sick of taking care of her.

She had wondered that about Bishop. Was he sick of it all? Part of Ellie had wanted him to leave her, so she could do what she needed to do. Sometimes she knew: it was Bishop that stopped her from actually taking her own life. She couldn't do that to him, not after everything he had suffered through for her. Ellie acknowledged, that there was but a thin veil separating her from taking that step. If he ever did leave, he'd take the last obstacle with him. She loved him more than anything. But part of her wanted him to go; just so that she wouldn't have to endure the resounding guilt of it all.

Then Bishop had died. Left her in a different way. And she couldn't think of anything else, but suicide, after that.

Prior to Bishop's passing, Ellie hadn't mentioned anything to Ruth. She knew she should have. *Who better to convey your thoughts of suicide, than your psychologist?*

But only if you wanted to be stopped.

Even today, Ellie wasn't sure if she felt the motivation to stay alive. Aside from pain, she didn't feel much of anything. Only fatigue. Numbness. Like a fall-down drunk. An outcast. Maybe neither mattered: dead or alive. Who cared? She was too tired. Ruth could see it too.

Just a few short weeks ago, as she had lain on the floor, gasping what she thought were her final breaths; that text message had come in. The message from Dr. Green's office, had confirmed an appointment Bishop had set up for her. It was the specialist he had found. In those fleeting moments, even as she could feel herself fading away, she could feel him calling out. As if it were a sign from beyond. An opportunity. And she hadn't found the strength to call back.

Both dogs were lying next to Ellie. Their presence brought comfort, and in some strange way, it brought Ellie some energy. Her eyes were able to regain some focus. She tried to feel gratitude. It didn't come easily. Still, she made her best effort.

"You said had a good memory today," Ruth said.

Ellie snapped back into the moment. "Sorry, what?"

"You said you remembered your last Christmas."

"A bit of it," Ellie said. "Yes."

"That's a good sign Ellie. Things are coming back. It's part of your healing. Even a little memory like that. So, did he like it?" Ruth said, directing the conversation.

Ellie opened her eyes and waded through the murkiness in her mind. "Did who, like what?"

"Bishop," Ruth said. "The guitar you got him for Christmas. Can you remember any more?"

Ellie thought about it for a moment. "Actually, he was really weird about it."

"Weird? In what way?"

"He just stared at it for a while. No emotion. I couldn't tell what he was thinking. I didn't know if he hated it or loved it. He just stared, like a stunned deer."

Ruth tilted her head down, and glanced at Ellie above her eyeglass frames. "What did you make of it?"

"He said he liked it, but his reaction didn't show that at all. I finally got it out of him, but it was like pulling teeth. He ended up telling me later that night, during dinner. And only when I pushed it. I guess the right word would be...*overwhelmed*. That's how he felt, he said. Overwhelmed."

"Why so?" Ruth asked. "Bit of an odd reaction to a gift."

Ellie tucked her hair behind her ears and pet Izzy's belly. "Because it had been his dream," she said. "You know how he grew up. They didn't have money. They didn't have anything. He was enduring physical abuse by his father. It was hard for him."

"I do," Ruth said. "He had spoken to me about it."

"He always loved music and as a boy had always wanted to play an instrument," said Ellie. "But they couldn't afford anything. Bishop had wanted to be in Boy Scouts, in karate. He'd wanted to play sports, but he couldn't do any of it, because it all cost money. His parents had divorced by then, and his Dad was in and out of jail. So, Bishop resorted to reading books from the library. He drew pictures and wrote stories, because those things didn't cost any money."

"How does that connect to the guitar?" Ruth asked.

"Because he'd given up on those childhood aspirations, subconsciously," Ellie said.

Ruth smiled. "And that guitar sparked something?"

"Funny thing about Bishop," Ellie continued. "When we first met, we were going through some old pictures at his mom's house. I'd seen an old picture of him at about eight years old, no shirt and carrying a broken tennis racket. It was a cute picture. When I'd asked him if he played tennis, he laughed. He had found that old broken tennis racket at the playground, and used it as an air guitar. I should have known. He'd had that imagination his whole life. It was a part of him, and it's what helped him survive. And, I know why he never liked sports."

Ruth chimed in. "His father."

"Bingo," Ellie said. "It's because his Dad wasn't around to teach him anything. It's because his mom couldn't afford to put him in any organized sports like his friends. So it faded away, and he naturally drifted towards the arts. I mean, the guy taught himself everything he needed to get by. From riding a bike, to fixing cars, to being handy around the house."

"That's interesting," Ruth said.

"When he saw that guitar," Ellie said. "I guess it brought back a torrent of those emotions. Of that loss. And of rediscovering what he thought he had given up on for good. He was in his forties, and that time came flooding back to him."

"I understand," Ruth said.

"I don't think he realized he'd given up the way he did," Ellie said. "That kid threw away that broken tennis racket and forgot. He moved on. Bishop needed to finish school. Get a job. Help with the bills. There wasn't room for him to explore those things he was passionate about, or his potential talent, or the things that brought him joy. His parents weren't exactly supporting him in *being anything he wanted to be*. They didn't know how. And they didn't have the means to."

"He told you all that?" Ruth asked.

Ellie let herself smile. "He did," she said. "I was proud of him."

"Giving up like that happens at a subconscious level," Ruth said. "It becomes a habit, especially as a child. Like you said, a means for his survival. You forget what makes you happy, because you're too busy trying to stay afloat. And that becomes your narrative. Funny thing about Bishop, is that people who are like him, *need* to be creative. They need it like food. Like water. Like air. And when they don't express themselves in that way, they begin to starve, and eventually they suffocate."

Ellie glanced at the rain through the window. "No one managed time like him for work," she said. "Yet he struggled to find the hours for himself."

"Did he miss a meal, or a night's sleep?"

"No."

"No," Ruth agreed. "No, he didn't. He found time, somehow, each day, to eat and sleep. And so, we should with these things too. We need our creativity; or whatever outlet makes us happy. Something to be learned,

Ellie. Whatever your passions are: rediscover them again. Did he play? The guitar?"

"It took him less than a week," Ellie said, quickly changing the subject. "Less than a week to learn two songs."

"I'm glad you remembered Ellie," Ruth said.

"Me too." Ellie glanced at the clock at the bottom of her laptop, and sighed. "I guess we're out of time."

"That's okay," Ruth replied. "I can stay on if you need."

"No, that's okay."

"Do me a favor? Make some time to do something for yourself today. Something to make you happy. Anything. Please."

Ellie smiled weakly. "I'll try."

"You have a good day, dear." With her last sentence, Ruth disconnected from their video conferencing session. Ellie stared blankly at the black screen for a few more moments.

Hearing a sudden noise outside, Winston coiled up from his slumber. His ears perked. "Lay back down, you vicious pup," Ellie said. "It's just Sean, from next door, mowing his lawn."

As if he understood, Winston stared at her, blinked, and gently laid back down on his side.

Ellie wondered what she was going to do today.

She rose from the bed and opened the blackout drapes in the bedroom. It had seemed so long since she'd done that. Light poured into the room, and she squinted. Although the sky was grey and dreary outside, the rain had stopped. The moisture in the air beamed effervescent light into the atmosphere; illuminating the day. It was pretty. She took a deep breath. The day seemed bright. Fresh. And hopeful, somehow. Now that her pain had slightly subsided, she was able to appreciate that.

Ellie winced as she passed the dresser, because the daylight emphasized the dust buildup on its surface. She made a mental note to get to it today.

Unless she was bedridden, most days were taken up with house cleaning anyway.

It's not like she had a job to get to. Her hobbies had been physical, and she couldn't pursue those anymore. She wasn't like Bishop: happy to be locked up in his office typing on a keyboard, fiddling with his camera for hours, or plucking away at those guitar strings.

"I need movement," she said aloud, to no one in particular.

There was no purpose for her. In cleaning at least, she felt purposeful; as pathetic as that sounded. But she worried. Sometimes, the most minuscule of activities would send her into a painful flare-up. Who could've known that cleaning a few toilets could send her into a tailspin?

Sometimes, she and Bishop would argue about how far she pushed herself, even if it was just housecleaning, or garden work. He didn't want her to do it, because he recognized the patterns. One thing was for sure: a day full of movement, would always be followed by pain. And for the week.

Despite this, Bishop never won the argument. He'd always do the heavy work outside, but conceded and let her stay in the garden as long as she wanted. He'd peek out to check occasionally, but it was important for her to be outdoors.

Gardening and toilet cleaning.

It was a far cry from her marathon days.

As she walked throughout the house, she methodically opened up each blind and drape to let the light gush in. At this moment, she realized that her aching had subsided. Ellie connected the dots quickly:

Wanting to let light in the house, meant wanting a better day.

Wanting a better day, meant she wasn't as down.

Not being as down, meant the pain must've waned. Even just a little bit.

It was subtle, but it was a fact.

Ellie joined her dogs in the living room, and in hugging them— she thanked God. First time she'd done so in forever. It was only when she stopped to think about the pain, or rather, the lack of it— that she subconsciously felt a little more human, when the agony would dwindle for a moment. Most people would be in bed for the day, at the slightest hint of pain. She thought for a moment: *it's funny what you get used to.*

Ellie lay motionless on the couch, trying to collect her thoughts.

Numb.

The only sound in the room was that of the air conditioner spewing its ever-frigid airstream. Ellie reached her hand past her hip, and scratched Winston behind his neck. He snored in soft undulation as he slept between her legs and the couch. Izzy remained in her usual spot, stretched out on the cooling hardwood floor, head relaxed beneath the sofa and just within arm's reach of Ellie.

Ellie's appetite had been steadily diminishing for some time, and the last few days, she remembered she had barely eaten at all. She'd already vomited twice that week, not knowing if it was from the vertigo, indigestion, or if there was yet another symptom cropping up. This was a fact she'd hidden from her father. The best she'd been able to do, was choke down a few occasional pieces of fruit.

She glanced at the plate of half-eaten watermelon on the coffee table, already beginning to gather fruit flies. Ellie had been drinking water, but mostly because her pain medications required her to ingest them with something. Even then, she'd spent hours each day swallowing back the nausea.

In contrast, she'd found herself giving the dogs more treats throughout the day; mostly because she wanted them to be happy. She had been feeling increasingly guilty about not having them absorb her emotional agony, which she knew Winston was sensitive to. So, she compensated with frozen blueberries, sliced apples, and the occasional store-bought peanut butter dog treat.

Abruptly, a thought popped into Ellie's head. She reached for her phone and lazily typed into the search engine. She didn't even have to finish typing, because the autofill kicked in: *How long can a human being...*

...live
...hold their breath
...stand
...run

There it was: *How long can a human being... survive on only water?*

Before the results could display themselves, she locked her phone and set it back down on the table. She had to get those thoughts out of her head. For her dogs, for her Dad.

For Bishop.

The moment she released the phone, it rang.

She grappled with answering it. She'd been hating people more and more. If it was important, someone would leave a message. If it was a telemarketer or a scam call, she would have dodged a bullet. They always block their calls, those bastards. It couldn't be any more bill collectors—once she figured out their finances, everything had been taken care of. No one but her Dad called her anymore. And Hannah that one time.

The phone rang again.

And again.

After the fourth ring, it started feeling like an itch. Just before she knew the voicemail would pick up, she sat up hesitantly, and answered it. She tried her best not to sound like she'd been sleeping. "Uh, hello?"

Ellie glanced at Winston, who silently blinked his thoughtful, dark eyes back at her.

"Is this Eloise Price?"

"Yes," Ellie said. "It is. And it's Ellie."

"Ellie," the caller corrected herself. "I'm calling from Dr. Green's office. We never heard back from you about your appointment next week, just calling to confirm again."

Ellie began to panic. Hope of getting better had long abandoned her, and the thought of going through this without Bishop was unfathomable. He was her support system. What was she to do? Her palms began to sweat. "I'll be there," she said quickly, surprising herself.

"Great," the woman said. "I just emailed you the confirmation. Everything you need, including the intake forms and address, are on there."

Ellie heard the email notification come through. She tried to control her pulse. "I'll see you then," she said, and hung up the phone.

Chapter Ten

Ellie sat alone in the doctor's office, squinting over the framed credentials on the wall. She had read as much as she could online, and wondered how in the hell a doctor so young had accomplished so much.

The office was large, clean, and well organized. Large gray slate floor tiles accented the stark white walls. There was a large bay window, opening up to a cityscape of majestic skyscrapers cutting through the sky. The minimalist artwork that hung around the office invoked peace and tranquility, in line with the overall Zen motif. A state-of-the-art air purifying system buzzed quietly in the corner of the room.

Ellie sniffed. The office atmosphere smelled of lemongrass, emanating in a ghostly mist from an essential oil diffuser sitting atop the doctor's desk. She inhaled deeply, and tried to let the scent bring her stillness.

Ellie occupied one of the four seats that were placed in a circle, surrounding a small side table next to the bookshelf. It amplified her loneliness, and she felt her husband's absence more than ever. Her Dad had offered to accompany her, but she hadn't wanted to burden him.

In the far corner of the room, close to the window, there was a large wooden desk with a laptop and two additional seats.

She looked around curiously, feeling her heart race with anxiety. To distract herself, she directed her eyes to process every detail; trying to interpret the person behind the design of the room. It was something she found herself doing often, while waiting. Anything, other than scrolling mindlessly on her phone.

From the neatly arranged remedies and supplements in the cabinets, to the plethora of books on the shelf— Ellie appreciated the systematic attention to detail, and used the bits of information she gathered to profile Dr. Green before she even walked through the door.

When Ellie had arrived at reception in the modern downtown office, she was greeted warmly and moved immediately out of the waiting room, and into the doctor's office; to her surprise. Although she was terrified, something about that gesture made her feel inspired, and a bit of hope fluttered in her chest.

As Ellie sat alone in the office, she imagined her husband asking if she was okay. Despite him being dead, and her being alone in the room— she nodded her head in response. He would know she was nervous, and he would have comforted her. He would have held her hand, and warmed the coldness of her skin. Anxiety had become part of Ellie's daily life, and she had made a habit of internalizing it all. But he would have loved her anyway. He would have encouraged her to fight on. Bishop would have tried to put her at ease by gently massaging the back of her neck. He had learned her process over time. Only time could help, and she needed to get through it. He just needed to be there.

Ellie stared across the room in silence, at nothing in particular— her leg anxiously fidgeting while she waited, the way she did when she flew. She remembered flying with Bishop for the first time.

The plane had been filled with fellow travelers on a six-hour flight, bound for the tropics. Enthusiastic banter filled the cabin space, in anticipation of the forthcoming cerveza in the warmth of the white sand beaches. Amongst the rows of excited faces, Ellie had stood out.

Her pupils were as big as hockey pucks, and her skin was as pale and cold as the surface of arena ice. Her fear of flying became apparent the minute the plane had started its ascent. Strategically, she had avoided disclosing this vital piece of information to Bishop, and had hoped she'd quietly get through it without him noticing. He had only realized her trepidation the moment the plane broke through the ceiling; when he had glanced over to see it on her face.

She had stared ahead silently, firmly clutching his warm hand.

Every time the plane jolted as it banked towards its destination, she tightened her grip. He had tried for the first hour to reassure her, but she remained stoic—never breaking her vow of silence.

Bishop had learned her process quickly: *sit, swallow, silence, internalize the panic, and wait it out. Hope the fucking plane doesn't crash. God help us all.*

He had chuckled at first. It worked for her though, and he respected that. *Better than utter hysteria*, he had said. When the rubber hit the tarmac and the plane taxied to a stop, she had let out a profound sigh of relief, and smiled. She would be okay, and he knew that. He was supportive through plain instinct, and he had known to step back to let her get through her process.

There was a soft knock on the door. The doctor leaned her head in. "Can I come in?"

Ellie stood. "Hi Doctor Green."

"Please, call me Grace," she said, gently closing the door behind her. Grace kept her jet-black hair tied expertly in a tight ponytail, and it bounced as she walked to her desk. She had a caring, youthful smile, revealing two front teeth that were slightly larger than the others. She radiated warmth and attractiveness.

Ellie swallowed, her own confidence deflating. Subconsciously, she tucked her red hair behind her ears, and adjusted her ball cap, wishing she had worn more makeup.

Grace placed a folder filled with stack of papers on the side table, and took a seat across from Ellie. She reached a slender hand towards Ellie, still smiling. "Great to meet you."

Ellie feigned a poised smile and shook the doctor's hand firmly, which Grace reciprocated with equal, but genuine confidence. "You as well," Ellie said. "Thank you for seeing me."

Grace glanced at her new patient, and leaned forward. "Is it Eloise, or Ellie?"

"It's Ellie," she quietly replied with a nervous smile. She felt herself go pale. "Only my mother called me Eloise."

"Ellie," Grace repeated. "Nice to meet you." She took off her half-frame designer eyeglasses and carefully folded them on top of the folder. She reached across and clasped Ellie's hands in hers. The gesture took Ellie by surprise, and immediately, she felt a rush of unexpected emotion. Ellie fought her instinct, and tried not to pull back. Her eyes watered, suddenly overcome with sentiment. "I want you to know you're in the right place," Grace said.

"Thank you," was all that Ellie could muster out.

"I've read your intake forms but I want you to tell me your story in your own words," she said. "And know that this is a safe space."

Ellie had had this same discussion with so many other doctors and specialists in the past, that it felt almost scripted at this point. Even she herself, sometimes doubted whether or not her pain was real. It was almost too hard to believe. Reciting the same story over and over, had always left her emotionally fatigued.

She would feel it later for sure. Reliving it, drained her energy like a brooding vampire. In the least, it would help her sleep. Anything was welcomed at this point.

"Start from the beginning," Grace asked.

Ellie spoke, slow enough to access her memory banks through the fog. "It's been nearly a decade," she recalled. "My husband and I had just started dating, and one day, I suddenly lost vision in my left eye. He took me to an eye doctor, where they found no cause. I was then sent to an ophthalmologist, who also found nothing of note."

"Let me guess," Grace said. "Your vision just came back after a few days?"

Ellie nodded. "Yes."

"Your list of symptoms is long, but I've seen other patients who are worse, believe it or not."

Ellie closed her eyes for a moment, imagining Bishop squeezing her hand for reassurance. "I don't want to overwhelm you," Ellie said.

Grace motioned for her to continue. "Not at all."

Ellie summoned her strength and took a deep breath, trying to control her tears. "Grace, you have to understand. I feel like I'm at the end. We burned through our life savings seeing private doctors, naturopaths, traditional Chinese medicine doctors, chronic pain specialists— you name it. Aside from my family doctor, none of these were covered by my medical insurance. We sold our house back home, and my car, to move here to be closer to better medical support. After all that, and almost ten years, I've seen nearly zero improvement. I'm not quite sure what's going on with me. I have no quality of life." Ellie felt her heart sink. "I am merely surviving."

"I understand," Grace said, placing a gentle hand on Ellie's knee.

"I won't end up like my mom," Ellie whispered.

"Tell me about her," Grace said.

"Why?"

Grace looked up from her notes. "Because it's part of the story."

Ellie painfully recalled the account for the doctor. She was only nineteen years old at the time—having to watch the most important person in her life slowly die. Her mother, Catherine, was diagnosed with a rare and aggressive form of multiple sclerosis, until it eventually took her life five years later. Ellie had tried to balance her mother's care, with her college, while simultaneously trying to maintain the care of her father, who was working through his own sense of loss, teetering on the precipice of alcoholism to numb his own pain.

At age twenty, Ellie had been shortly hospitalized for depression. She had recovered through therapy and heavy amounts of prescription drugs, which she remained on for many years— only for the depression to return in recent years, with her own illness. She'd vowed to never put that kind of poison in her body again.

"There are nearly a hundred symptoms I have Dr. Green, and I listed them all in the intake form," Ellie asked. "You don't want me to list them all?"

"No, but talk to me about the severe and constant ones."

"I'm going to overwhelm you."

"You won't," the doctor said. "I promise."

Ellie looked to the ground. "Sorry."

"No need to apologize."

"There is the constant feeling that I have the flu," Ellie said. "Body aches, debilitating fatigue, numbness in my extremities, vertigo, tinnitus, and severe pressure headaches. At its worst, I was bedridden for three months. Now, I walk with a cane sometimes."

Grace nodded along. "It must feel like your whole body is shutting down."

Ellie held back her tears. "There are then the resulting and compounding psychological symptoms from all this."

"Go on," Grace reassured.

"My body can't cope with the trauma, and in trying to manage, I get vibrating of my muscles, and the constant feeling of passing out on a daily basis."

"Have you ever fainted?"

"Yes," Ellie embarrassingly nodded. "I'm also losing my hair, if you haven't noticed— and my skin is riddled with cystic acne and eczema. I have unexplained bruising. I feel caught somewhere between an old lady and a teenager."

"How do you sleep?"

"I don't," Ellie said sadly. "I am up all night, exhausted. When I do, I suffer from night sweats. Nightmares, sometimes."

"And your eating habits? Digestion? Any discomfort there?"

"I'm a vegan now, have been so for the last few years."

"Can you not tolerate meat?" Grace asked.

"It's all of that," Ellie responded. "It's the inability to digest a lot of foods, but it's about the welfare of animals too. I made the switch in order to try and manage my symptoms with diet."

"Has it improved or helped?"

"I shudder to think what state I'd be in if I ate poorly."

Grace nodded in agreement. "Elaborate on your digestion issues."

Ellie paused. She missed Bishop so badly in that moment. He knew her well enough to understand that the same song and dance they'd recounted so many times before, felt futile. He would have understood how she felt. They'd consult with a new doctor, and leave feeling hopeful— only to find zero answers, and in more financial debt than when they'd started. Bishop would have leaned his forehead against hers, and patted her back, driving her to continue. Urging her to find her hope.

Ellie took a deep breath in, channeling his energy. "I have a lot of GI discomfort: bloating, severe pain and inflammation, mucus in stool, IBS issues. I can feel like passing out when I eat larger meals, and I have the inability to swallow food at times. I've actually had to start preparing for my meals by going through a short meditative breathing exercise. I've always had healthy teeth, in the last six months, the gum lines have started to recede and the enamel is wearing away, resulting in extreme sensitivity."

Embarrassed again, Ellie recoiled. Grace reached out a comforting hand.

"I'm overwhelming you, sorry," Ellie said.

"Not at all," Grace replied. "I can't imagine what you're going through. No need to apologize."

Grace walked across the room and retrieved several bottles of water from a mini fridge. The diffused scent of lemongrass followed her back.

Reliving her pain, and reciting out her list of symptoms out loud, made Ellie feel defeated. Less than human. She reeled in a state of utter despair, and unable to control it.

Grace sat back down. "So, what is your official diagnosis?"

"Fibromyalgia," Ellie answered. "I've come to learn over the years, they give that to sufferers of chronic pain with unknown causes."

"More widespread in women," Grace said.

Ellie nodded. "Auto-immune disease. It's the only thing that our family doctor could offer, to somehow categorize my condition. Of the over ninety symptoms that plague my body, a handful of them were found to be most commonly associated with fibromyalgia. The diagnosis has never put me closer to finding relief."

Grace changed the subject. "How have you been getting by?"

Ellie sensed Bishop's ghost. "It's been tough," she replied. "We had burned through our savings seeing private doctors, and it took almost two years of appeals to finally qualify for long-term disability. During that time, we managed as best as we could, on only my husband's salary. We spent carefully, lived meagerly, yet we continued to spiral into the debt we'd always tried to avoid. Our hands were tied. And now he's gone."

"I'm sorry Ellie," Grace said solemnly.

Ellie could only nod her head. She used the back of her hand to feel the increasing heat on her forehead. She became dizzy, feeling herself spiral again. She cupped her neck. "Can you help me?" she pleaded.

"I'd like to take some additional serological testing first, and we can go from there. And know, that it's certain that we have a long road."

Ellie clenched her shaking fists, conjuring up as much courage as she could. "I want to start today," she said.

"Good," Grace smiled. "We'll start some testing right now. I'll be right back."

Ellie let out a long breath as the door closed behind the doctor. Instantaneously, she unlocked her phone, scrolled through the contacts until she found the right one, and pressed the dial button. Her heart pounded like a thunderstorm while she waited.

Finally, a voice answered. "Hello?"

"Is this Hannah?"

"Ellie," Hannah said with immediate recognition. "Is everything okay?"

"Yes," Ellie said, getting right to it. "Remember that trip you mentioned?"

"Of course," Hannah said.

Ellie let out the longest exhale of her life. "I think I'm ready."

Chapter Eleven

Ellie drove down the unfamiliar road with both hands vice-gripped on the wheel.

Although she'd been driving on the long stretch of highway for hours, she hadn't seen many other cars, even when she passed through the odd sleepy town. She kept a close eye on the cell reception, which seemed to fade in and out every fifteen minutes.

Even when she passed through a patch of inhabited land, the signal was shoddy at best. Thank God, she had printed off the directions Hannah had given to her on paper, just in case the vehicle's navigation failed.

Like Bishop used to say, *always have an analogue backup.*

Most of the mountainous landscape was comprised of densely forested rocky terrain, and every once in a while, she'd catch a glimpse of the raging river that paralleled the highway through the trees. She tried not to be hypnotized by the river's deep blue-gray tendrils crashing over the jagged rocks, brewing its foamy white concoction. The road ebbed and flowed in elevation: sometimes down at river level, and other times so high she couldn't make it out any longer. She'd unexpectedly find herself lowering gears to climb the soaring heights; the forest getting thicker with the elevation. Impenetrable in some places.

She felt a mix of both fear and exhilaration; the adrenaline in her blood pushing and pulling like the different altitudes of the roadway. Ellie tried to control her dizziness, holding onto the steering wheel like the safety bar on a roller coaster. She swallowed, suppressing the nausea.

As her vehicle descended and rounded the next curve, ahead of her, she could glimpse an approaching tunnel.

Her chest constricted in panic.

The highway bottlenecked into a single lane, and she gently merged into the left one. She inhaled, and eased the foot pressure off the gas pedal.

The vehicle slowed.

She glanced in her rear view, and counted three cars in line behind her. There could have been more, but the curves of the mountain road blocked her view. She looked again. The silver pickup truck directly behind her was close.

Too close.

"*Fuck*," she muttered to herself. "*Barely any cars, and now I'm leading a parade?*"

She squinted her eyes.

The tunnel entrance widened like the open, toothy mouth of a menacing clown, as she reached closer, and closer. She gripped the steering wheel tighter, nails digging into the leather. Her eyes darted between the lines on the pavement and the rear view.

The truck behind her flashed its headlights.

Ellie glanced at the speedometer and noted that she was travelling well below the speed limit. Steadfast, she kept her pace. The truck increased its speed, and inched nearer, closing the gap.

"Get off my ass, redneck," Ellie whispered.

She locked her eyes where they needed to be.

Road.

Rear view.

Road.

Rear view.

Still, maintaining her resolve, she kept the vehicle steady. Ellie removed her sunglasses with a shaky right hand and carelessly threw them onto the passenger seat, with a little too much force. Her Burberrys rolled across the seat, banged on the passenger door, and fell into the oblivion in between.

"Shit!" she shouted.

Suddenly, she reached the tunnel, and was thrust into darkness. She jerked her neck straight forward, and held her breath. Her temples pulsated.

Ten and two.

Ten and two.
You'll be fine.
Steady.

She tried not to think of passing out. She tried not to think of the darkness. Or her car rolling onto itself in a crumpled mess. Just ahead, she could see the faint light of the exit. The tunnel was much shorter than she'd anticipated. She stepped on the gas, and her car lurched forward, creating a distance between the redneck behind her. He too, increased his speed.

Closer, now.

She could start to make out the rocky mountain face and evergreens, as the opening widened on her approach. Ellie sped through, passing the threshold into open air. Barely thirty seconds had passed within the tunnel, but to her, it felt endless. As she exited, the highway once again split into two lanes.

She let out a deep sigh, and guided her vehicle onto the right side.

Ellie watched the truck floor it, and quickly gain speed until he was driving in parallel.

She told herself not to look. That's what he wanted, to engage. He maintained his speed to match hers, and she could feel his stare through her peripheral vision. She locked her gaze directly in front, and refused to give in.

Impatient, he sped off.

Finally.

As the sunlight passed through the windshield of his pickup, she could make out a silhouette through his back window. Exactly what she'd expected: male, trucker cap, and a middle finger.

She scowled and shook her head.

He sped forward, as if he needed to make up for the precious minute he'd just lost. As he disappeared over the horizon, she finally let out a sigh. Ellie maintained her hand position at ten and two, but eased her grip. Her fingers were still shaking.

The highway began to descend at an acute angle.

She watched the minutes pass on the dash clock, suspended somewhere between a single second and eternity. With each passing mile, the mountain began to fade behind her, and the landscape opened into a wide vista. River on her left, and acres of lush green farmland, far in the distance.

Immediately to her right, there were huge patches of blackened trees, passing her vision like gravestones. Her heart sank. Every few years, a wildfire would overtake the area. Although she lived hours away from the interior of the province, where she currently found herself, smoke from the fires would overtake the city for weeks at a time, reaching as far as Vancouver Island in really bad years. She didn't remember wildfires and smoke being a problem when she was a child. Now, it seemed like it was happening every other year.

Thankfully, this year, there had been just enough rainfall to keep the fires at bay. Still, there didn't seem to be any regrowth of vegetation on this particular stretch of the highway. The dark forest of burned trees called out to her like ghouls.

Her sternum felt like it supported a hundred pounds of coal.

Without thinking, she quickly slowed her vehicle and pulled over, swiftly tapping the hazard lights switch, and engaging the emergency brake in a single fluid movement.

Car still running, she opened the door without even checking if she'd had enough clearance, and bolted to the shoulder of the highway, leaning her back against the passenger side. Ellie placed a hand on each hip and hunched over, desperately trying to fill her lungs with air. Her red hair slung over her face.

She heaved the passenger side door open and rummaged through her purse, until she found her phone. Her fingers worked in autopilot, unattached from the rest of her body, unlocking and speed dialing with ferocity. She listened to the ringing with bated breath.

Finally, he answered.

"Dad?" she whimpered.

He responded with immediate and heightened concern. "Ellie? Are you okay?"

"I…I don't know," Ellie choked out. "I'm having a panic attack."

"Where are you?"

Ellie felt the blood drain from her face, keeping her back steady on the car to keep from falling over. She could feel the engorged veins pulsating in her temples. "I don't know," she gasped. Cars passed loudly, chaotically passing gusts of wind through Ellie's hair. "I think I'm about an hour away still. Just on the side of the highway."

"What happened?" her father shouted into the phone. "Is everything okay?"

"I don't know," Ellie answered. "Why are there so many burned trees?"

Confused, her father tried to sound confident. To be her beacon. Her lighthouse. "Take a breath. Take your time. Count, like we do. Four in, five out. Okay?"

Ellie inhaled through her nostrils in short bursts.

The oxygen enveloped her dizzy brain. She turned and peered at the raging river across the highway, trying to find an anchor point. Her eyes scanned until she honed in on a large, flat black rock, protruding from the rushing water. She focused on it intently, hearing the river crashing violently. She tried to maintain a balance of breaths, somewhere between emotional control but without actually passing out from the dizziness.

"Tell me where you are, and what happened," he calmly asked.

Ellie steadied herself. "It's nothing Dad. I'm sorry," she sheepishly offered, her heart still racing. She inhaled, and took control of her diaphragm. She placed two fingers on the side of her neck, just under her jaw.

Steady.

Tibetan monk on a mountaintop.

Calm waters.

Puppies.

God-damned, fucking rainbows and unicorns!

Her BPM lowered a fraction. She could feel her pulse slightly slow in her neck. Ellie closed her eyes for a moment, and reopened them, still laser-locked with the rock. That little bit of control was all it took. She used the opportunity to wrangled her terror towards the direction it needed to go.

Downstream.

Let it pass.

"Sorry," she finally repeated.

Her Dad spoke softly through the phone. "No need to be sorry."

"I don't know," Ellie said, now exhaling deeply. Slowly. "I was fine. Driving. Everything happened at once. I went through a tunnel. A guy was tailgating me. I passed a bunch of burned, dead trees. And for some reason, I just started panicking. Maybe I shouldn't have come. I don't know. Everything started closing in. I couldn't breathe. It's so fucking stupid." Ellie slumped her shoulders. "I can't even do normal things."

"You're not the only one," her father said. "Happens to me too, every other day. It's okay. You have to tell yourself you're fine. That you're okay. That you're not going to die. That's the essence of it, yeah? That somehow your subconscious thinks you're not going to make it. Your nervous system lit up, from your disease. You have to just wait it out. What else can you do?"

"Thanks for trying to help, Dad. I should go."

"You gonna be okay?"

"Yeah," Ellie lied to herself, angrily wiping away her tears. "I'll be okay." She hung up the phone, with an overwhelming sense of shame flooding over the anxiety.

Ellie screamed as loudly as she could into the void of the empty highway. The sound echoed across the expansive landscape, and then returned to complete silence, as if nothing had occurred.

Chapter Twelve

As Ellie drove down the steep, gravelly driveway towards the cabin, she could see Hannah standing at the foot of the wooden stairs, waving. Behind her, the lake shimmered like a flawless pane of glass. Ellie waved back with exhilaration, and shouted through her open window, barely able to contain her relief. "Hi!"

Abruptly, she felt a swell of emotion arise from her stomach at the site of Hannah and the cabin; a byproduct of finally arriving, of finally letting go of the tension in her body. And instantly, she could feel the spirit of her dear departed Bishop, who loved that place so much.

She could see why.

Through her expression, Ellie's lips quivered. The unexpected sensation arose like a volcanic eruption: a cacophony of relief, happiness, and anxiety. Ellie cupped a right hand over her mouth, and suppressed it as deep as it would go, quickly drying the few tears through a forged smile before Hannah could see.

Ellie parked the car.

Hannah opened Ellie's door, and barely waited for her to stand to give her a warm hug. Ellie embraced it and let herself fall into Hannah's arms. With both arms on Ellie's shoulders, Hannah looked into her new friend's eyes. "You okay, sweetheart?"

"I'm okay," Ellie sniffled. "I'm glad I'm here."

From behind the house, a large yellow Labrador Retriever came trotting towards the girls. Ellie bent down to greet the smiling dog. "And who is this?"

"This," Hannah responded, "Is Millie."

"How old?"

Hannah scratched behind Millie's ear. "She just turned twelve. Getting a bit slow, but she's doing her best to keep up. You didn't bring your pups with you?"

"Dad's got them," Ellie said. "It would have been too much for me."

Hannah smiled. "Yes, same with my daughter. Mom's got her. Next time."

"Next time," Ellie agreed.

"What do you think?" Hannah asked, gesturing towards the lake.

Ellie closed her eyes for a moment and inhaled a chest full of fresh air. "It's perfect."

From behind, Ellie heard the door creak open from the house. She turned to see a familiar face standing in the doorway, smiling, with her arms crossed. Without thinking, Ellie ran as fast as she could up the patio stairs, to hell with the pain; and embraced the waiting woman wholeheartedly. Ellie hugged her so hard, they almost toppled over. When she finally caught her breath, she looked into the woman's eyes.

"Ruth."

"Hello, dear."

The evening sun hung low on the horizon, casting brilliant pink and orange hues over the tops of the evergreens, and across the sprawling sky. The scene reflected just as impressively on the lake, as Ellie watched the gentle ripples dance across its surface in silence, absorbing all that she could.

Ruth, Ellie, and Hannah sat on red Adirondack chairs, arranged in a circle around a large brick fire pit, while Millie, the Labrador Retriever, lay fast asleep on her side in the soft grass. Once in a while, her tail would wag, even in sleep— fondly reminding Ellie of Izzie back home.

Ellie watched plumes of gray smoke drift high into the atmosphere, filling the air with the pleasantly familiar scent of campfire: a smell that she had known to bring her husband peace. She let it help her drift into nostalgia.

Ellie slouched in her comfortable chair and stared lazily into the sky, bundled in a woven blanket, watching the horizon darken minute by minute. She tried to relish in the moment; to focus on the stillness in her sternum, even though she knew, the beast of panic lay dormant somewhere down there.

She had eaten her dinner vigorously, something she hadn't done in nearly a year. But something had shifted today.

Maybe it was the exhaustion. Maybe it was the lake. Maybe it was the feeling of being safe around these two women. Ellie felt their connection like Saturn's rings, revolving around some kind of spiritual center.

But maybe it was the red wine.

Either way, it was the first time she'd felt protected since losing Bishop.

"How was dinner?" Ruth asked.

Ellie glanced over. "I'm out of words. I don't remember the last time I had a meal like that."

Hannah took a sip of her Merlot, watching the wine legs flow down the inside of the glass. "Me too," she said. "It was amazing. I need to get the recipe from you. I've never had lasagna that good before, and vegetarian to boot."

"It was my mother's actually," Ruth said softly. "From the old days. I've been altering it over the years into something healthier, while keeping its original roots." She smiled. "I'm glad you enjoyed it."

"This whole time," Ellie said. "I've been able to let go a bit, something I haven't done in a long time." Her eyes welled up. "I have you two to thank."

Ruth reached across a supportive hand. "Of course, dear."

Ellie used her sleeve to wipe her eyes dry. "I've been so overwhelmed since I got here," she sniffled. "I never stopped to ask how you two even know each other."

"We met at Bishop's funeral of all things," Hannah answered. "We had a short conversation, and that was that. But when I saw you at the hospital, I could tell how much Ruth means to you, and how much she's helped you. So, when I planned this trip, I Googled her. Found her business listing. Thought it would be a nice surprise."

"I hope you don't mind, dear," Ruth said.

Ellie smiled, succumbed with emotion. "Not at all," she said. "It's been… perfect. I can't thank you both enough. I really needed this."

"Are you comfortable," Hannah asked Ellie. "Can I get you anything? Tea? How's that blanket?"

"I'm good," Ellie smiled. "Thank you."

"How's your pain?"

"It's fine," Ellie said. "Believe it or not, it's settled down since we ate. It's there, but low-grade. I expected it to be a lot worse, especially after that long drive."

"Do you feel anxious?" Ruth asked.

"I always feel anxious, to some degree." Ellie folded her arms. "But overall, no. It's okay tonight. You don't have to check in. It's okay."

"It's connected. The anxiety to the pain, I mean."

Ellie exhaled. "I know."

Hannah got up and carefully placed two more logs into the fire. The logs hissed as the flames engulfed the wooden fibers, ejecting hot embers into the dusk. For a brief moment, the light from the campfire illuminated the three faces, then died back down. Hannah rubbed the particles from her hands. "Which stage are you in, Ellie?"

Ellie paused. "Stage?"

"Yes, stage. Of grief."

Ellie looked down into the fire. "Oh."

"I went through that with my cancer. You've been through so much. Your illness. Bishop. There are generally five stages of grief: Denial. Anger. Bargaining. Depression. And acceptance. It's stupid to say, but I have these memorized, because I spiraled through them myself. I had to do a lot of work to get through. Survival tactics."

Ruth leaned in. "Hannah, it was not *your* cancer. Remember that. It was cancer, yes, but never *yours*. It was never personal, or because of something you did. You let it go. The association of words are important."

"Right," Hannah agreed.

"And there is a sixth stage," Ruth said. "That usually comes with anger: *blame.*"

"To be honest," Ellie said. "I think I'm rotating through at least one of those stages every other minute."

Hannah took another sip. "I don't blame you."

"But it is getting better." Ellie let out a deep breath. "I usually live in the stage of depression, even before Bishop. From my...from... *the* illness that consumes me. I haven't reached acceptance yet."

"There is time yet, dear."

"I know."

"You know, as well as I do," Ruth said. "That we will live our entire lives working on ourselves. It won't end. But we *will* move forward. It's natural for you. You are not lazy. You want this. You have the ethic. You've worked hard. And there will always be a new day."

Ellie felt her eyes swell. "I'm still angry too. About everything. About my mom, about Bishop, about this... *thing* in my body."

"I know," Ruth said. "That's natural. You can allow yourself to feel angry, furious even. Scream if you need to. Thinking about losing such a vibrant human being, at such a young age, naturally makes us feel pissed off. Yet I'm sure Bishop and your mom, both of whom were so kind-hearted and compassionate, would urge you to find meaning in their loss."

Ellie almost choked, raising her voice unexpectedly. "Meaning? What meaning could I possibly find?"

"Whatever your beliefs may be," Ruth said calmly. "Open to let them guide you in knowing that both your husband and mother made an impact in your life. Their light remains with you still. When someone has completed their purpose, they are summoned home— wherever that may be. That is, however, a hard thing to accept. We walk by the simplest of things in life. Because we think there is always plenty of time. It takes a conscious effort to stop and notice the subtle sounds outside, to be open, to laugh, to learn, to remain centered, and to love someone so unequivocally. We all forget these things. But they can help you to remember. When you lost Bishop, when you lost your mother— here, you wept. But, the angels rejoiced."

"Why?" Ellie asked.

"Because Bishop and your mother came home, that's why."

Ellie wiped her tears. "I'm utterly broken in pieces."

"We all are. You will one day, my dear, stop resisting the reality of the situation. And we call this, acceptance."

Hannah took another sip. "Ever hear of Kintsugi?"

Ellie and Ruth shook their heads.

"It's something they do in Japan," Hannah said. "To fix broken pottery. Instead of throwing it away, they repair it using gold. What you are left with, is a ceramic bowl seamed with little golden rivers. There is beauty in that which is imperfect. A history of scars, an acceptance of change. Renewed strength. There is… a story."

Ellie's heart sunk, at both the despair and inspiration of it all. "I'm trying."

"You're doing good. Give yourself that time," Ruth said. "There is no timeline."

"I'm having trouble remembering him," Ellie said. "Remembering, us." She closed her eyes, trying to conjure the ghosts of her past. "Being in the hospital reminded me of *that* smell," Ellie said. "That smell I was so used to. I definitely don't miss coming home from work smelling like that."

"Do you miss it?" Ruth asked.

Ellie looked down. "What? The hospital? Sometimes. It's part of who I was. Without my career, I don't have an identity anymore."

Hannah took a sip of wine. "You're more than just that job, Ellie."

"I helped a lot of people."

Ruth reached out a hand. "I know you did, sweetheart."

Ellie smiled, remembering her husband's face the first time she'd told him that she was an X-Ray and MRI technologist. "It was our first date," Ellie chuckled, thinking about his smile.

That first night, they had found easy conversation over great wine and unexceptional pub food. When he had asked about her job, Ellie had shyly divulged to Bishop the many interesting items she had witnessed inserted, *accidentally*, in people's orifices throughout her career. A glass Corona bottle topped her list, with the remnants of a lime wedge still inside. The disturbing image had been burned into her memory. Most people wouldn't think that about an X-Ray job, but it was more common than one would guess. Bishop had sneered when she told him that, and he had almost spit out his wine in laughter.

She was shy by nature, and reticent about sharing those stories, but Bishop was persistent; even though the subject made him slightly squeamish. He used his humor to charm her, and they'd had a wonderful night laughing together.

When thinking about what she did as a career, Bishop had imagined patients lining up to get routine scans for broken bones from playing sports, filing through the imaging wing of the hospital, grasping at their elbows in makeshift slings. Ellie had been trained not only film technology, but also in fluoroscopy, angiography, CT, and mammography. Since there were limited MRI jobs in town, she had taken the first X-Ray position that had come up at the time.

The reality was, she spent most of her shifts in the emergency operating room, assisting surgeons in real time: gunshot wounds, stabbings, workplace accidents, vehicular crashes; you name it. Plenty of blood, body fluids, and verbal abuse to go around.

Terminally ill patients were the hardest.

She had ushered many on their way to the other side. But it wasn't all like that. She focused on what she needed to— helping people. It was why she chose the profession she did: a delicate balance between science and spirituality.

Ellie treated her patients with thoughtful empathy and kindness, and in their moments of uncertainty and fear, she had an ability to put them at ease, and they gravitated towards her. But in all this, she absorbed their energy, something Bishop would learn to be true, even if she didn't.

It would be an impossibility to not bring that kind of work home.

Sometimes, the terror and panic that emanated from patients lingered in the air, awaiting a compassionate host. A natural empath like Ellie, would come along and subconsciously soak it up.

Her only fault— she'd been trying to ease someone's distress.

"I remember when I stopped working," Ellie recalled, gazing at the lake. She relished the moment in the outside world, of which she rarely took part in anymore.

She evoked the memory from all those years ago, when she had worked the night shift, opposite of Bishop. She had been suffering silently, the symptoms increasing exponentially each day. She pushed to get through her days, her shifts, suppressing the depth of her pain. He had known something was wrong, just not to that extent.

She and Bishop passed each other like ghosts each day.

He'd come home from work in the late afternoon, and would connect with her shortly before she'd have to leave for her own shift, able to hug one another only for a few brief moments. Despite the limited time with his wife, he tried to make each moment count, if nothing else, lingering on the embrace.

They'd hand off the dogs, catch up to coordinate dinners, and discuss which household chores needed to be completed.

It was exhausted, domestic bliss.

By that time, Ellie and Bishop understood wordlessly that they were establishing a future together. In their late-thirties, and immersed in their careers, it was the right time to put their heads down and get to work. They had pooled their savings and come up with just enough for a down payment on their first small townhouse. They both dreamt of better things, and real estate was a feasible way to get there, even if that meant they couldn't fully furnish their new home.

Building a home took time and effort, and an empire had to start somewhere.

Ellie despised the sight of a partially furnished home. It reminded her of her childhood in an empty house, eating on the floor because they couldn't afford a dining room table.

For this to work, both Ellie and Bishop would have to grind, like their parents had done before them. It was all they had known, and all they had been taught: *Work to climb. Ascension happens one step at a time.*

Ellie had watched her mother do the same as an LPN, as did Bishop, whose mother cleaned hotel rooms for over thirty-five years. Coincidentally, both had had electrician fathers.

Shortly after moving into their first home, Ellie's health began to decline rapidly. Strange symptoms had begun to appear the year prior, but they began changing and increasing by the day. It was something she couldn't deny.

Although she never spoke of it, she feared she'd succumb to the same fate as her mother. Out of guilt, and to spite her mother's path— she pressed forward. She refused to accept that kind of suffering for herself. She made do; sometimes releasing her emotions by sobbing in the car on the way to work. She did it in concealment from Bishop, like a guilt-ridden adulteress.

Despite her best efforts, Ellie's sick days were adding up. Her pain increased and her mobility decreased. She had found herself slowly deteriorated into a woman who needed to cry every day, to experience any sense of deliverance.

That particular day, dressed in her light blue scrubs, she was leaving for work. When she reached the landing of the stairs, she stopped, unable to find the energy to take another step. It was an impossibility to hold back the tears. She didn't have the energy to hide them anymore.

Bishop was on his way into the kitchen for a snack, when he saw her on the stairs. She was hunched with her head in her hands. He rushed to comfort her, and had made the decision for both of them, instantly, and without debate. She needed to stop working, and she needed to do it in that very moment. It was perpetuating her sickness.

They would find a way to manage, somehow.

Bishop phoned the hospital himself, and told Ellie's manager that she wouldn't be back to work until they'd figure things out. She'd felt the release of the burden she'd been carrying, and wept in Bishop's arms. He carefully tucked Ellie's copper hair behind her ear, kissed her on the forehead, and cried with her.

They were directionless.

That was nine years ago.

The illness had in fact, continued to worsen since then. By the time she received her long-term disability approval, she had been robbed of partial mobility and had to rely occasionally on walking with a cane; a far cry from what other women Ellie's age were posting on their Instagram feeds.

She was young, and nothing could have made her feel less of a woman.

Ellie took a deep breath of lake scented air; the crackling of campfire bringing her back to attention. She immediately began fiddling with her wedding ring. The elegant piece of jewelry complimented her delicate fingers, and even in the dim moonlight, it sparkled.

Ellie looked down at the shoulder bag propped against her chair. "I've got Bishop with me," she suddenly blurted out.

Hannah looked surprised. "Sorry?"

"Bishop," Ellie said. "He's in my bag. Well, part of him. I brought some of his ashes with me. I don't know why. I just did. For reassurance maybe. To not feel so alone. I don't know."

Ruth and Hannah remained silent. Ellie stared into the open flames, in a trance. "Part of me wanted him near me," she continued. "Part of me wanted to bring him to his favorite place. To let him feel joy again."

She began to quietly sob. Hannah started to get up to comfort Ellie, but Ruth stopped her with a subtle gesture of her hand. Hannah remained seated.

"I want him to feel that forever," Ellie said. "I hope that he isn't in pain, or worrying about me."

"He feels only love, my dear," Ruth said.

A sudden thought came into Ellie's head. She reached for her bag. "I need you two to let me do something."

"Anything," Hannah said.

They watched, as Ellie unzipped the bag and carefully extracted a container wrapped in craft paper. She gently tore it open and tossed the paper into the fire, where it was quickly consumed. In her hands, she held a small white oval ginger jar. Over its surface, ornate hand-painted cherry blossoms, in dark blue. It reminded Hannah of the Kintsugi pottery of which she had just been speaking of.

Ellie stood and began walking towards the lake.

The two women followed.

Hannah lit Ellie's path with a flashlight as they trekked towards the water's edge. Millie followed curiously.

Ellie walked until she reached the end of the dock.

Beneath her feet, she could hear the gentle sloshing of lake water. Although Hannah held the flashlight spotlight steady, the lake was illuminated by silvery moonlight. Ellie knelt near the edge of the dock, peering into the dark water below. She held the ginger jar firmly in her hands.

Carefully, she removed its lid.

"Bishop helped me with my mom. We put some of her remains into the ocean near our house. We go there, on the anniversary of her death each year, and place flowers. We throw them into the water, and let the current carry them away. He took me there sometimes when I was having bad days. Sometimes I couldn't get out of bed, and sometimes on days when I didn't *want* to go on. But now he's gone, and I'm lost."

Ellie turned to Ruth. "But you're right. Only love now. I want him to be reconnected to this place, that he loved so much. A place I can come to visit, if that's okay, Hannah."

"Of course," Hannah said through her tears.

Ellie used both hands to gently tip the contents of the jar into the water. Fine ash poured into the lake. Part of it sunk along the dock, part swirled within the gentle waves, and part was carried off with the wind. She watched the gentle current take the remainder away into the darkness. "You're free now," Ellie said.

She closed her eyes, and felt the tiniest bit of weight move from her sternum, into her stomach, and out of her body.

Still kneeling, Ellie's muscles loosened into a heap, and she wept harder than she had in her entire life.

Part III
Ascent

Once you choose hope,
Anything is possible.

– Christopher Reeve

Chapter Thirteen

The U.S. Customs agent stared at Ellie, and repeated his question. "Ma'am, are these all yours?"

Ellie tried to focus, and not sound visibly annoyed. "Correct."

She responded to his line of questioning with direct answers: no bullshit, no fluff, no extra words; just like Bishop had taught her so long ago.

"These too?" he asked.

She calmly answered. "Yes."

Prior to meeting her husband, she couldn't remember ever getting stopped going through the border.

It seemed, however, it was standard operating protocol for Bishop.

The first time they'd taken a drive across the line for the weekend, Bishop had warned her, that they'd have to leave early because they'd be delayed while he was checked at the Customs crossing.

Ellie had laughed, and called him paranoid.

She didn't think it was so funny, after spending three hours in a check room that first time. They'd waited for their vehicle and belongings to get thoroughly inspected, and answering dozens of questions. She was upset, and had felt so utterly violated. Her husband had been treated like a criminal. She'd attempted to make a complaint, but Bishop had stopped her with a reassuring hand.

No use, he had said, tranquil as ever.

Ellie would come to realize that he was right. Bishop was stopped almost every time they crossed after that. They always called it a *random* check. But she knew better. They both did.

He wasn't white.

She had felt hurt for her husband. But Bishop always stayed patient, polite, and answered every question without hesitation. He had been groomed to do so. It was less trouble for him. So he had taught her the same. She could remember his smile.

Be cool, Bishop always said. *Be cool.*

And so, she tried to be, while she currently underwent her own actual random check. This time, for the plethora of medications she'd had to carry. This time for once, it was justified. Still, she answered as she'd been taught by her husband.

"All of this?" the Customs agent asked.

"All of it," Ellie confirmed.

"There are a lot of pills and liquids here. What is this all for? Are they supplements? Are you some kind of health nut?"

Ellie overheard a man a few tables over, agitated at being inspected, and loudly voicing his contempt.

She watched the agent go through her personal items with disdain. He picked through each bit of medication that she had carefully packed in Ziploc bags. He'd already tested a few through his illicit drug identification machine. All came back negative for narcotics. Still, he scrutinized each one.

He held up a tincture with his latex-gloved hand, and read the tiny label through squinted eyes. Ellie made a mental note to clean everything with alcohol wipes when she reached the hotel, because she was certain he didn't change his gloves between each suitcase he checked.

She felt her face go flush.

"I have an illness," she confessed to the officer. "Here is my doctor's letter. I'm allowed to travel with these."

The Border Protection Officer quickly reviewed the letter, set her things back into the bag, and zipped up the luggage— all the while scanning her with suspicious eyes. He placed it on the ground, extended the handle, and handed her back her passport. He broke his eye contact, and instead stared past her at the next victim in line. "On your way."

She retrieved her luggage, and headed towards the exit, without another word. Asshole didn't deserve a thank you.

Ellie pulled the luggage through the crowd towards her waiting friend in the bustling airport. "Jesus, Hannah."

"Everything okay? You were in there forever."

"Yeah," Ellie said. "Let's get out of here."

Hannah chuckled. "Agreed. I poked my head out while I was waiting for you. We have to take a shuttle to the car rental building. It's five minutes from here."

Suddenly, Ellie was bumped from behind, and nearly dropped her purse. She turned to find a tall man in a navy suit walking away.

He had slicked blonde hair. Square jaw. Cold blue eyes. She noticed his red necktie wrapped in a full Windsor knot.

His shoulder clipped Ellie as he walked by, while he exchanged angry words with whomever was on the other end of his cell phone. He barely acknowledged her. Instinctively, Ellie stepped behind her suitcase, trying to place some distance. She was taken aback and tried to maintain her breathing. Nervously, and quite subconsciously, she looked around for a security guard.

"Hey!" Hannah shouted. "Watch where you're going!"

The man turned mid-stride, and slowly lowered the phone; glaring at the two women. He took his time to size them up from head to toe. Ellie noticed his intense grip on the phone. A vein pulsated on his forehead. "What's the point?"

Ellie watched Hannah plant her feet firmly on the ground and lean forward, silently staring back, wordlessly. Her eyes shot laser beams into his.

Ellie's heart raced.

She wiped cold sweat from her hands onto her jeans. She hated confrontation. But she admired her friend in that moment. Was jealous even.

Hannah had metamorphosed into a fierce lioness.

"How about an apology?" Hannah growled under her breath.

The man gritted his teeth with hostility, but kept his voice low. "What's the fucking point of it all?"

He raised the phone back to his ear and continued walking towards the exit. Discretely, Ellie unlocked her cell phone and typed a sentence into the notepad, placing it back into her purse.

Ellie and Hannah stood there for a moment, and stared at each other in confusion. Hannah shrugged her shoulders, and smiled at her friend, declaring victory.

Ellie grinned back.

Ellie shouted into her cell phone. "Dad, can you hear me?"

She lowered the screen and counted the five full bars on her signal. Her father's voice cut in and out, like a malfunctioning robot. She strained to hear.

"Dad? Are you near the grocery store? I told you not to call me from there!"

Ellie cupped the phoned and glanced at Hannah behind the wheel. "For some reason, he always waits to call me until he drives past the only area in town with shitty cell signal. Fuckin' old man," she quipped.

Hannah laughed out loud, keeping her hands at ten and two. Ellie smiled at her friend, admiring the way the breeze rustled her blonde hair from the open window, dancing around her Prada sunglasses. Ellie captured a mental image of the brief, but beautiful moment, and logged it into her memory bank.

Ellie could hear the sound clear up. "Can you hear me now?" her Dad said.

"Yes, finally."

"I'm just driving to get a coffee."

"And you've just passed the corner store on seventy-second street, right?"

Her father gleamed with utter surprise. "How'd you know?"

"Just a guess."

"How was the flight, everything okay?" he asked.

"Good, and the dogs? Did Izzy get her medication, and Winston— is he okay? He doesn't like change." Her heart swelled, thinking about her little ones.

Her Dad laughed. "Yeah, they're okay. Happy. They miss you. I'll give them a kiss from you. You all settled in? How's San Diego? How's the hotel?"

"San Diego is beautiful Dad. It's warm. But we're not staying here, remember? We're going to Del Mar, where Bishop and I had our honeymoon. Same place. It's not a far drive from San Diego, though."

"Oh right," he said. "What car did you end up renting?"

She answered, acquainted with his short attention span and familiar with his common disinterest in anything truly important. "A white, Genesis GV70," Ellie answered. She glanced uncertainly at Hannah, who confirmed the car's make and model with a nod.

"Ooh, nice. Luxury."

Ellie massaged her aching wrists. "Dad, I gotta go, appreciate you calling to check in. Listen, thanks again for staying with the dogs and taking care of the house. I really appreciate it. This was really important to me."

Ellie turned, and subconsciously scanned her suitcase in the back seat. Next to her luggage, the handle of a telescopic cane jutted out of her open shoulder bag. She peered at it with contempt, trying to ignore the reminder. "This trip is important. It's something I have to do."

"I know Ellie, don't worry about anything here."

"Love you."

"Love you too," he said, hanging up the phone.

Hannah made a left onto the long private road, towards the hotel; considered one of the most luxurious in the country. They entered through large open gates, which opened up to a long windy road ahead of them.

Ellie felt as if they'd crossed through an invisible threshold into someone's peaceful dream; the highways and buildings of the city dissolving into the rear view. Her heart filled with gratitude, remembering her first and only trip here with Bishop so many years ago. They had saved for a year to be there. She had felt young. Optimistic. Naïve even.

Unbroken.

Before any of *this* had happened.

At the time of their honeymoon, she'd had only a few symptoms. But that was a lifetime ago. Surely, it was something that would go away. Some kind of temporary malady, they thought— but not something that would consume her life like a wildfire.

That thought had never even crossed into their minds. Wasn't even in the realm of possibilities.

Bishop had wanted to go to Mexico for their honeymoon, to stretch out their dollar. But eventually, they opted for a shorter, but more expensive trip to California. She rolled the window down and lavished in the warm breeze, cherishing her precious memories.

The private, narrow road looked upon meticulously kept golf greens, enveloped on all sides by lush vegetation. Palm trees peppered the landscape amongst magnificent Torrey Pine and Monterey Cypress trees. These latter species remained so incredibly special to the area. The kind a child might draw when asked to conjure up the perfect tree from their imaginations. Ellie tried to absorb the image of each one as they passed.

As they reached the top of the hill, the paved roadway melted into cobblestones. Ellie smiled at Hannah, as she watched her friend take in the glorious cast-stone fountain at the center of the roundabout, leading to the resort's entrance. Her heart fluttered. The Mediterranean-style building radiated beauty and grace against the backdrop of blue sky, like a classic Hollywood starlet in a premiere spotlight.

Hannah parked the car. She removed her sunglasses. "Ellie, we came a long way," she said. "And I think this is the most perfect place on Earth, to do what you have to do."

"I think so," Ellie agreed. "I really hope so."

Chapter Fourteen

A dark figure stood silently in the corner of Ellie's hotel room, next to the mirror.

Camouflaged in the shadows.

She couldn't make out its eyes, but instinctively knew that they were peering directly into hers. Paralyzed from fear, Ellie could barely bring herself to blink. She was helpless in every way.

Ellie wished Hannah's room was closer, and not a few doors down.

It's a dream, she repeated to herself. *It's not real.*

It's the sleeplessness, the stress, the pain. The sadness.

I'm stuck in some kind of insomnia-driven purgatory, she thought.

Still, the looming figure looked on. Too dark to make out any features. Unsure if it was even male or female: it exuded a kind of androgynous energy. But she could sense its malevolent eyes. Watching.

Ellie lay on her back in the darkness, bunched up in the covers. Too frozen to even cry. She despised being alone in that moment. She missed Bishop. She missed her dogs.

Ellie struggled to orient herself. She was unable to look away from the corner; even though every cell in her body told her to run.

Sleep paralysis held her down like a prowler, even though she was aware of being conscious. Her heart exploded in her chest. Unmoved, Ellie was forced to look on at the dark apparition observing her from its shadowed corner, unaware of its intention. She managed to close her eyes for a few moments. She focused again.

Still, the phantom watched her intently.

It wasn't the first time it had visited.

This *being*, this…*thing*, had been with her since she'd been a little girl. An ever-changing entity, who appeared when she felt most vulnerable. It chased her in her dreams.

In her logical mind, she knew who it was.

It was the personification of her *fear*, her *trauma*. It was the nameless and faceless *boogeyman* who came to see her when she was hurting.

Ellie had never kept it a secret. Bishop knew, and she'd spoken to Ruth about it. She had a sensitivity; a propensity even towards these things. That's why Bishop always said that she absorbed too much around her. From her patients, her dying mother.

And he was right.

She had woken him up on countless nights, often consumed with terror. When she'd had enough energy to break through the threshold and exhale a scream.

Ellie could never be sure what it was: *a nightmare, a ghost, an energy of some sort?*

She wasn't sure if Bishop even believed her. But he'd try, God bless him. Anything to ease her mind, anything to get her to sleep.

Once the lights came on, it was always gone.

Bishop would get up and walk around the house with a bat, shouting throughout their empty home, demanding the spirit leave their home. That it was not welcome.

That they only allowed *love* and *light* into their home.

In the morning, they'd sage the house together.

Ruth had provided Ellie some explanation, although the jury was out on that too. In these counselling sessions, Ruth had switched her hat from psychologist to that of spiritual practitioner, something that she'd had a long and rich background in. The dark energy had to do with a combination of things, and not any one— she had said.

There are energies all around us, not necessarily good or evil. Just, energies. Angels even. And Ellie, you are sensitive to them. You are a conduit, and they are attracted to you, because they know you will listen; that you will empathize.

Sometimes, these energies float around, searching endlessly; and they find you. Sometimes, they are bound to the land around your home, perhaps in your house itself, or tied to both you and Bishop. They may be passing, or they may want something.

When you are in trauma or pain, you are particularly vulnerable, because fear and sadness create an opening that can attract negative energies. It's not your fault. But when this happens, you must find the courage to ask it to leave. You must visualize a protective shield.

You can't walk around open all the time, dear.

Ellie called out into the room, as defiantly as she could. "You are not welcome here."

She closed her eyes, trying to regulate her breathing. Four seconds inhaling, and five seconds exhaling. She counted carefully, and repeated; over and over.

Energy in, through my nose.

Panic out, through my mouth.

Eventually, she opened her eyes.

The sun was starting to come up. There was just enough light to dissipate the darkness in the corner of them room. She focused.

Nothing there. No beast, lurking in the corner.

She let out a sigh of relief.

In that moment, pain swelled around her sternum. She ran into the bathroom, and vomited into the toilet.

Chapter Fifteen

Ellie solemnly walked around the hotel grounds. It was still early; the sun had barely come up, but it was already warm. Ellie sauntered forward both aimlessly and with purpose— simultaneously, trying to find a spot that spoke to her.

She discreetly massaged the muscles just above her knees as she walked. Already, her body was aching. She cursed her cane before she'd left the room, and condemned it to remain imprisoned inside the closet.

She wouldn't give it the satisfaction. Not today, anyway.

The horrible sleep last night had caused a flare-up. Today, it was body aches. Tomorrow, who knew.

She had haphazardly tied her red hair into a ponytail before she'd left the room, for once, not caring as much how she looked. Almost no makeup. By the time she reached the lobby, she immediately regretted her decision.

I shouldn't have come. I'm not ready. I should be home.

A young blonde woman in her twenties walked by with a coffee, talking into her phone, and Ellie's low self-esteem erupted again. She almost turned around, and instantly took a detour to avoid the pool areas, afraid of seeing other beautiful women in their bikinis.

As usual, she was covered up as much as possible, despite the sun. Ellie concealed her body at every turn, *especially* in California: land of beautiful people. Ellie's body wasn't anywhere near where she'd wanted it to be. Not like when she was a marathon runner. She glanced at her wrist and pulled on her sleeve. Her skin was devoid of any summer color. Subconsciously, she tucked the hair behind her ears, wondering if anyone could notice her thinning spots. Immediately, she regretted leaving the room without her hat.

She pleaded with her anxiety; with her racing heart.

Please.

Let me do this.

Ellie increased her pace and walked further into grounds, past the courtyard and marble fountain. Out of sight. Trying not to hobble. She adjusted her shoulder bag, discretely feeling for the contents inside, to ensure she hadn't lost her precious item.

The gardens behind the hotel were impeccably maintained. A stately manor, fit for royalty, designed with Tuscan influences in mind. Lush and soundless; save for the rusting of the vegetation and singing of the morning birds. With acres and endless paths to choose from, Ellie could do what she needed to do in privacy, she was sure.

Her cellphone buzzed a text notification. It was Hannah. *U up?*

Ellie welcomed the interruption, embracing the buoy in her sudden loneliness. She stopped to type: *Yes, just on a walk. Going to do that thing.*

You okay?

I think so.

Do you need me to meet you?

I'm okay.

Going for a quick run. Text me when ur back. I'm starving. I'll keep my phone with me. LY. Hannah.

Thanks. LYT.

Ellie returned the phone to her bag, and walked another twenty minutes. She embraced the feeling of being lost in a garden paradise. When she finally looked up, she was faced with her destination.

It just felt right.

She was face to face with a soaring Monterey Cypress tree. Thick trunk. Old growth. Deep, rich foliage. Ancestral.

Ellie could barely make out the top of it. Its wingspan marked off its surrounding land, creating a safe haven from the sun. Instantly, Ellie's heart bonded with it. The landscape designers must have also recognized this special place, because they had installed a park bench directly underneath. A place Ellie could return to visit. To find peace.

It was perfect.

Like a thief, she peered around to confirm her solitude.

No one.

She walked towards the tree, and knelt at its base. Ellie unslung the shoulder bag, and removed a small tin. Removing the lid, she used it to clear the grass, and dig a shallow cavity where the trunk met its roots.

She poured some of Bishop's ashes, and carefully covered up the hole.

Ellie sat at the park bench, feeling numb. She tried to think of something apt to say to memorialize him. Something profound and timeless. But nothing would come. No more than, *I miss you*. It hurt too much to think about anything else; to think of their memories, or his loss.

Ellie imagined what Bishop would want. What Ruth may have suggested. She intuitively knew that she should visualize love. To think about her time with Bishop. Imagining herself healing, bathing in light. Connecting to God. Manifesting her future. But nothing would come. Only numbness. And dizziness, and nausea, and pain. She bowed her head in defeat.

"Sweetheart?"

Ellie snapped up. A woman stood, the sun casting a halo behind her head. The light illuminated her long grey braids. She had rich black skin, and sensitive brown eyes. The woman's face glowed with vitality against her pastel lemon-yellow blouse. She exuded matriarchal energy. Like a queen. Like an angel.

Ellie was taken aback.

The woman repeated herself. "Sweetheart? Is everything okay?" She pronounced it *every-ting*, through a thick Caribbean accent.

"Ye…yes," Ellie stuttered.

"You look upset, love."

"I'm sorry," Ellie offered.

"No need to apologize."

Ellie looked to the ground, and discretely wiped her tears. The woman was balancing herself with a cane, and Ellie stared at the grey boot at the end of its chrome tip. It reminded her of the cane she'd left back in her own hotel room.

"Don't mind this thing," the woman smiled. "I'm old, but not that old! I had knee surgery a few months back. Soon I'll be getting rid of this God forsaken thing."

"Oh no, I didn't mean to…"

"It's fine," the woman laughed. "Mind if I sit?"

Ellie slid over and placed her bag onto the ground. "Please, of course."

"Where are you from?"

"Vancouver," Ellie said. "Yourself?"

"Barbados originally. Been living in Chicago for the past thirty-odd years." The woman reached out her hand. "I'm Ophelia."

Ellie nervously adjusted her hair, and smiled. "I'm Ellie. Nice to meet you."

"I surely don't mean to intrude, darling," Ophelia said. "But I just want to make sure you're okay."

"I am."

Ophelia leaned back against the bench and admired the tree. She looked lovingly into Ellie's eyes. "What's troubling you? You can talk to me, if you need."

"I lost my husband," Ellie revealed. A surprise even to herself. People, were not her thing. Strangers, even less so. Opening up to anyone— impossible.

Still, she trusted this woman. This stranger.

Surprisingly, Ellie's every spoken word brought instant catharsis. "I'm here because it's a special place for us," she said. "Where we had our honeymoon. The last place I can remember feeling any joy. I came to leave some of his remains. To try and find some closure, maybe. I left it under that tree."

Ophelia put a hand on Ellie's shoulder. "I didn't mean to interrupt sweetheart."

"Not your fault. It's okay," Ellie said. "I'm glad you came."

"That's a nice thing to do," Ophelia said. "For your husband. What was his name?"

"Bishop."

"Bishop," Ophelia repeated, as if savoring sweet tea. "That's a good name."

"He was a good man," Ellie said.

Ophelia looked to the blue sky. "The poet Dante Alighieri said: *'There is no greater sorrow than to recall in misery the time when we were happy'.*" She turned to Ellie. "Ain't that the truth."

Ellie pondered Ophelia's words. "I was thinking about how long I have left, on this Earth. When you came by. That's what I was thinking about."

"Nonsense, dear. You are a young woman. Time will heal. And you have a lifetime, still. But you know that."

"I'm sick. I have an illness."

Ophelia took Ellie's hands in hers. "Yet here you are. Now. Don't squander your time. None of us know."

Ophelia squeezed Ellie's hands. Her heart sank at the stranger's support. At a mother's love. "I'm sorry," Ellie whispered. "I shouldn't be burdening you."

"You are not burdening me, love. This is my honor. The Almighty put us together today, for a reason."

Ellie's throat quivered. "Bishop, my husband. He used to say that I wear this disease around my neck like an albatross. Like a burden. That always stuck with me."

"A dead albatross, yes," Ophelia said. "It's used as a metaphor for burden, yes. But there is another thought to it, sweetheart. A *living* albatross symbolizes innocence and hope. It can mean God's creation. One who is blessed with a divine spark. That's you too, love. Your albatross can mean both things. I can see it in you."

Ellie felt her throat constricting. Her face flushed. She took a deep silent breath, and released. "How do you know all this?"

"I was a high school teacher," Ophelia beamed. "Literature. These are all themes you're describing. A great book can change someone's life. And the church, of course. Every once in a while, all the things I've read, the things I can still remember— I can impart in my old woman's wisdom."

Ellie squeezed Ophelia's hand back. "Thank you."

"I'm here with my daughter," Ophelia said. "We are celebrating my retirement." She closed her eyes and let the sun warm her face. "It's our last day here. That's why I'm walking today. To create one last memory of this beautiful trip. I want you to join us tonight for dinner."

"I'm here with a friend," Ellie said. "Is that okay?"

"I insist," Ophelia said.

Chapter Sixteen

"You sure you don't want any wine, honey?" Amara asked Ellie, pouring herself another glass.

"I'm good," Ellie smiled. "I'll stick with my tea."

Amara turned to her left. "Mom?"

Ophelia nodded in gratitude, accepting a refill.

Ellie self-consciously shuffled in her green dress, trying to not be obvious. It was the same one she'd worn on her first date with Bishop. The one that made him light up. He told her that it brought out her eyes, and that it complimented her red hair. Most importantly: it accentuated her butt, which had always made his heart race. The dress was special to her; had made her feel beautiful, and so she'd put it on for this special occasion— not noticing that it no longer fit as well as it once did. The muscle she'd lost over the years, caused the dress the droop in areas that previously hugged those precious curves. She didn't realize the fit was off, until it was too late, and by that time— they'd already been seated.

She tried to ignore the thought, and averted her eyes; wishing she could partake in the drinking; in the mood of the table. But she feared it would interfere with her medication. The illness, never missed a chance to remind her of its grasp. Something so ordinary, yet so out of reach, as a sip of fine wine. Something so uniquely human. And something else, Ellie would have to do without.

The hotel restaurant buzzed with patrons, attracting elegantly dressed guests to celebrate the weekend. It was well deserved of its Michelin stars, and getting reservations without waiting weeks was almost impossible. Ophelia and her daughter, Amara, had generously invited Ellie and Hannah; extending their special last-night reservation to include their new friends. Ophelia couldn't be more thrilled.

Ellie sat uneasily, nervous that she wouldn't be able to get her food down, as impeccable as it looked. The lump in her throat was getting in the way. She feared that it might seize entirely, and that she'd be unable to breathe, much less eat.

Slow down, she corrected herself.

Slow. The. Fuck. Down.

Ellie took an anxious breath. She thought of Ruth, who had given her the technique to take the time to be grateful before she ate. No religion, no rules: simply a method by which to deliberately decelerate her mind, so that she could nourish her body.

And exist in the moment.

The act of feeding oneself was a sacred ritual, and should be respected.

Ellie folded her fingers beneath the table and repeated an internal mantra, trying not to stand out. She spoke the words in her head. *Be thankful,* she thought. *Food, to heal.*

Ophelia glanced over at Ellie with comforting eyes.

"I don't have to ask *you* if you want a refill," Amara laughed, turning towards Hannah, who held her glass up high.

"Ladies," Ophelia politely interjected. "Will you join me in saying grace?"

Ellie looked up and caught eyes with Ophelia. She smiled with relief.

"Of course," Hannah said.

Ophelia extended her arms and clasped Ellie's hand in one, and Amara's hand in the other. Amara and Hannah did the same, forming a perfect circle.

"Thank you, Lord, for our blessings," Ophelia began. "For this food, for this love, for our family, our community, and our friendships. Give us balance and guidance, in times of uncertainty, and help us move forward with determination. May we all be fed. May we all be healed. May we all be loved."

She opened her eyes and looked deliberately at each individual woman around the table. "Amen."

"Amen," the women repeated.

Ellie was taken aback. She squeezed Ophelia's hand in gratitude. "That was lovely."

Ophelia smiled. "Let's eat."

Ellie hadn't tasted a meal like that in years. Even better than the last time she and Bishop had visited. She savored each flavor. In between bites, she tried consciously to put extra effort into not adjusting her hair, and outfit. Trying to be comfortable in her own skin. Trying not to get lost in her lack of confidence amongst all of these beautiful strangers; amongst her wonderful new friends.

Instead, she discretely used her breathing exercises to bask in gratitude, as she chewed. Ellie looked around, thankful to be there. Thankful to be amongst new people. Trying to be present.

And for once, it was working.

For just a split second, a beacon of light felt like it had broken through the gloom. An underlying grin rested on Ellie's face, even if she was unaware it was there. She wholeheartedly embraced the momentary sense of happiness, something she hadn't felt in a long time. She listened to the after-dinner conversation, soaking up the laughter; refilling her vessel.

Ellie admired Amara's striking elegance from across the table. She watched in wonder, at Amara's amazingly confident and sophisticated energy; letting herself be inspired. Amara reminded Ellie of the actress, Danai Gurira, and effortlessly personified what a goddess would look like in Ellie's imagination. Her body was athletic, and her dark skin was flawless. No need for a woman like that to wear much makeup. Amara's short-cropped, natural hair highlighted her modelesque bone structure, and somehow, her heritage shone through. Ellie could see Amara's ancestry defined in her face. She looked like an exquisite sculpture. Like a picture-perfect photograph.

Like a *warrior*.

She tried not to stare.

"I meant to say," Hannah said, seemingly reading Ellie's mind. "Amara is such a beautiful name. Does it have a meaning?"

"It means *grace* in African, and *bitter* in Italian," Amara quipped. "I guess it's apt," she laughed at her mother.

Ophelia rubbed her daughter's shoulder. "All *grace*, darling."

Ellie's heart shuddered with envy. She could never escape the longing for her mother; in any situation. Imagining what it would be like if her mom was sitting at the dinner table with them. She would have loved Hannah, Ophelia, and Amara. She would have laughed along with them. She would have enjoyed the food. And she would have appreciated the moment.

Ellie knew her mother had lived a life, never having tasted a really fine wine. Never having seen the sun rise on another continent. Never having stepped foot in another ocean. Never having observed the different beauty of another culture.

But she deserved to. And Ellie's heart ached because of it.

"Do you have any kids?" Amara asked Ellie, while she refreshed her lipstick.

Ellie flushed. "No."

"One day?"

Ellie couldn't imagine that place, as hard as she tried. "It was never quite a thought with my husband and I," she said. "We were preoccupied by my illness."

What she left unspoken, was how big that hole was for her. In a perfect world, she would have wanted to be the kind of mother that Catherine had been to her. In her version of paradise, Bishop was alive. They'd have two or three children. A career. Health. She would run marathons until her muscles couldn't carry her any longer. It wasn't too much to ask. She glanced back at Amara. "One day," she lied. "I hope."

"This is from the gentleman at the table over there," the waiter suddenly interrupted. He set down a bottle of Merlot, and a cup of hot peppermint tea in front of Ellie. The four women glanced over.

Across the dining room, sat three men. The two in suits were discussing some paperwork on the table, while the young one in a navy blazer and white t-shirt offered a polite salute. Amara nodded back graciously, but with suspicion, on behalf of the table. She turned back to the women and raised her eyebrows, smiling.

"He's handsome," Hannah said, tipping her glass.

Ophelia grinned. "He sure is."

"Got a *Keanu* thing going on," Amara snickered. "I'll give him that."

Ellie took a sip of tea, and inadvertently met the stranger's stare. Even from that distance, she could make out his piercing green eyes. She quickly averted her gaze.

Hannah made a toast. "Ladies," she said. "I want to say thank you for inviting us to dinner. And congratulations to Ophelia on her retirement. Meeting you both has definitely been a highlight of this trip."

"Thank you," Ophelia raised her glass. "I think we all have something to celebrate; something to be thankful for."

"I love you, mum," Amara said. "I'm so proud of you, and you deserve this."

She turned to Ellie and Hannah and raised her glass even higher. "And strange as it sounds, we're also here celebrating the finalization of my divorce."

Hannah reached a hand across the table. "I'm sorry."

"Don't be," Amara replied. She took a sip and grinned. "Something to be thankful for, like mum said. I'm happy it's over, and I'm grateful to be able to move on. We have a son, Elijah, he's six. It was affecting him. His Dad and I are better apart." She turned to her mother, who returned the gesture with an approving nod. "It's better for all of us," she continued. "He's a better father, and a better business partner now."

"What do you do?" Ellie inquired.

"We own a design studio. He's a general contractor and I'm an interior designer. We started with small projects, one room at a time— just the two of us. Kitchens, bathrooms. We've since moved onto designing entire homes, and in the last two years, have expanded into commercial spaces and offices. It's a dream, really."

Ellie's heart swelled. This woman was living her best life. "I love interior design," she said. "Something I wished I'd pursued."

"Never too late, love," Ophelia encouraged.

Isn't it? Ellie thought, shaking her head, dismissing the idea.

Amara reached into her purse and slid Ellie a business card. "Please keep in touch Ellie, I'm happy to answer any questions. I agree with mum; you should think about it."

"You've been quiet Hannah," Ophelia said. "What about you? What are you celebrating?"

Hannah's eyes welled. She didn't need to think about it. "My daughter," she said. "Like Amara, her Dad and I have split. But I'm thankful for her. And the remission. This was Ellie's trip; I was tagging along. But I've since realized how much it was mine too."

"It's *ours*," Ellie said. "I'm thankful for *you* Hannah. You came when I needed you most, and you're helping show me the way out of a dark place. And I can never repay you for that, except to say, I'm here for you too. And you, Ophelia and Amara. Any more inspired, I could not be. You were right, Ophelia. There was some divine purpose into us meeting. I feel that."

"I can see what's underneath your veil," Ophelia said. "And I know you're in pain. But you are not alone. There is a saying: *The pain you feel today will be your strength tomorrow.* And all four of us know that all too well." She stopped to savor her wine. "You are here for your husband," she said. "To scatter his remains. To help him find peace, to show him love. And that's good. But this is your life too, Ellie."

Ophelia glanced around the table. "All of you. If there is one thing I've learned, it's that we must follow *our* passions. This life is about *us*, and we women, are the heroines in our own stories. Everyone else is a supporting character. We have commitments, to raise our children. To take care of our husbands, our parents, our families. But that shouldn't come as a sacrifice. Take care of business, ladies. But pick up when you need to. You go, Ellie. All of you. And chase what's important to you. Find your passions, and heal yourselves."

Silence befell the table. As far as the women were concerned, it was as if they were the only four souls around for hundreds of miles. Each within her own realm, manifesting their destinies. Visualizing their hope. They smiled at one another, knowingly.

"Ladies," Ophelia broke the silence. "Please accept my apologies, but this old lady is tired. And the wine didn't help. We have an early plane ride tomorrow."

Hannah and Ellie stood to exchange hugs with Amara and her mother. "You two keep in touch," Ophelia said.

Ellie took Ophelia aside and warmly held her hands. "I cannot thank you enough. For, everything. I appreciate you being there when I needed you."

"And I, you. We will meet again in this life, I hope." Ophelia hugged Ellie tight. "Today is the oldest you've ever been, and the youngest you'll ever be. Find your joy, knowing that. Yesterday to tomorrow, love."

"Bye Ophelia," Ellie choked out.

"It's not *goodbye*, my dear— it's '*I'll see you later*'."

Ellie was surprised at the depth at which her heart stung, having to say goodbye to a stranger she hadn't known twenty-four hours ago. She and Hannah watched Amara carefully escort her mother into the elevator.

"She's right, you know," Hannah reflected, untying her ponytail.

"About what?"

"About everything. About how we put everyone's needs before our own. That we neglect ourselves in the process, trying to be perfectionists. We don't accept help enough, and we undervalue ourselves, living in a subconscious state of self-deprecation. Do you feel that?"

Ellie sighed. "Every day."

"We neglect our own care and mental health, and reject when someone tells us we're doing well." She took another sip of wine. "Why is that? Why do we do that?"

"I don't know," Ellie replied. "Something I've been speaking to Ruth about."

"It's made us sick," Hannah said. "It's not all of it, but it's contributed."

"But days like this heal us too. Refill the tank," Ellie said. "I'm slowly learning that, I guess."

"Amen, sister," Hannah smiled.

Ellie looked towards the men at the other table, and caught eyes again with the man who had sent the wine. He smiled and nodded. This time, she let the connection linger for a moment longer, before breaking eye contact. She tucked her hair behind her ears.

"Keanu can't keep his eyes off you," Hannah laughed.

Ellie dismissed her comment and flushed. The man stood to his guests, who were packing up. As they shook hands, he nervously glanced at Ellie again.

Hannah watched them interact. "Here he comes," she whispered into her wine glass.

The man headed towards them, confident, buttoning up his navy blazer. Ellie noticed his retro black-and-white Air Jordan's, as he strode across the dining room. He moved with poise, even through his tall and lanky frame. He reached out a hand. "I'm Tom."

"Thanks for the wine, Tom," Hannah said, shaking his hand. "I'm Hannah."

"And thanks for the tea," Ellie said, feeling her ears getting red. She shook his large hand, and subconsciously scanned. Thin fingers, no wedding ring.

Instant guilt.

She shut the thought out. "I'm Ellie."

Tom combed his dark hair back with his hand. "Mind if I join you? Can I get you a coffee, or another tea?"

Hannah turned to Ellie, and put her purse over her shoulder. "Actually, we were just heading out."

She paused to read Ellie's expression, and winked discreetly at her friend. Tom was too busy gazing into Ellie's eyes to notice. "But if you want to walk us to the front desk, that's okay," Hannah said.

They stood in the center of the quiet and opulent hotel lobby, in an awkward triangle. Ellie could feel the heat emanating from her face. Her left hand nervously fidgeted with the leather of her purse strap.

Ellie tried to think of something to say. "Were those your friends?" she asked, instantly feeling stupid.

"Those two suits?" Tom chuckled. "No. Those were business associates. We were finalizing a contract."

"Are you a hitman?" Hannah joked.

"Not exactly," Tom laughed. "I'm a musician."

"Well Tom, it was nice meeting you," Hannah said. "But we should be getting back. And thanks again for the wine."

As they began walking away, Tom called out. "Ellie," he said. "Can you hang back for a second?"

Ellie nodded at Hannah. Hannah shot an astonished glance back at Ellie. She raised her voice to ensure Tom was paying attention. "I'll head back then. I'm only down the hall, and a phone call away." She drew Ellie close for a hug and whispered in her ear. "You sure? Will you be okay?"

"I'll be okay," Ellie said, hugging her back and receiving a kiss on her cheek. "I won't be long, and I've got my phone."

"Text me when you're in your room. You've got five minutes," Hannah winked.

Ellie reassured her. "Okay."

Hannah nodded sternly at Tom and headed for the elevator, her heels clacking along the floor until they faded into silence. No one else was around. Tom waited for the elevator doors to close, and bell to sound, before he spoke. "Ellie, I was hoping maybe I could take you out?"

Ellie was taken by surprise. "What?" she said in shock.

"Dinner, maybe?"

She let out a nervous laugh, clutching at his forearm. "Tom, I'm sorry. I didn't mean it like that. I didn't expect that," she said, trying not to make him feel bad. A few weeks ago, she didn't want to live. She'd only recently started to feel like a human being again. She felt horrible, looked horrible. She was a mess. And now this stranger was asking her out? "Why?" she blurted out.

"Because you seem kind," he smiled. "You have good energy. I can't quite explain it."

Ellie smiled. Her heart fluttered, and she tried desperately not to cry. She looked to the ground, unsure of what to say.

He nervously reached into his jacket and handed her a business card. "I can pick you up in the lobby here tomorrow evening?"

She only contemplated for a few seconds before answering, hearing Ophelia's voice in her head, telling her to take the chance. "Okay," she said, feeling the air leave her lungs.

"I'll meet you here at six," he smiled confidently.

"Great," she said.

Tom waved goodbye, and walked towards the front entrance of the hotel. Once Ellie reached the elevator, she turned over his business card:

Thomas King. Composer/Musician. San Diego, California.

Chapter Seventeen

Ellie watched the soft blue ocean waves roll onto the sandy beach, letting the crashing sounds bring her peace before they receded back towards the horizon. She tried to be present in the moment, even though she felt terrified. She clasped her sore fingers while she nervously waited for Tom to return from the kitchen, and delicately sipped the lovely Cabernet Sauvignon that he had poured for her.

The air was warm, so she had removed her sweater. She watched the setting sun illuminate the evening sky with pretty pink and orange clouds. Even though the neighboring houses were relatively close, the private beach was empty. No sounds, except for the wind and waves. She had never in her life seen a house so amazing.

It wasn't mansion-sized, but was much more than what was needed for just one person; that was for sure. She hadn't taken a full tour yet, but could sense its expansiveness from the entry alone. If she imagined the perfect home, it would be this. Modern, clean lines— open concept. A beach house to be envied; like the kind of home you see when you close your eyes.

It had an infinity pool next to a gas fire pit, filled with rocks that looked like diamonds. They sparkled with every lick of the flame, and Ellie sat hypnotized at its beckoning.

She was situated on the elegant wicker patio set, just a few steps up from the white-sand, private beach. Dancing palm trees lined the landscape as far out as she could see. It was luxurious paradise. The only thing missing, she jokingly thought, was a helicopter pad. She'd wondered if all this was really his and had spent the evening so far, trying to figure him out. Ellie wondered why a man so handsome and successful would be single. And more importantly, why he would have asked her out.

She placed her palms together under the table and discreetly sent a prayer into the universe, begging that he wasn't a serial killer. She also prayed that her ribcage pain wouldn't get any worse. That she'd be able to eat without feeling nauseous. And that her brain fog would let her get through a conversation without slipping up and looking stupid. Lastly, she gave thanks for the momentary, but joyful moment— something she'd been aching for. For this second anyway, most of her pain had subsided; emotional and physical alike.

"I hope you're hungry," Tom said, placing a plate in front of Ellie.

She looked up at him in utter surprise, inhaling the appetizing aroma. "You made this?"

"Linguini with vegetables in a Roma tomato and basil sauce," he said. "I'm glad I called this morning and figured out you were a vegan, before I accidentally cooked you a porterhouse steak."

Ellie laughed and took a sip of wine. "I might have eaten it anyways," she flirted.

He had picked her up from the hotel, right on time, and had driven her along the scenic Pacific Coast highway with the panoramic sunroof open, until they reached an incredibly swanky neighborhood. It seemed every house had gated entrances, four-car garages, immaculate gardens, and rooflines that reached into outer space; obscuring the majestic ocean views that hid behind.

Ellie hadn't protested too much when Hannah had insisted that she setup the *Emergency Location Sharing* app on her cell phone. "If you haven't reported back," Hannah had said. "I'm kicking that fucking door down." Ellie had laughed with Hannah at the remark, but felt a lot better that she'd had such a good friend to watch her back. Now that Bishop was gone, she'd been feeling more and more vulnerable.

When they pulled up to Tom's home, Ellie's jaw had dropped. She had assumed that perhaps he'd been renting it, until she noticed framed pictures of he and his mother in the living room. He'd shown her the stunning main floor, expansive chef's kitchen, and custom recording studio in the basement— which housed his vast collection of plaques, crystal pyramid

Ellie's Albatross

awards, and gold records bearing his name. And of course, the pool and backyard. She hadn't seen any of the bedrooms yet.

"We could have gone out," Ellie said. "You didn't have to cook, really. Although I really appreciate it. It looks amazing."

"That makes me happy," he said.

Ellie wasn't kidding either. The meal was spectacular, and she couldn't get enough of it. "This home. This view, Tom," she said, taking a bite. "It's unbelievable. You should be proud." As she scanned his handsome face, her thoughts swirled back to wondering how he was so well put together, waiting tentatively maybe, for the other shoe to drop. When he made eye contact, she broke the gaze and nervously looked into her food. She hadn't been on a date since meeting Bishop, all those years ago. Part of her knew she wasn't ready; it was too fresh still.

Another part of her, wanted to explore the possibilities; guilty as she felt.

She'd tried to take her own life not long ago, and her circumstances hadn't changed since. However, her sense of gratitude was starting to. She'd been forcing herself to. Knowing that her father was there to support her, and her dogs were there to love her back unconditionally. She was luckier than most other people. Ellie felt deep remorse in that moment, chewing her food— thinking about what she had almost done to them.

When it couldn't get any worse; all of a sudden, the universe had opened up. She'd been making new friends. And now, found herself on a date with a stranger; in California of all places. In that moment, while the sun set, the wine breathed, and the steam emanated from her pasta— she reflected on these things.

As the darkness of evening took hold, Tom served her tea and a side plate of fresh strawberries, smothered in dark chocolate. She was thankful that she'd managed to make it through dinner without getting any tomato sauce on her light-blue floral sundress. It had been one of Bishop's favorites. She hadn't been shopping for herself in so long; everything she had, reminded her of him.

"This is for you," Tom said, placing a neatly folded knit blanket in her lap. His movements were patient and gentle. Although the air was warm and still; the blanket provided some additional comfort for Ellie.

She looked up. The cloudless night sky beamed with stars. Ellie reached for his hand in gratitude. "Thank you," she said.

"Do you need anything else?"

"I'm okay," Ellie said.

He stared into her eyes, smiling. She tucked her hair behind her ears again, praying he wouldn't notice the thinning patches. Ellie hoped he wouldn't make out her skin blemishes in the dim light, and tried to stop her heart from racing with insecurity. She tried to slam it below the surface with a sledgehammer. He made eye contact. The moment he did, she started thinking of ways to make an exit. Any excuse. He wouldn't like her anyways. She was too damaged.

Who was he anyways? Can I trust him?

"Where did you grow up?" Tom asked.

"Vancouver Island," Ellie said. "In a small beach town. We moved to the city a few years ago. My husband and I."

Tom stopped chewing his dessert. His eyebrows leaped in shock. He looked like he'd been caught shoplifting. Immediately, his eyes moved to her left hand; obvious, that he'd missed her wedding ring. Ellie looked down at her finger. She'd forgotten she was still wearing Bishop's commitment to her. She gasped.

"Husband?" Tom asked, placing his hands on the armrests, as if he was about to bolt away. "I didn't realize. Is this okay, us eating dinner?"

"My *departed* husband," Ellie corrected herself. She caressed her ring. "I forget that I'm wearing it sometimes."

Tom eased his elbows, and settled back into his seat. "I'm so sorry Ellie, I didn't know."

"I'm the one who's sorry," Ellie reassured him. "It wasn't long ago, and I should have mentioned it." She quickly read his expression and changed the subject. "And you? Where are you from?"

Tom shone with pride. "Here. San Diego. My parents are from Ireland, originally. They came to the U.S. in the seventies. And I was born here shortly after."

"You said you were a musician. What do you play? Anything I'd have heard?"

"Maybe," Tom said. "I play a few instruments. Drums, piano, guitar. I started with a few local bands when I was a teenager, and studied music composition at UCSD. When I was twenty, a friend from college asked me to score his directorial debut. The movie went on to break some box office records. I've been scoring movies and animated films ever since; the rest is history."

"Those guys you were with?" Ellie asked.

"Those were producers from Hollywood." Tom's green eyes lit up with excitement in the firelight. "Possible new movie deal. Big, movie deal."

Ellie beamed. "That's great, I'm happy for you."

"Well, I'm terrified," he said.

"Why?"

"I still get nervous," Tom said.

"That's not a bad thing."

"No," Tom said. "I guess not. Keeps me sharp. I'm afraid of failing. Guess that's it."

Ellie looked around. "I don't think you need to worry about that, you're doing fine," she said. "My husband was like that. He pushed himself to be the best that he could. But it got in his own way sometimes."

Tom smiled. "I can relate." He reached for his espresso. "What are you doing here, so far from home?"

Ellie sighed, gathering her confidence, trying not to overwhelm him. "I'm not exactly sure, to be honest," she said. "I suppose I'm looking for some sense of direction, after his loss. A change of scenery. Hannah came to support me, which helps."

Ellie hesitated. Suddenly, the momentary self-assurance deflated like a swirling hot air balloon, heading for a crash landing. Her face felt hot. Ellie second-guessed herself. She felt stupid. "I'm sorry," she said. "It's heavy, I know. I shouldn't have said that. We just met."

Tom laughed. "What? No. It's good to be honest, I appreciate it."

Ellie looked to the sky, and focused on the stars, embracing the night breeze. She listened to the sound of the wind rustling the trees. She searched for her grounding. Ellie wondered how long it would take for Tom to run. She was unsure of his intentions anyway.

"Listen," he reassured her. "It's okay."

Jesus, he does look like Keanu.

Ellie wanted to let her guard down, and be vulnerable even. Trust, was a locked door for her these days.

"If we're being open," Tom said. "I lost my mom six months ago. Breast cancer. I've been thinking about her tonight, because she would have been proud of me. She was the one who encouraged me to pursue my passion for music. Everything I have, is because of her. I've been trying to come to terms with it, like you, for your husband."

"Your Dad?" Ellie asked.

"He shut down on me," Tom said. "He's dealing with it in his own way."

"I'm sorry," Ellie said.

"Shit, maybe I need a vacation too."

"I'm sorry about your mom," Ellie said. "I understand what that feels like."

He nodded. "Sometimes I take my acoustic guitar and play at the palliative care center, where she was. At the end, I mean. Feels like I'm playing for ghosts sometimes. But it helps people, I guess. I hope. I have to do *something*."

Ellie released a breath.

Something stirred. White-hot energy. A mix of instant raw emotion: hurt, love, admiration, guilt, excitement. Maybe even lust. All at the same time.

Ellie felt her jugular throbbing. She wanted to kiss him so badly in that moment, but repressed her urge, as deep as it would go.

Still, it nagged. She hadn't felt that feeling in a long time. Those electric butterflies. She'd given up on it. Didn't realize it was there.

For a split second, Ellie fantasized herself lunging across the table and holding Tom's face, kissing him on the mouth. Hard. She imagined a hissing fire igniting between them. Maybe it would take his hurt away, and maybe he would do the same for her. Maybe everything would be okay, if she just did that. Ellie wished she'd had the courage to release her inhibitions. To fling her reluctance and angst to the wind, and truly just live in the moment.

More wine might help, she thought, reaching for her glass.

Ellie crossed her legs. Her heart fluttered.

"Did I say too much?" Tom asked, leaning forward.

Ellie felt like she'd fallen from the sky, and splattered down to Earth. "What? No. Not at all."

"I wasn't sure where you went for a second there," Tom said.

"It's just..." Ellie said. "Well, I'm a bit of a mess right now. I'm not sure why you asked me out."

"Because I think you're beautiful," Tom said without hesitation. He smiled. "To me, you were the only woman in the room."

The comment was so unexpected, that it knocked the wind out of Ellie. *Beautiful*, was the last thing she felt about herself right now.

"Something about you," Tom continued. "Maybe it's an energy thing. It resonates. It was an instant attraction. You're a good person; I can feel that. That's what matters to me. I just wanted to be near you the moment I laid eyes on you. I couldn't let you walk away," he said. "Even now, I'm nervous." He looked down at his feet. "You're making my heart race. That doesn't happen often to me."

Ellie wanted to be closer to him too and she couldn't redirect the thought. But it was met with instant guilt. About Bishop. She hadn't been with anyone else. This wouldn't go further than just one night; of that she was sure.

How could it?

Ellie wasn't here looking for a relationship. She couldn't pull someone else into her whirlwind, taking him down her spiral— like she had poor Bishop. This sickness, it was too much to put on anyone else.

He took her hand in his. "That's a lot to say, I know," he smiled. "But you asked."

She glanced at the moonlight shimmering on the ocean. Each thundering wave crashed onto her heart. As if suddenly possessed, she leaned in and clutched his jacket collar with both hands. Despite her brain telling her otherwise, Ellie opened up; allowing her body to succumb to the impulse. She let herself be taken by the current.

Ellie stared into Tom's green eyes, and kissed him.

Fuck it, she thought.

She let herself be vulnerable, even unsafe for a moment... if that's what it meant to live life happily, for just a second. Without pain. And with a little bit of joy, fleeting as it may be.

She kissed him softly at first. But her primal hunger grew. Ellie bit his lip, feeling it swell, and unearthed a passion that dredged up from a place of deep slumber. One that she'd long assumed had perished, with Bishop. It awoke in her like a star going supernova, bursting energy in every direction. She could feel her skin come alive; blood throbbing just beneath the surface.

Tom kissed her back, lightly holding her cheeks. He returned her embrace with intensity, but still somehow maintained a sense of tenderness. Of adoration.

She felt her heart drop.

He kissed her on the forehead. And then her neck. Tom took a long, deep breath and inhaled her in. Ellie could feel his pulse as they embraced.

She recalled his voice again. *I wasn't sure where you went for a second there.*

"I'm here," Ellie finally said.

Tom took another stunned breath, and touched her forehead with his. He held the back of her head with his hand, grasping her red hair. "That caught me off guard," he said. "It was nice."

She straightened her dress. "It was."

"I don't know what's going on," Tom said, holding his chest. "I feel like I'm being electrocuted. I don't want this night to end."

Ellie stood and clasped Tom's hand, leading him silently towards the house. He followed for a few steps until they reached the threshold of the great room, and then took the lead. As Tom led her towards the master bedroom, her heart raced with so many emotions. Exhilaration and fear at the same time. Excitement and uncertainty. He turned towards her. "You sure?"

Ellie nodded and continued to follow him along. She didn't take notice of anything in the bedroom; the impeccably ironed white duvet cover, the expensive hand-crafted furniture, the high-end finishes, the spotlessness.

She saw only him.

They stood in the center of the room and undressed each other, still standing. Ellie undid the buttons on his shirt and let it fall to the floor. She gently ran her fingers over the sunflower tattoo on his muscular shoulder. From the brilliant yellow color, Ellie could tell it was fresh ink. Instinctively, she knew it was to commemorate his mother. He held her on both sides, just above the hips.

She looked up at him, and he lowered to her— decreasing the immense height difference between them, and kissed her. Tom held the small of her back and lifted her onto him. She wrapped her legs around his torso, and he gently sunk her onto the bed. He kissed every inch of skin he could, and she felt his warmth; his kindness, his care. Ellie pushed her head back against the pillow, and inhaled— mouth wide open.

Ellie felt her twinge of passion turn into angst. You could love someone for a minute, or a lifetime— then in the next instant, fear losing them. She took another deep breath, and let herself be free of the guilt. Instead, she plunged head-first into their desire for one other, and relaxed her body. She breathed, surrendering herself to him. He pushed his hips forward.

Even as they connected so intimately, she knew: this would be the last time she'd see him.

Chapter Eighteen

"Are you *ever* gonna tell me about Tom?"

Despite the unrelenting tinnitus ringing in her ear, Ellie grinned. "What is it that you want to know?"

"Everything," Hannah laughed. "Every last, filthy detail. You can't keep that shit to yourself."

Ellie felt her face flush, and tried to keep from smirking. She rubbed her ear with the palm of her hand. The ringing persisted.

"Let me read this text from Dad first," she said, turning to Hannah. "Turn off the car. I don't want you to go yet. We can sit in the driveway for a bit, if you can't come in. I know you have to get back to your little girl. But we'll make it quick."

Hannah cut the ignition.

Ellie glanced at the dash clock. Early afternoon: her favorite time of day. Glad to be home. Glad to be inhaling the British Columbian fresh air.

She unlocked her phone.

> *Hi Ellie. I got your message from the airport. Was out walking the dogs. I left the house at 11. Dogs are fed. They should be good. I'm sorry I missed you, but I had to rush to catch the ferry, otherwise I'd be home too late. Text me when you're home. Be back next week. LOL. Dad.*

Ellie chuckled. "My Dad," she said. "He always ends texts with 'LOL'. He thinks it means 'lots of love'."

Hannah roared out a deep belly laugh, bracing her hands against the steering wheel. Ellie joined her friend, until tears were rolling down both their cheeks. Hannah finally caught her breath and wiped her red face. "You ever tell him what it really means?"

"A couple of times," Ellie said, still chuckling. "But he forgets. It cheers me up, seeing him type it out of context. So, I just leave it now. Sometimes, he sends it in the worst moments. Like one time, he said, 'Aunt Esther passed away, poor lady. LOL'."

Hannah could barely contain herself, and laughed so hard, she went silent for nearly a minute, mouth agape. She waved her hands in the air in surrender, still shrieking with laughter. "I shouldn't laugh," she exclaimed in between breaths. "I shouldn't laugh."

"I know," Ellie smiled, massaging the sore muscles in her abdomen.

She typed back a response to her father and locked her phone.

> *Hi Dad. Thanks for everything. Home now. Will call you later. XO*

Ellie's vertigo swelled. Not surprisingly. The trip, the plane's altitude, the hotel bed— even laughing as hard as she did just now.

The illness, never let up. Never let her have a moment.

Her smile slowly faded.

She squeezed her forehead in frustration, resisting the urge to bash her head onto the dashboard to make the lightheadedness go away.

Hannah looked concerned at the sudden change in Ellie's demeanor. "You okay?"

Ellie peered through her passenger side window and nodded. Her heart sunk. "It'll pass," she said. "Thanks for putting up with me Hannah. I know it gets in the way. I know it kills the mood sometimes."

Hannah placed a reassuring hand on Ellie's shoulder, wordlessly.

Ellie closed her eyes.

Reset, she thought.

It will pass.

Don't resist it, it only makes it worse. Open the door. Let it come in and then leave in the other direction. Focus on something nice while you wait for it to go.

She opened her eyes.

The vibrant green grass was cut short, thanks to her Dad. In fact, the entire yard looked amazing. He could never stand still, and had taken it upon himself to trim everything for her while she was away. Every topiary was immaculately formed, and not a single leaf sullied the front lawn. The house looked immaculate, just like when Bishop took care of it.

Watching the autumn breeze move the leaves, she felt some energy shift.

It was her favorite time of year; the first few weeks of September, and she took a moment to revel in the scene outside through her open car window. Kids were back at school. God love them, but it made the neighborhood a little quieter. Heat from late summer was still afoot but the leaves had started to turn to shades of deep red and orange. It was a balance of past, present, and future converging in a perfect nexus.

Ellie made a mental note to thank her Dad for taking care of everything so well.

"So?" Hannah pressed. "We were in California for a week, and I didn't ask a word about Tom. We flew to Vancouver, not a peep. We drove home from the airport, and still nothing. At least tell me if you're going to see him again. Before I go. Are you going to keep in touch? Give me that much."

Hannah paused. "And most importantly: was it… *good*?"

"No, no, and… yes."

"What?" Hannah laughed.

"It was good, yes," Ellie said. "Different. I felt a lot of remorse afterwards, you know? I haven't been with someone other than Bishop in a very long time, in any way. But it was nice. Something I have to wrap my head around. Tom was kind, gentle. Caring. Everything I could have hoped for. I was lucky."

"It's okay to be with someone else, Ellie. There has to come a time when your life returns to being about you again."

Ellie hesitated. "I know."

"So, you're not going to keep in contact?"

"There were sparks, yes, but this doesn't have to be about him. I don't want that. He made me feel a little confident again. Made me remember who I used to be. Who I am. Helped me to see, that maybe I could love again. Maybe. But I don't need Tom to do that," Ellie said. "Does that make sense?"

"It makes sense, Ellie."

"He held up a mirror, you could say, so that I could catch a glimpse," she said.

"I agree you shouldn't jump in, but *nothing*?" Hannah asked, tying her blonde her back. "No number, no email, no Facebook, no Insta? *Nothing*?"

"Nothing. It was a moment in our trip. In my life. I'm okay with that."

Hannah winked. "Sometimes they're supporting characters."

Ellie nodded, reflecting on Tom. "But he *did* look like Keanu, didn't he?"

Before Hannah could answer, a white Volkswagen SUV pulled into the neighbor's driveway. Both girls cocked their heads to see. Her neighbors Sean, Elias, and their son Roland exited the vehicle and began carting groceries into the house. Ellie shouted through the open car window. "Hey guys!"

They all turned their heads and smiled. The taller of the two, Sean, called back.

"Ellie! We missed you, welcome back!"

The boy waved. Ellie blew him a kiss. He shyly smiled.

"We just pulled up," Ellie said, leaning her head back. "This is my friend Hannah. Hannah, this is Sean and Elias. And that handsome young man over there is Roland. No school today, kiddo?"

"It's Saturday," Roland smiled.

"Oh yeah," Ellie said. "I forgot."

Hannah leaned over and waved. Roland blushed, and ran into the house after Elias, who had an armful of brown paper bags.

"Need help with your luggage?" Sean asked Ellie, rummaging through the cargo space of the SUV.

"No, thanks."

"We stopped at Pottery Barn on the way home from the grocery store. Elias is on this mid-century-modern kick. He's redecorating the whole house. It'll take me an hour to unload this damn car."

"I'll see you later," Ellie chuckled.

He nodded back, and carried on.

She turned towards her friend. "Hannah. Go home, get settled in. See your daughter. If you're up for it, let's do dinner this week. These last few months have meant everything to me, and it's all because of you. I want to take you out." She reached for Hannah's hand. "I can't ever repay you for what you've done for me. I was in a horrible place. But *someone* sent you to me. And now? Now, I'm in a *less* horrible place. It's one more step I'm thankful for."

Hannah leaned across and embraced Ellie as hard as she could. She didn't say a word. Ellie could sense her softly whimpering. She squeezed back, thanking God for her friend.

Ellie unloaded the luggage and watched her friend drive away. Before she reached the door, she could hear Izzy and Winston whining. With each ascended step, the sounds turned to moaning, and then to frenzied barking as she unlocked the door.

Mama was finally home.

Izzie stood on her hind legs, like a perfectly balanced ballerina, awaiting her attention; half-stepping around the rug. Winston ran in circles. Both displayed toothy canine smiles. Ellie smiled back at them, truly happy to be home. She knelt and hugged both of them, caught in a frenzy of tail wags and doggy breath.

She quickly closed the door behind her so they wouldn't bolt, and dropped to her knees. Ellie cried tears of happiness at seeing her fur babies. Winston shrieked so loud, that it pierced Ellie's ears, on top of the tinnitus. Smiling, she hugged him tight, while Izzy danced around the foyer, wiggling her butt.

She calmed them down and carried in her luggage. Izzie and Winston, now content their mom was home, lay together on the couch; their black and white fur intertwined like a natural yin-yang.

As Ellie walked through the entry, she noticed an unfamiliar shape through her periphery. It jolted her for a second, until she realized it was an inanimate object, and not a looming attacker.

In the corner of the room, there was a walnut-colored, upright piano. It was in good shape, but an ancient instrument; she could tell that right away.

Carefully resting, where a music book would go, was an envelope. She opened it, to find a hand-written letter inside. She recognized the neat hand-writing instantly. It was from her father.

Ellie,

This was your grandfather's piano, as you might remember when you were little. It's been in uncle Jim's basement collecting dust for decades. The family thought it would be nice to have it restored for you. I picked a spot, but can help you move it next time I come by. I hope you play it.

LOL.

—Dad.

Chapter Nineteen

Ellie stood in the center of her new office, hands on her hips, proud of what she'd accomplished. She was wearing blue jeans and one of Bishop's striped collared shirts, with the sleeves rolled up. On her hands: a pair of blue nitrile gloves, and on her head: a white bandana to keep the dust from getting in her hair.

Light poured in from the window. She looked around, feeling it breathe new life into the space.

It had once been Bishop's office. The place he worked, where he practiced playing guitar, and where he wrote his unpublished short stories.

The ones that only Ellie had read.

She'd spent the entire morning carefully boxing and labelling up his belongings. But only those things that she couldn't reuse, for the moment. Files and papers mostly. Everything that reminded her of him, stayed. Even the black guitar she had given him for Christmas. It rested against the corner wall, where she'd left it after wiping it spotless.

She had made two stops the previous day: one to the local home décor store, and the other to the Office Superstore Warehouse.

It was time, that she started to make the room her own.

She'd gotten up early, to start tackling the house, afraid that she'd struggle to find the vitality. There was a ton of cleaning and organizing to do. But…it was a new day. Little bit at a time, if that's what it took. She glanced at the desktop calendar, pausing to realize it had been nearly a year since Bishop had died. It had taken her this long to build up the mental energy to even step in the room.

Ellie coiled up the guitar cables, and packed them with a stack of picks and instrument accessories into a small box. She opened the closet door, scanning for a space to put them, when her eyes caught something she'd missed. A wrapped cardboard box. Looked to be a gift of some sort.

How could I not have seen this?

She reached for the mysterious package, hands shaking; not quite sure why. Ellie examined the box. It was eloquently wrapped in expensive black paper, and sealed with a white silk ribbon. Out of sorts for Bishop, who couldn't properly wrap a present if his life depended on it. This was professionally done.

Bishop had no secrets. *Did he?* Christmas had just passed when he died. Their anniversary was in April, and her birthday wasn't until September. So who could it have been for? Odd. She had a flash in her head. *Did he have a mistress?*

She thought about the possibilities; the suspects: *Someone from work? Someone he met online? Someone she knew? One of their friends?*

Judy. Nora. Oh my God— Hannah?

Please God, not Hannah.

Ellie leaned her back against the wall and slid down, cradling the box in her lap. She pondered whether it was right to open it; that maybe it wasn't meant for her. She shook it against her ear: no sound. It barely had any weight, just enough to know there was *something* inside. It was her house, and the belongings of her husband— yet she felt as if she'd be betraying him by opening it up.

She gently tugged on the ribbon and it came undone in a single movement. Ellie opened the lid of the box. Inside, was a plain white card inscribed in Bishop's handwriting: *Ellie. Love Bishop.*

Her heart dropped.

Curious, she set the card aside and carefully removed the pink tissue that concealed its contents. Inside, was a wooden picture frame with a photograph of Ellie as a teen. Maybe thirteen or fourteen. It was a moment in time, that she struggled to recall. Gone, from her memory bank.

She was sitting atop a beach blanket on the sand. Ocean behind her, wind blowing her bright red hair. Laying contently on the blanket next to her, was her beloved childhood pet, Toby: her first Miniature Schnauzer.

The little girl's eyes were transfixed upon a dragonfly that flew near the edge of the frame. She smiled naturally, as if someone captured the moment after asking her what she wanted to be when she grew up. There was wonder in her sparkling green eyes. And hope. She looked happy. Ellie stared at the picture, trying to remember who she used to be.

Maybe that was the point.

But she'd never be able to ask Bishop, and her heart ached at that thought. She wondered about the moment the picture was captured. Surely, Ellie's mother must have taken it, but she couldn't remember. In the moment, she recalled what Bishop had often said to her, that she would've made a good mom. Ellie had cast that thought in concrete and flung it into the ocean. She would never have imprisoned a child with her illness. She could never bring a child into the world, knowing they'd be burdened to take care of their mother, like Ellie had had to do for her own. It was enough that Ellie's period was a day late when she'd returned home from California. She'd panicked, thinking about those things. And when it finally came, she felt heartbroken at being reminded she'd never be a mother.

She stared at the object in her hands. Beneath the picture frame, was a small jewelry box. Ellie set the photograph aside, and opened it. Inside, was a gold chain, attached to a gleaming pendant, encrusted with Blue Sapphire.

A dragonfly.

She held the box against her chest, and kissed the pendant, remembering her husband. She recollected the bond they shared, and felt overwhelmed by his love in that moment. She was breathless. Somehow he was managing to speak to her from beyond the other side. She whispered into the open, empty room. "Thank you."

Ellie stood, with a renewed sense of energy.

She stepped back and examined the room. Still, a lot to do, but it was a good start. And the fresh white roses in the glass vase were perfect. Bishop would have been proud of her. Of what she had done with the space.

Ellie had managed to fasten a large corkboard to the wall, using Bishop's drill and level. She'd done a pretty damn good job too. She could visualize the finished product, and knew exactly what she wanted to do with it. She'd get back to it, but ached to christen the bulletin board right away. It would only be right.

Ellie closed her eyes and tried to find inspiration. Tried to visualize a peaceful place. One with good energy. She scribbled a few words on a piece of blue cardstock with a black felt pen. She hated her handwriting, and crumpled it into the garbage. She reevaluated, and slowly wrote again; this time, satisfied with the outcome.

Ellie used a tack and pinned up the card on the wall.
She stepped back and read.

Travel more.

Good enough for now, she considered. She'd make some time tonight to add more. But those two simple words, strung together, were powerful enough to ignite the possibilities. And that was the point. She read it again.

Travel more.

Her default inner voice set in. *Yes, but where? How the fuck am I going to afford that? Who am I going to go with?*

Her computer beeped. Ellie turned and squinted at the clock on the bottom right of her monitor.

Shit!

She had almost forgotten her session with Ruth.

Quickly, she stripped off her gloves and bandana, and tried feverishly to straighten her hair. Ellie sat at the desk, peering past the screen. She adjusted her angle to catch her reflection in the glass. She checked her face and makeup. She looked tired. Saggy eyes, swollen face. Not that Ruth wasn't used to it by now.

The computer beeped again.

Ellie clicked the *Join Meeting* button.

Ruth's image appeared on the monitor, radiant as ever. Ellie felt instant gratitude at seeing her face. Ruth peered closer into the lens, looking past Ellie. "Wow, my dear. New space?"

"Yes," Ellie confirmed, glancing hesitantly around the room. "You like it?"

"I love it," Ruth said. "Looks like you've been working hard, being productive. You should be proud."

"I've got a lot more to do," Ellie said.

"Don't diminish the work you've done, dear. There's always more to do, but I hope you've stopped to acknowledge all of this. This is a major step."

"Thanks Ruth. It was Bishop's old office."

"I figured," Ruth smiled. "And look at that light. Gorgeous. Those white roses are a lovely touch."

Ellie smiled timidly, and adjusted the vase. She tucked a few loose copper strands of hair behind her ear. "They remind me of my mom."

"Lovely," Ruth repeated. "Are you ready to begin?"

Ellie swallowed. "Yes."

"First, let's start with your pain today, to level-set; and go from there. Your symptoms. How have they been?"

Ellie answered without hesitation. "Same."

"Is that right?" Ruth asked. "Don't just answer out of habit, Ellie. Take a moment to *really* think about it. Microscopic movement, is still movement."

Ellie paused, and reconsidered. "Well," she said. "Actually, maybe it's been a little less so lately. Or maybe I'm managing it better? I don't know."

"List them off, as best as you can."

"Joint pain, a lot of intense anxiety, dry mouth. Dizziness mostly," Ellie said. "And nightmares. That, thing again. Found me all the way in California."

Ruth nodded. "Uh-huh. Are you surprised? About the nightmares?"

Ellie shook her head.

She heard soft thudding sounds coming from outside. She leaned over and discretely glanced through the white sheers. Roland was outside bouncing a soccer ball on his knees. Ellie leaned back in her chair, and thought for a moment. "No, I'm not surprised."

"Your symptoms, have they been front and center?"

"They're there. But they've been dwelling in the background. Now that I think about it."

"That's good. Normally, they're in the forefront, and it's you that mentions them first. Have you thought about why?"

"Why, what?" Ellie asked.

"Why your symptoms have taken a back seat for the moment?"

Ellie pondered the thought for a moment. "No, actually."

"The trip have something to do with it?" Ruth said. "Your time with Hannah.

Unplugging from *life* for a moment? Spreading more of Bishop's remains. Added release and closure, perhaps? There is a reason people take vacations, dear. But for you, it's likely deeper than that."

"I don't know exactly."

"Some homework, then. It's important to understand when there have been positive changes. You should think about journaling, to track the ups and downs. Make connections."

Ellie wished Bishop was around. He'd have made her a sophisticated Excel sheet. She smiled at the thought and picked up a pen, scribbling some notes while they spoke.

It was odd. Now that she'd considered, the pain had felt lessened today, even though she'd been cleaning all day. That, in and of itself, was a miracle, because even the smallest physical exertion flared her up.

It had been so long, that she hadn't paid attention.

But there was always tomorrow.

She looked down at her fingers and balled them into fists, releasing them again. She did this several times. Pain shot up from her knuckles, but it was significantly diminished than usual. "Huh," she whispered to herself.

"I've been thinking about your mother, Ellie," Ruth said.

Ellie looked up.

Ruth smiled, and continued. "I've been studying a lot about grief lately. You came into my thoughts. I've been thinking about how her loss may have affected you, and what role that plays in your life. It was Bishop really, that got me thinking. After our trip to the cabin. That his death, must have opened up some old wounds. And that now, you're reliving that trauma all over again."

Ellie's throat quivered, but she repressed. "I feel that way," she said.

"I know dear. It's expected. You are human, yes?"

"Yes."

Ruth put on her eyeglasses. "I want us to try something, if you're okay with it."

Ellie nodded her approval.

"I want us to walk a path," Ruth said. "I will guide you, but you will walk alone. Backwards. Through time. And I want you to think about your lineage, your past."

Ellie closed her eyes and sat back in her chair. Through second nature, she began breathing consciously, without direction from Ruth.

Four in, five out.

She began steadying the trembling of her cells, one body part at a time, until she was in a calm state.

Ruth spoke softly after a few moments. "We are going to take steps, one after the other. The setting is whatever you want it to be. A completely empty room. A forest path, a quiet palatial library, or an open white-sand beach. Doesn't matter. It's your place. Whatever feels good." Ruth focused her words intently. "But I want you to move," she said. "To walk. Don't stay put. Walk until eventually, you have cleared your thoughts. Until there is no sense of time: past or present. In some ways, it should all blend into one. I want you to think about your life, and your loneliness. I want you to think about the important times in your life, the milestones."

Ellie took deep, slow breaths and envisioned the scene, as asked by Ruth. She thought about the things Ruth had asked her. She thought about her childhood friends. Graduating from college. Her wedding day.

She thought about some of her darker days. Her mother's death. Bishop's. The last day she'd worked. The last time she ran.

Ruth asked another question. "Who was there during those times? There is no right or wrong answer here."

Ellie swallowed.

"What I'm asking," Ruth said. "Is, who was prominent?"

Ellie answered without hesitation. "Mom was there, and later, Bishop."

"No one else?"

"My Dad, sometimes. But not as often as I'd have wanted. He's trying now."

"That's a good thing," Ruth said.

"I guess."

Ruth took a sip of her tea. "It's important that you understand something, dear. That you've never been alone. None of us are. I want you to see yourself. However way you want. See yourself on that path, on that journey. Glowing with energy."

Ellie focused. She tried to see herself in her mind's eye.

"Now," Ruth said. "I want you to imagine yourself leaning back. Throwing caution to the wind, even if you might fall. Prepare for it, even. I want you to outstretch your arms, and I want you to lean back all the way, while you are standing. In your vision; in your imagination."

Ellie was unsure. "Okay," she whispered.

"Are you letting yourself go?"

"Trying to."

Ruth waited a few moments. "Have you fallen yet?"

"Not yet," Ellie said, surprised. She moistened her lips, and forced her quivering eyes to stay shut. Her heart rate increased. She was leaning far back in her mind's eye, but her actual body paralleled the movement. She grasped the armrests of her chair, preparing for the inevitable tip backwards.

"Not ever," Ruth said. "And do you know why?"

Ellie shrugged, and pressed her eyes shut.

"Because it took a lot to get you here, sweetheart. Many things had to occur over millennia for you to be able to exist, here and now. Therefore, it is not an accident. You have a right to be here, and you deserve to be here. And, as I've told you before, you have the right to exist happily and with health. Your body wants to get better. This visualization is a metaphor. To understand your support system, even when you are alone."

Ellie's heart sunk at hearing that word: *alone*.

Ruth removed her glasses. "When you lean back, you are surrounded by all of your ancestors. Generations of them. They gather around you, to hold you up. Your mother is there; your husband is there. But they are not alone. And when they cannot bear the weight, there are hundreds of hands on your back, making sure you don't fall. Even your father, although he is still alive. He is a part of your support system. And when he cannot be there, or doesn't know *how* to be there— there are many others to take his place. They all play a part. Your father is on his own life's journey and is learning himself. And so, they all share this responsibility. For you."

Tears fell from Ellie's eyes. She felt weightless. She tried to envision the warm touch of her family's hands around her. She tried to reach back. She could feel her mother's presence, but was terrified to see. It would be too much to let go of her, something she could never do.

Not again.

Ellie found herself mute, able to only observe; as if she were underwater. She moved in slow motion. Floating, in the absence of time and in the blackness of space.

Yet, she could breathe. Quite easily, too.

"Do you understand this concept, Ellie?"

"I understand," she whispered.

"You're getting better at this, my dear," Ruth reassured her.

Ellie tried to smile. "I'm starting to understand I need to get out of my own way, maybe."

"Indeed," Ruth said. "You have to understand as well, the role that you, yourself, have played. There is some accountability here, but I'll help you with that. Plenty of time.

"And above all else, you must know— and *always* remember: it's not your fault. You and your mother, had a deep and symbiotic relationship. So much so, that you created a sense of emotional connective tissue with her. One that remained after she died, like an ethereal umbilical cord. And no one can blame you. Because you were a little girl.

"But that decision has affected you, ever since. You created a spiritual tether with your mother, which binds you together. She has moved onto the *next* place, but you remain here, in *this* one. And you have to acknowledge what that attached cord does to the human body. That it may have contributed to making you sick. Because you are in a state of stuck energy, for lack of a better term. Your body is in a constant state of deep distress."

Ruth paused, letting her last few words sink in. "That choice," she said. "To not let go, has created a causality, and may have led to devastating consequences for you."

Ellie was silent. She felt hurt. Like she was somehow to blame. For her mother; for the state of her own health. Like it was her, that had opened the door and let a serpent into their house. She hadn't meant to. All because she loved her mother too much; because she missed her too much.

That wasn't fair.

Ellie couldn't squeak out a single word. Her throat was clamped shut. She tried as hard as she could to maintain presence in her meditative state. To not get lost in the despair. Or anger. She took a breath and tried to feel the support of her ancestors, and simultaneously, tried to connect with Ruth's words.

Finally, her voice came through again.

"Ellie," Ruth continued. "Loving your mother wasn't wrong. Missing her isn't wrong. And grieving her death wasn't wrong either. Nor Bishop. Your grief will remain until you, yourself, pass on one day. That is your right, and also your privilege. And no one is taking that away from you. You shouldn't ever stop, because that kind of love, *is* who you are. That is your purpose. At the same time, it is important to understand and recognize, that there is a difference between grieving, and longing for something that can never be. You have created a world that always asks: *what if?* What would life be like if mom was here? Why can't Bishop be here? In *this* moment, or in *that* moment. And in doing so, you have created a void that can never be filled. Over time, it has become an abyss."

Eyes still pressed shut, Ellie tried to choke out a breath. She felt like she was weighted down at the bottom of the sea, chains bound to her body. This was something she would not accept.

Ellie willed the shackles around her ankles to disintegrate into powder.

She pushed her feet on the muddy bottom and thrusted herself towards the surface, where she knew there was air. She swam in the darkness as hard as she could, until finally, she began to see light.

She broke the surface and exhaled.

Suddenly, she jolted forward in her office chair, and opened her eyes. Realizing where she was, she began to weep. She pressed her face into her hands, and sobbed from the pit of her stomach.

"I wish I was there with you, sweet Ellie."

Ellie cried until her tear ducts ran dry. She was a bubbling mess, and embarrassed at the sudden release. It would have been better to come to this realization in solitude.

She dried her face with a tissue. "What am I supposed to do, Ruth?"

"Just knowing this, can be enough. Enough to shift the energy. Remember, that it is simply stuck. And to move it, takes practice. You told me that you were a competitive marathon runner once, yes?"

Ellie grit her teeth. "Yes."

"Then you know more than most, that it takes practice. Every day, you had to train. You slept right; you ate right. You pushed harder than the day before, to gain… but, an inch. That's how you moved forward. It's no different here. In order to make progress, you must practice. Each day, each moment. Without fail."

"How, Ruth?" Ellie pleaded. "Where do I even begin?"

"The notion of self-care means more than hair and makeup," she said. "It means taking care of yourself, and it means living your life, striving for those things you want. It means finding the will to move forward, especially on your worst days. Knowing there is something out there for you. Practicing stillness of your mind, positivity about your self-worth. All of those things. Whatever you need to remind yourself of, even if it feels clichéd."

"No storm can last forever," Ellie sniffled, rolling her eyes and drudging up an apt expression.

"Exactly," Ruth said. "I'm sorry to say, dear— but you'll only reach enlightenment at the *end*, if you catch my drift. Until then, be easy on yourself. Forgive yourself. It's what you already know, Ellie."

"What's that?"

"*Love*, Ellie," Ruth said. "It's always about love."

Ellie glanced through the window, where Roland was still at it, kicking around the soccer ball. She watched him, intently focused on not letting it fall to the ground.

"I understand Ruth, she said. "And thanks."

"Think about these things, and I'd like to hear your thoughts. Some more homework," Ruth said. "Let me leave you with something. Something to think about. If you'd had a daughter, and she was sick. How would you handle it?"

Ellie tried with futility to stop the onset of tears. She was so sick of crying. And yet the tears came every day. It was uncontrollable. "I'm not sure what you're asking," she said.

"What I mean," Ruth said, "Is if your daughter was sick, would you punish her? Would you pressure her to get better, quicker? Would you tell her she wasn't good enough?"

Ellie jumped back. "Of course not!"

"Why is it okay to do that to yourself?"

The air left Ellie's body. She slunk in her chair. The realization came spiraling like a windstorm. She looked to the floor.

"My dear," Ruth said. "You would only show her love. And you would support her, wherever that journey took her. And I ask the same of you. Speak to yourself, as if you're speaking with that little girl. Can you do that?"

Ellie nodded her head, succumb with emotion.

"What you're doing at home, in that office, rebuilding? It's a good thing, and I'm proud of you."

"Thank you," Ellie said, wiping her cheeks.

"I'd like to see you again this week for a check-in, no charge. Is that okay?"

"Yes, thank you."

Ruth waved and disengaged the meeting. Ellie stared at the blank screen for a few more seconds, while listening to Roland bounce the ball outside.

Ellie stood, and turned to the corkboard.

She removed the cap from the felt pen, and wrote four words on a blue card:

Take care of yourself.

Ellie tacked it on the top left side of the board. She moved the card that she'd filled out earlier, Travel more, to the left side of the board.

Ellie cleared her mind to access her memory, and began writing excitedly, placing each completed card on random places on the corkboard. Ellie forced her mind to think in basic terms and not overthink. First things that came to mind. She thought about the things she wanted to accomplish, jotting each one down:

Take a course
Learn piano

Find a new career
Volunteer

Ellie tacked those up on separate cards. She stepped back and let the words absorb into her consciousness.

Good, she thought. *I like this.*

Ellie grabbed another card and wrote in smaller font: Stop calling it a bulletin board. It's my "INTENTION" Board. She tacked that card in the top center.

Ellie fondly recalled something her husband used to say, and wrote it down:

"How about we start with saying *good morning, before anything else?*" – Bishop

Ellie thought about Ruth, and penned more recollections:

"Love and light."

Bishop & mom were summoned home, and the angels rejoiced.

It's not *my* sickness.

She thought about her dear friend, who came to her in a time of need:

"There is beauty in that which is imperfect."- Hannah

Ellie remembered a kind stranger that she'd met in California:

"This life is about us, and we women, are the heroines in our own stories."- Ophelia

She laughed out loud, as she wrote a few random ones:

"What's the fucking point of it all?" - Man in airport

"No need to constantly say sorry." – Everyone

"Lots of love." – Dad

She listened to her heart, and wrote down what came to her:

Be grateful. Every damn day.

With her heart full, Ellie set her pen down.
She rummaged through some of Bishop's boxes until she finally found what she was looking for. Ellie held up an incense stick, and inhaled the bright aroma of lemongrass. She took it into the kitchen and set the tip aflame, watching the wispy smoke dance through the air.
She put her palms together and gave thanks. For anything she could think of.
That her pain was slightly diminished today. That she had a roof over her head. Her friends, her family. Her dogs. And most of all, that she was simply here another day. Despite the pain. She prayed, and gave thanks that she'd at least had her mom and Bishop; even if for a short while. And she gave thanks that her father called an ambulance, and stopped her from taking her own life.
That she'd somehow found the resolve, so far.
It had been a long time since she'd done something like that, and she felt whole in that moment.
As she placed the incense holder on the counter, she caught sight of Izzy and Winston peeking at her from behind the couch. Realizing how intense the smell must have been for them, she opened up a few windows.
She looked through, letting the gentle breeze baptize her skin.
After spending some time petting her dogs, Ellie pulled a jug of iced-tea from the fridge, grabbed two glasses, and headed to the front porch. "Roland," she called out. "Come sit with me."
Roland was still underneath the immense red maple tree in his front yard, practicing his soccer skills. He immediately caught the ball he was bouncing, and smiled at her.
She took a seat on the top step. "Want some iced-tea?"
"Yeah," he said softly, joining her on the stairs.

Sean poked his head through their front door, and glanced over. "Hi Ellie," he said. "I heard the ball stop bouncing. Was my queue to check." He chuckled. "I'm trying not to be a helicopter parent, though."

"Join us," she smiled. "You want a glass?"

"Anything stronger?" he winked.

"I wish."

He grinned as he headed over, dressed like a distinguished Hollywood actor. His kindness always brought a smile to her face.

"You're glowing," Ellie said. "Tell me your secret."

Sean took a seat on the last step, but still towered over Roland and Ellie. He gently slapped her shoulder, and pursed his lips. "Oh stop, you."

She smiled.

"Getting settled back in?" he asked. "Trip was good?"

"Yes," Ellie said. "Starting to clean and some much-needed organization in the house."

"Make sure you let me know if you need help," he looked at his son. "I can send Roland over."

"Yes!" Roland said. "I can help."

Ellie's heart swelled. "You're a good kid, Rollie. Thank you."

She poured him a glass and handed it over. Roland used both his small hands to gulp it down. He lowered the glass and set his large brown eyes on Ellie.

"How old are you now?" she asked.

"Eleven."

"Getting strong."

He wiped his mouth with his forearm. "Yup."

Ellie refilled his glass, to which he accepted with enthusiasm. "Ellie?" Roland asked.

"Yes, kiddo?"

"Have you ever been on a plane?"

"I have," she said. "In fact, I was on one very recently."

Roland turned wide-eyed to his father. "Whoa."

Ellie laughed. "You taking a trip?"

"This Dad is from England. And my other Dad is from Iran," Roland said. "They told me I was from the Phil…the Philip…"

"The Philippines," Sean helped him along.

Roland carefully sounded out the words. "The… Phil..i..ppines. And, we're going to go there one day. We're gonna fly. In a plane."

"I hear it's amazing," she said. "Do you remember Bishop?"

Roland nodded, and turned to his father, as if he needed the permission. Sean nodded to him and smiled.

"Well," Ellie said. "Bishop spent some time there, for work. He lived there for four months. And he loved it. Said it was a beautiful place, with lots of friendly people. Did some volunteer work too."

"I can't wait," Roland said, taking another sip.

"He's old enough, and starting to understand the atypical family he's in," Sean said, speaking as if Roland wasn't there. Roland was, however, and listened intently; happy to be the subject of one of his father's stories. "Elias and I are starting to slowly tell him about his own background. *His* story. He just figured out he was adopted, on his own. I guess that should have been obvious, even though we tried to sit him down and explain it our way. We want him to experience our heritage, in its diversity. Something different for all of us. To understand where we he comes from. It's time."

Ellie squeezed Sean's hand. "He's lucky."

Roland politely interrupted the tender moment. "Can I go play soccer again?"

"Go," Ellie said. "Your Dad and I can catch up."

They watched Roland return to his favorite spot under the tree, resuming his bouncing. Sean turned to Ellie. "You know, for some reason I forgot that Bishop spent time overseas for his job. What type of volunteering did he do over there?"

"His company sponsors a lot of charity work over there, and they have quite a large operation. They invest in the community; same as here. While he was there opening up a new office, he spent a few days volunteering to help build low-income housing. *Digging and carrying lumber mostly*, he had said."

"Ah."

"I remember when he got back, he was really excited. Volunteering or helping with something that was close to him. It sparked something in him."

"We all should. We're taking the kid to the food bank this Christmas. He's old enough now. Usually, Elias goes on his own, while I stay home with Rollie."

"It's hard you know?" Ellie said. "We all feel like we should have our shit together first, before helping someone else. But I'm not sure that's how it works. I'd talk to Bishop about that a lot. We don't have to be millionaires with perfect lives, to be able to help someone else. I'm stuck with my illness, and feel like I couldn't help someone else, still drowning in my own hurricane."

"What do you think Bishop would have done?"

Ellie thought about it for a second. "I know he wanted to be involved in helping children and mothers that were victims of domestic abuse. Alcoholism. It's not like he was open about it, but he knew first-hand what it was like. It was the environment he grew up in."

"He would have been good at helping with that," Sean said.

She paused for a moment, and cupped her neck, just below the chin. Sean held her other hand in both of his. "I just wished he had more time," Ellie said. "He would have done something good. You know?"

"I know," Sean said softly. "I knew Bishop, and you're right. But we can do it for him. In his honor. We can remember him through that, by realizing his potential. By achieving the goals, he set out for himself, and making them our own—we can find our own fulfilment, maybe?"

Ellie gazed into Sean's deep blue eyes, finding comfort in his kindness. "You're right. I'm sorry I'm turning into a blubbering mess again."

Sean shot her a questioning look.

"I know," she said. "Don't apologize so much."

He hugged her, and held onto her shoulders. "You are never alone."

"Thank you."

"Which reminds me," Sean said. "Elias is in there finishing up his mid-life crisis redecorating project. Thank God. He's been at it for months. I let him do what he wants, because he actually has a great sense of style."

"I know he does," Ellie agreed.

"As a compromise, I've negotiated the sunroom as *my* space. We've moved in the infrared sauna from the garage and we've redone the floors. White candles, fresh linen, gorgeous orchids. It's my spa and yoga space. As fuckin' Zen as you can get."

Ellie chortled.

Sean reached into his pocket, and pulled out a key— handing it to Ellie. "This is for you, darling."

Ellie furrowed her brow. "What's this?"

"It's the key for the sunroom. I want you to use it anytime you want." He placed a gentle hand on her arm. "I know what you've been going through. And we want you to feel like you can come to a little mini-retreat anytime you want. It'll be good for you. We can do yoga together. And the sauna is great for detoxing."

Ellie leaned over and hugged Sean, taking the key. "Thank you. I would love to. This means a lot."

"Anytime. Oh, by the way, I spoke to your Dad a few times while he was here taking care of the place. He was out in the garden quite a bit." Sean raised his eyebrows and nodded his head, smiling. "Saw a big delivery coming in."

"Oh," Ellie said. "The piano. You know about that? It was my grandfather's."

"Your Dad told me."

Ellie thought about her Dad. "Was really sweet."

"Do you play?" Sean asked.

Ellie looked to the ground. "Not anymore. My grandfather tried to teach me when I was a kid, but it never stuck. I didn't have the patience. I regret that now."

"Never too old, Ellie. If you need lessons, my cousin is the best in town. He's splendid. I'll text you his number."

"Great," Ellie said.

Suddenly, a thought swirled into her mind. An inspiration. "Wait here. Don't let Roland go anywhere."

She ran into the house, not waiting for Sean to respond, and returned holding a heavy object in her hand. When Sean saw what it was, he stood and placed his hands on his hips, shaking his head. "No, Ellie. You can't. You don't have to."

"Roland!" she hollered. "Get over here."

Roland caught the soccer ball and turned. "Whoa," he said. "Cool!"

He ran over. "Is that yours?"

"No kiddo," Ellie said. "It's yours."

Roland turned to his father for approval. "Ellie," Sean said. "We can't accept this."

Ellie ignored him. She crouched, and handed the boy Bishop's black guitar with both hands. "This was my husband's," she said. "And I want you to have it. He would want you to have it. This would have made him happy."

Sean nodded to his son. Roland reached out and carefully grasped the black guitar with both hands, as if it were a priceless artifact. King Arthur, clutching Excalibur itself. He let his legs slowly fold beneath his body and sat on the steps, admiring the instrument, headstock to bridge.

"Thank you," Roland said. He carefully handed the guitar to his Dad and rushed into Ellie's arms, burying his face in her stomach.

"You're welcome" Ellie said. "I have a ton of stuff that goes with it. Cables, an amp, a stand. You come over later and I will have it packed for you."

Roland nearly screamed. "Dad, can I start playing tonight?"

Sean laughed and lovingly straightened his son's hair. "Yes, you can start tonight. But you can bet on this, Roland. You'll be over here helping Ellie with whatever she needs."

"Deal," Roland said.

Ellie said goodbye, and watched them head back into their home, after promising Sean she'd join him for a yoga session soon.

She returned to her office, dogs in tow.

She was glad that she had given the instrument to Roland, and was certain: Bishop would have beamed, seeing the kid's face.

Ellie was proud to pay it forward for her husband, who didn't have the opportunity when he was a boy. It felt right. And she knew, a kid like Roland would commit, and not just let it sit in the corner un-played, collecting dust.

He was special; gifted maybe. She knew Roland enough to know he had heart; she felt it in her gut. He would do good things.

Ellie sat cross-legged on the ground with her dogs, looking around the office. Izzy and Winston both fell to their sides, and laid on the rug, accepting the belly rubs their mama was offering. Izzy, fell asleep almost instantly.

Ellie thought about her morning. The session with Ruth; her visit with her neighbors. And she realized the support she had around her. She felt lucky.

So blessed and so loved.

Ellie gently arose, careful not to disturb her sleeping dogs. She picked up a blue card and the felt pen. She wrote an inscription, and tacked it to her *Intention Board*.

She stepped back, still smelling the sweet citrus scent of lemongrass incense permeating her home. Ellie read the blue card with pride.

> You can honor and remember Bishop, by realizing your *own* dreams.

As she pondered the words she'd just written, the laptop beeped, indicating a message had been received. She opened the email:

> Ellie,
>
> Hope you arrived home safely, and hope you are feeling okay. I'm sure the dogs missed you. Wanted to say hello. I haven't stopped thinking about you - Tom.

Ellie looked through the window, reveling in the stillness outside. She watched the red and orange leaves fall from the branches one-by-one, as she closed her laptop screen.

Chapter Twenty

"Thanks for seeing me again, Dr. Green."

"Please Ellie, call me Grace," she smiled.

"Grace, yes," Ellie smiled back.

"How have you been?"

Ellie struggled to focus. She wasn't feeling good. Her knuckles were throbbing. Back to the dissociation, and memory fog. A far cry from the day before.

More, she'd been thinking about the note she'd received from Ophelia. The message had really moved her.

Ellie had rushed to Dr. Green's office that morning. As usual, she'd spent a bit too much time on trying to cover up her skin, and making sure her hair was as best as it could be, despite its steadily diminishing state and the fact that most of it was hidden beneath her hat. She caught herself slipping back into her routines, as hard as she'd been trying, and running late in the process. Her self-assurance was back at zero. And seeing the attractive and vibrant Dr. Green, never helped much out in the confidence department either.

At least I'm being honest with myself, Ellie thought, staring into space. *That's a step, isn't it?*

On her way out, she'd grabbed the stack of mail that her Dad had carefully piled up on the entryway sideboard table. He'd taken the time to sort through and discard the junk mail, so all that she was left with were letters that were actually addressed to her.

Ellie had driven to Dr. Green's office in a mad panic, speeding through side streets. Every time she ran a yellow light, she glanced in her rearview and had said *sorry* out loud, waving to no one in particular.

Her racecar driving had resulted in her arriving ten minutes early; and she celebrated her small victory by re-checking her makeup. A few minutes early still, she sifted through the mail that she'd had piled on her passenger seat.

Bills, bills, bills, advertisement— and then. Something she hadn't seen in a long while. She might've even been a teenager.

A postcard.

On the front, a photograph of a sprawling skyline, on the shores of Lake Michigan, with a caption that read: *Greetings from Chicago!*

Her heart fluttered.

She turned the card over and read the message. It was written in beautiful cursive handwriting.

> *Ellie,*
>
> *I hope you have arrived home safely. Been thinking about you. Some words below, I thought you could use.*
> *—Love, Ophelia.*

Ellie kept reading, just below Ophelia's handwritten note.

> *"You may encounter many defeats, but you must not be defeated. In fact, it may be necessary to encounter the defeats, so you can know who you are, what you can rise from, how you can still come out of it."*
>
> *- Maya Angelou*

Ellie had stopped cold, thinking about those words. Inspiring in one sentiment, and yet, her eyes focused on a single word: *defeat.*

She didn't know whether to cry happy tears, or scream at the top of her lungs in frustration. So many emotions arose at once: anger, at feeling defeated at every turn, and yet encouragement, from the gratitude of blessings she did have. *How much goddamned adversity does a person need, to pass the test? How many fucking trials and tribulations does a person have to go through?*

Ellie sat in a daze until she realized she was a minute late for her appointment, and quickly ran up to the doctor's office.

"Ellie," Grace repeated. "How have you been?"

"I'm sorry," Ellie said. "I'm a bit unfocussed today. Brain fog."

"That's okay. Take your time."

"A lot has been going on, and to be honest," Ellie said. "I'm not sure how I'm doing. It's been bouncing back and forth. I have been having days with less pain, and some clarity. It starts to feel like I am making some headway, but I fall back into the rabbit hole again. It's like this little bit of hope, you know? Then it all comes crumbling down again."

Grace looked up empathetically from her chart. She removed her eyeglasses.

"Ellie, you're not the only one. Healing isn't linear and it doesn't happen in a day. Part of this journey for you, is to really understand and accept that. We have a lot of work to do. And I'm not going to lie to you, this is something you may be dealing with for the rest of your life. Have you thought about that?"

The room blasted back, as if Ellie was inside the vacuum of a kickdrum. Her head buzzed, hearing those words. *Rest of my life?*

"I can't. I won't end up like my mom."

"I can't guarantee that, Ellie."

"I know," Ellie sulked. She looked through the window at the towering Vancouver office buildings, remembering the first time she had met Grace not long ago. She'd had her blood drawn that day; for testing, overseas. She couldn't remember where. Was it Spain? Switzerland?

The sky was overcast, and Ellie knew it would rain soon. She wished she could just float away and disappear in the forming mist.

"Tell me about one of your recent good days," Grace asked.

Ellie hesitated, and tried to remember. She closed her eyes. "I just got back from a trip with a friend. We scattered some of Bishop's ashes. Tried to unplug. Met some new friends. I had a few good days there, in amongst the bad. I had a really good day yesterday. Felt energized, hopeful. And then…"

Ellie's Albatross

"Those are the moments you have to hang onto, Ellie. It makes all the difference in the world. Human nature; sometimes we bond to the bad days, and the good ones fade away. The outlook you have, the sense of hope: these all have effect."

"Everyone keeps telling me."

Grace nodded her head. "You have to follow the trail of breadcrumbs, and find the pattern."

"I'm lost."

"Remember the blood test you took," Grace said. "Last time you were here? The one we sent to Germany?"

Germany, that was it!

"Yes," Ellie nodded.

"The results came back," Grace said. "The good news is; we better know what we're dealing with now."

Ellie sat up, mouth wide open. Not a single doctor, in over a decade, had been able to say those words to her. She'd been crawling around in a pitch black cave without a flashlight. Suddenly, there was a glimmer. Ellie stared into Grace's eyes, wordlessly.

"Chronic Lyme disease," Grace said. "Well, not just Lyme disease, but several tick-borne co-infections."

Ellie fell to Earth from ten-thousand feet, and splattered onto concrete. She gulped. "I don't remember being bitten by a tick."

"You don't have to," Grace sighed. "You told me you were an avid marathon runner and hiker, correct?"

Ellie nodded, bewildered.

"Spent every waking moment that you could outdoors," Grace continued. "Could have happened at any time. You may not remember getting bit, and maybe you don't remember seeing a bullseye rash. Just symptoms, then getting worse. It's where it may have started."

Ellie paused for a moment. She could feel her skin getting flush. Panic set in. Every bone in her body told her to run.

"From your test results, we know you have tick-borne coinfections, and there is a high probability that there are parasitic elements that we may be dealing with, from your previous travel, and what your testing has shown. All of this may have kicked off this road you're on, but these only make up a fraction of the story. There are toxins from daily living, resulting fibromyalgia. The list goes on and on. All we know is, you're not feeling well. I can help with supplements and medications to help bind and clear. To detoxify. You are handling it from the dietary perspective. But, what we are really talking about, is strengthening your *terrain*."

Ellie massaged her right temple. "Terrain?"

"*The pathogen is nothing; the terrain is everything.* Part of something called 'germ theory'; the basics of which, is that if you take care of the foundational elements of the body, then it can combat external pathogens; because the body *wants* to get better. We know to eat well; we know to get adequate rest. We think about macronutrients and vitamins. Exercise. But what you have, after this long: is a *chronic* illness."

Grace paused for a moment to let things sink in. "Do you want some water, Ellie?"

"Keep going," Ellie said, holding her stomach.

"We get into those abstract ideas which we all know about," Grace said. "And how they can affect the body, but struggle to manage. Namely, trauma and stress."

Grace stood and walked towards the large plate-glass window. As she moved, the orchid on her desk danced with the slight breeze she generated, as if it were bowing. She stopped at the bookshelf, seemingly searching for a title. She turned back to Ellie. "Are we really taking care of those things?" she asked. "Think about what we are bombarded with every day. Do we think about external factors such as EMF, and how that affects us? Pesticides. The processing of our foods. Or, how our modern world is so detrimental to our mental health. More than it was, even as little as a decade ago. Social media? The more connected we are, the more *disconnected* we are. The pace at which we work and live?"

"I'm not sure I follow," Ellie said, more confused than ever.

"I know you're ahead of the game when it comes to food and exercise. You could probably school me. But we have to think about how everything else has been affecting you, during the course of your entire life. And how you have been handling things. *Terrain*," she repeated. "The idea is, when two different people get infected with the exact same pathogen. One gets better, while the other does not. Because one has a more robust terrain. That person, perhaps, has not suffered the same traumas. Or they have not been subjected to the same environmental exposure. Maybe they perceive the world in a different, more positive way? In other words, misery can beget more misery."

Ellie swallowed, feeling the air leave her body.

"Ellie, it's not just you. It's all of us, me included. And I know you're doing your best. We can get the body stronger to rid your body of any unwanted bacteria. The rest though is up to you, and is going to take an incredible amount of work. Think about it this way: if for example, you smoked for twenty years, how can you expect your lungs to clear, in just a few days? It took time for the damage to accumulate, and it could take equal time to heal."

Grace sat next to Ellie, and held her hand. "Same goes for trauma—for stress," she continued.

"We would all love to spend the next twenty years on a beach with no worries, but that's just not reasonable. And so, we have to fit in those moments of Zen, where we can. Through stress management, meditation, gratitude. In our surroundings, in our actions, in our thoughts, in our outlook; and in our practices. In order to work through our trauma, we have to first identify it, and confront it. Then, we can move forward. And it takes will and courage. But I believe that our brains never come out of a state of plasticity. That it can continue to rewire, to mold and adapt, based on the direction we give it. Bit of a *chicken* and the *egg* scenario."

She stopped for a moment to let it sink in. "Does that make sense?"

"I think so," Ellie lied, unsure if it did.

She felt overwhelmed, like she did so often. That helpless idea of *David versus Goliath*. She tried to picture her strength, but only found herself shrinking even more. Ellie fought the urge to self-doubt, but it came like a gentle tide; so long as the moon and Earth continued to exist.

Could it really have that much effect?

"And there's those things on the peripheral," Grace said. "Things we all have to work on. How much pressure we put on ourselves to be perfect? Trying to pursue happiness by getting back to putting ourselves first, and chasing those things that are important to us. Exploring our talents. Finding something bigger than ourselves even, whatever that means to you. It's about the pursuit of these things, that brings purpose and meaning."

Ellie rotated the wedding ring on her left hand. Her circulation seemed to cease. She rubbed her cold fingers with her thumbs. "Easier said than done."

"Tell me about it. If it were easy, we'd all be chasing our bliss. There's work involved. And not everyone has to do it, nor do they want to. They go on, just existing. But that's okay. That's not your path. Your path is bigger."

Ellie forced a smile. *"Free your mind, your ass will follow."*

"Come again?"

"Something my husband Bishop used to say."

"Exactly," Grace laughed. "What one does, affects the other. A kind of quantum entanglement, if you will. All the more reason, to continue seeing your therapist. We're all working as a team here."

Ellie nodded. It was much to think about.

Her eyes widened when Grace returned to the office with a tray full of pills and tinctures.

Beginning of the regiment. "We are going to start you off very slow," Grace said. "Very slow. To minimize the Herx reactions, which is what happens when you detoxify too fast. This booklet explains your medications, your dosage, and what to expect."

Ellie's mind raced. She wondered if this new protocol would work. She thought about how much they'd cost, and how she'd be able to afford it. How long would it take to see results? How could she fit all this in her day? Would it make her nauseous?

She stopped herself.

Too many *what ifs*.

"First step," she said to the doctor. "Right?"

Grace shook her head. "No Ellie," she corrected. "*Next* step."

Chapter Twenty-One

Ellie exited the medical office building, with much less energy than she came in with. As she walked to her car, she could hear the clinging and clanging of the glass bottles in her shoulder bag, which was loaded with a plethora of medications that Grace had prescribed.

Her shoulder burned from the weight of it.

Ellie approached her car, and stopped to look around.

The traffic on the street had nearly doubled since she'd been in Dr. Green's office, and she groaned at the sight of it. While at her appointment, rain had begun pelting the city, and every surface was thoroughly drenched.

It was September after all, so right on queue.

Ellie sniffed the air, and the earthy smell of petrichor infiltrated her nostrils like an arrow. It emanating from the asphalt in waves. They'd gone the last month without any rain at all, and the first sprinkle of it, changed the entire tone of the city. Almost immediately, the wardrobe of its inhabitants would change. Shorts and tank tops yesterday, turning to rain jackets and umbrellas today. As if scheduled, the vibe went from optimistically happy, to dreary survival mode.

And it would stay this way for almost the next eight months.

There were always concessions to the gloom, and Vancouver was no exception. Two things broke the monotony of the rainy season, which extended well into the spring: a bit of collective joy around Christmas, and overweight men who wore shorts and flip-flops, even in the snow— and socks optional. To them, the bleak weather seemed to have no effect, and they were a permanent fixture in the city year-round.

Ellie wondered if unhappy people wore shorts and flip-flops. She didn't think so. Bishop had always rolled his eyes at the sight of one of these snow-shorts offenders, while it always made Ellie giggle. If he timed the traffic lights just right for the getaway, Bishop would yell through the window: *"Put on some long pants, motherfucker!"*

Ellie would burst into hysterics, which would always make Bishop happy.

He loved hearing her laugh.

Ellie sat in her car, with the engine running. She leaned back on the headrest and watched the windshield wipers swipe back and forth. She reached over and pressed the power button on the radio, and switched it off again.

Ellie let out a deep exhale, watching people hopping over puddles.

She looked through the passenger glass to see how much time she still had left on the meter. Two hours. She checked her watch. The appointment must have gone a lot quicker than she'd thought.

I'm out, she thought. *I should do something.*

Ellie picked up her phone and Googled the closest bookstore. Fifteen-minute walk, or a four-minute drive. She wasn't sure if the pain in her body would afford her the round trip. She was achy today; pain concentrated around the joints. This little act of walking, could throw her into a tailspin for the next few days. Or, the fresh air would be good; she'd deal with the pain.

She glanced at the postcard from Ophelia on the passenger seat.

Ellie shut off the car, and headed down the street on foot.

By the time she had reached the bookstore, she was completely soaked. A steady stream of rain ran down her neck, but she didn't care. It felt good against the warm, humid air. She read the sign on the front door.

The Last Chapter: books and café.

The door chimed with the sound of little bells as she walked through, cementing its status as local bookstore. Big chains never implored such analogue methods of customer notification. She smiled at the sound when she crossed the threshold.

As Ellie dried off her boots on the mat, she reveled in that new-book smell. It reminded her of the Scholastic book club of her youth. Something about that smell: a scent that both she and her husband adored. Coffee and fresh print, signaled magic to them.

A new world.

An escape.

The store was much larger than it looked from the outside, transcending its exterior dimensions. It was moderately busy, with most of its patrons seated near the small café to the side, thumbing through pages and pages of literature.

Near the front of the store, stood a thin, young man at the checkout counter. He was seated on a round stool, and clicking away at the computer. His dark brown hair was untidy, and he fiddled at his striped sweater with his thumb. His eyes darted back and forth while he read words across a computer screen. A pile of textbooks were strewn across the tabletop.

Ellie neared closer. "Excuse me," she said. "Where is your poetry section?"

He barely looked up, chewing on a fingernail. "Huh?"

"Poetry," Ellie stared, trying not to make a face.

He used a thumb to gesture behind him, and avoided any eye contact. "In the back."

Ellie stared at him in disbelief for a moment. She considered commenting on his horrible customer service skills, and thought against it. She'd rather avoid the confrontation.

Like he'd care anyways.

A woman's voice called out from Ellie's left. "Ma'am? Maybe I can help?"

Ellie turned to find a petite woman, wearing a knit black shawl over her blue dress. She appeared to be stocking books from cardboard boxes, that were sitting atop a wheeled cart. As she walked towards Ellie, her chestnut ponytail danced back and forth. She put a soft hand on Ellie's forearm. "That's my son," she said. She blinked slowly as she spoke, as if to say *I'm sorry* with her eyes. "He's studying for his mid-term," she said. "And I'm afraid he's not being very helpful at the moment."

The last part of her sentence came with an increase in volume, and a glance in his direction, so that he could hear. He squinted at her for a moment, and went back to his reading. She may as well have called him an imbecile— but she didn't. Instead, she turned her attention to Ellie and said, "I'm Cora, I own the place. Welcome."

"Nice to meet you, Cora. I'm Ellie. Nice little spot."

Cora adjusted the thick black frames of her cat-eye glasses. "First time here?"

Ellie nodded.

Cora smiled through light pink lipstick, "I heard you say poetry? An author in particular you're looking for?"

"Yes. Maya Angelou."

"Ah yes. The reigning queen of American poets. Our hero."

Ellie felt relieved she was dealing with Cora, and not her inconsiderate little shit of a son. As Cora led her towards the back of the store, Ellie looked around. "In fact," she said. "I'm hoping you can point me in the direction of a few different areas. I'm looking for *inspirational writing, overcoming adversities, Lyme* disease, *dealing with illness*. Stuff like that."

Cora stopped walking, and turned to face Ellie. Her expression changed.

"I'm sorry," she said.

Ellie was confused. "For what?"

"For whatever you're dealing with."

Oh yes, Ellie thought. *Overcoming adversities, dealing with illness. I've been living with it for a decade. How alien it must sound to some people?*

Ellie tucked her damp red hair over her ears, and adjusted her ball-cap. "Thank you Cora, I appreciate it," she said, trying to half-step forward, and continue the quest; signaling to Cora to return to their objective. It worked.

"Well, here we are," Cora said. "Poetry is over here, and books are sorted by author's last name."

She used her index finger to slide down the spines of the books, like she was playing a scale on the white keys of a piano. She whispered each author's last name as she went, until… "*Angelou*, right here."

Cora looked up through her eyeglasses, and pointed. "Regarding anything more on the inspirational side of the house, the entire non-fiction section is on that side. I'd say look through *Educational, Self-Help, and Health.* If you think of a specific title, the search computer is there, or you can come find me. Good?"

"Good," Ellie smiled, and dove into the Poetry section, feeling her heart flutter.

She left the store with a canvass bag, full of books, and waved at Cora on the way out. She'd be back, for sure. Ellie felt excited.

Next Step, Grace had said.

Indeed, Ellie thought.

The rain had stopped for the time being, and the sun began peeking through the dark clouds, turning the air into a haze of steamy humidity. She trudged along the sidewalk, towards her car, passing dozens of storefronts. As Ellie weaved in and out of the sidewalk pedestrians, she imagined being connected to those around her. Perhaps, in some kind of higher energy exchange.

Take what you need, and give what you can.

She'd been spending too much time being isolated, and the change felt good. The vitality, felt good.

A glint of sun reflected off of an unassuming mirrored door, across the street. Ellie stopped, and squinted. Her eyes made out the sign: *Ministry of Family Services.*

She felt drawn to the building—drawn to the energy. Ellie stood for a moment, frozen where she was. She glanced down both sides of the street, and waited for a break in traffic. She darted across, and approached the door, dodging a few speeding cars. As she drew closer, she noticed the full sign on the door. Beneath the larger navy-colored words that read *Ministry of Family Services,* written in standard government font; there was another declaration printed in a smaller typeface: *Domestic Abuse Victim Services.*

Ellie stared at the door, and the sign.

The reflective surface on the door didn't allow a view inside the building, as if it were a one-sided mirror in an interrogation room. She pulled the door open, and walked in. Immediately, a voice called out from behind the plexiglass partition. "Can I help you?"

The room was empty, save for the woman. Ellie walked across the low-pile gray carpeting. There were chairs arranged around the perimeter of the waiting room. In the far-left corner, there was a pint-sized red table with matching yellow chairs. In a basket next to the little table, were an assortment of toys and cardboard children's books; to compliment the piles of magazines for the adults. On the right wall, was a clear plastic shelf with support and resource pamphlets, ranging from domestic abuse to drug treatment.

"Can I help you?" the woman repeated herself.

"Hi, yes," Ellie said, approaching the window. "I'm hoping you can."

A heavy-set woman appeared on the other side of the glass, and relayed her voice from behind a brushed stainless steel speak-through, located in the middle of the partition. Her hair was jet-black, and tied expertly in a tight bun. She looked to be in her fifties, and when she smiled, small crow's feet appeared near the corners of her eyes. She wore a black blazer, which matched her hair, over a bone-white blouse. On the blazer, Ellie noticed a silver lapel pin in the shape of a small bird.

"What's your name?" she asked.

"Ellie."

"I'm Liz," she said. "What can I help you with sweetie?"

Liz raised on her tippy toes, tilted her head, and subtly looked Ellie up and down through the glass. Ellie could tell, she was making a polite assessment. She felt like an imposter.

"Actually," Ellie swallowed. "I'm here to ask about volunteer opportunities."

Liz closed her eyes and leaned her head back, as if she'd remembered something important. She smiled. "Of course, yes, give me a moment."

She picked up the desk phone, and dialed an extension. When someone answered, she politely asked the person on the other end if they could cover her for. Within a few moments, another woman appeared. This one was much younger, perhaps a volunteer or an intern of some sort. Liz pressed an unseen button beneath the desk, which produced a loud buzzing noise. She made eye-contact with Ellie and nodded to the metal door on the right. "Come through there, I've unlocked it."

Liz led Ellie down a corridor into an open office area with cubicled desks. From behind the soft partition walls, Ellie could hear a few quiet conversations being spoken in gentle voices. Liz looked back at Ellie and gestured the universal *quiet* pantomime, with a single finger over her mouth. Ellie nodded and followed silently.

Liz opened the door to a small secluded office, and shut the door behind them, once Ellie took a seat. "Tell me about yourself," she said. "And what you're looking to do."

"I want to help," Ellie said.

Liz smiled. "We do take donations."

"That's great, and I'll do my best," Ellie said. "But I'd like to do more than that."

"Do you know what this place is, and what we do here?"

Ellie looked around the office. A desk, a computer, but not much of anything else— save for a few unassuming government posters tacked to the wall.

"Actually," she said. "I was just walking by and decided to stop in. I saw the sign. I'm not exactly sure what you do here, though."

Liz removed her eyeglasses. "Well," she said. "We offer victim and trauma support to families. Those suffering from domestic abuse, and mostly to women, and their children. Do you have any experience with this?"

Ellie paused for a moment. "With volunteering, or being a victim of abuse?"

"Both."

"Neither," Ellie said.

Liz nodded. "We work closely with the courts, as well as other Ministries. Family Services has nearly four-hundred staff, including volunteers; many of whom work out of this office. However, we do have remote offices, as well as safe houses."

Ellie nodded along.

Liz leaned forward. "What is your background?"

"It's in healthcare," Ellie said. "X-Ray and MRI specifically, but I'm currently on leave. Have been so for a while." Ellie looked to the ground. "I have an illness."

"Well, we appreciate you coming in," Liz smiled. "We take pride in the diversity of our staff, and take applications from all sorts of people. What we look for are kind, compassionate people, first and foremost. That's all that matters."

Liz opened the drawer to her desk, and pulled out a business card. On the back, she wrote something, and slid it towards Ellie. She used her pen to point. "Go to that website, and there is a section to download volunteer application forms. Once complete, email them to me directly. Minimum you need is a grade-twelve diploma, and you obviously have post-secondary education. Also, as you can imagine, we'll need to do a criminal record check."

Ellie nodded. "What types of roles do you have?"

Liz rose from her seat and peered through the blinds into the office area. She turned to Ellie. "It's sad to say, but there's no shortage of families coming through here that need help," she said. "There are plenty of roles. Reception or administrative is always needed, to help check in. That's what's going on out there," she pointed. "I might start you there."

"My availability may be a bit tricky," Ellie said self-consciously. "Because I have good days and bad days." She hesitated for a moment. "Because of my health, I mean."

"We'll work something out," Liz assured her. She took her seat again. "If I can get you familiar with how things work, I could use you in one of the transitional units."

Ellie furrowed her brow. "Transitional unit?"

"We have temporary housing off-site to help families while they transition into permanent ones, safe from their abusers."

"What would I do there?"

"There's plenty," Liz said. "We need people to check women in, get them settled. Reception. Child care. Cleaning, watering plants, stocking food and supplies. Don't worry, there's many things to keep you busy. In effect, it's a home for these women and their children, and we maintain it like any other home. Most are really good people, just scared. If they are deemed at-risk youth, have a history of substance abuse, or deal with significant mental health issues— there are other types of housing for that."

"Is it safe?" Ellie said.

"As safe as we can make it."

"I'd like to help, then."

Liz smiled. "That settles it. And, really, Ellie: you are there to help women connect with each other, and to provide support. I've been here for over twenty years, because I get just as much out of it, as I put in. It's extremely fulfilling work. And that's the truth. It brings me a sense of…"

"Purpose," Ellie said, completing Liz's sentence.

"Purpose," Liz nodded her head. "Exactly. It brings me a sense of purpose."

Liz walked Ellie back to the foyer of the building, where she held the door open. On the way, she stopped at the wall of pamphlets and took her time to find the one she needed. She handed it with a nod to Ellie. "Take it."

Ellie turned it over to read the top: *Chronic Illness Women's Support Group.* "Thank you," she said kindly.

"You'll be surprised; how much it can help."

Liz reached out a hand. Ellie returned the gesture, and they shook hands firmly. "I meant to ask you," Liz said, before Ellie could step out onto the sidewalk. "Why us? Was it random?"

"Finding this building was random, yes. But this organization was not," Ellie answered truthfully. "My husband and I used to talk about doing more work, to help others, and to try and find fulfillment outside ourselves. Waiting for things to be perfect in our own lives, before being able to help others, is, well…bullshit. We waited too long, because our lives were complicated. But that was a mistake, and I realize that now. He suffered through domestic abuse as a boy, so it's important I'm here helping now. For me. And for him."

Ellie could see that Liz understood the hurt in her eyes. She didn't have to ask if Ellie's health would get better; nor did she have to ask if Ellie's husband was still alive. She seemed to just know. She had the intuition. Liz leaned forward and hugged Ellie. "Get those applications done, Ellie," she said. "I'm looking forward to seeing you."

"Will do," Ellie said. Before she turned to walk away, a question loomed. Ellie turned. "And by the way," she said. "I meant to tell you. I love your pin. The bird."

"It's a sparrow," Liz said, looking down at her lapel.

"Does it mean something?"

Liz held the ornament gently between her thumb and index finger. "It does," she said with pride. "They work very hard, these birds— as small as they are, to achieve great things. They don't sit idle. This little sparrow of mine, symbolizes *empowerment.* For all of us."

Ellie thought about that for a long while after she'd left Liz; on the walk back to her car, and on the drive home. It had stuck in her head.

There were those women that carried burdens, and others, who found liberation.

Some women wore albatrosses around their necks, while others wore sparrows on their lapels.

Chapter Twenty-Two

"How long have you worked here?" the boy asked Ellie, turning his head towards his mother for approval.

Ellie thought about it for a moment. "I think it's been about five months," she said. "And, I don't really work here. I'm a volunteer."

She smiled at him. He was small for his age. Thin, and short. His little stature gave his teeth the appearance that they were much larger than they actually were; causing him to light up the room when he smiled. He sat on the bed next to his mother, red winter coat still on, but he had left his snow-covered boots on the doormat by the front door. His feet dangled from the bed.

"What's the difference?" he asked.

Ellie quietly chuckled. "I don't get paid."

"What?" he shouted in surprise. "No pay? Why are you here?"

His mother gave him a stern look, and he slumped his shoulders. "Sorry mama," he said.

His mother straightened his thick black curls with her fingers, and softly rubbed the back of his skinny brown neck. "It's okay," she reassured him. "Just try to keep your voice down. We have to be polite."

Ellie listened to the woman interacting with her son. Her English was quite good, despite the relatively thick accent. Indian, maybe? Ellie wasn't sure. Her hair was long, and as dark as her son's. It was obvious where he'd inherited the curls from.

She was trying her best, considering the state she was in, and trying to hold it together for her children. Ellie could tell. The mother didn't want to let them see her upset. Her face was swollen with tears, and Ellie had been watching a dark bruise rapidly forming beneath the woman's right eye. She had a deep scratch on her neck. Still, she spoke with poise and an unwavering tone in her voice.

The boy nodded and turned his attention back to Ellie. His younger sister, sat silently on the other side of their mother, bundled up in knit winter clothing, and listening intently to the conversation she was too young to fully understand.

"What's your name?" Ellie asked the boy.

He answered without hesitation. "Benjamin. But I like *Benny* better." He smiled a toothy grin. "That's a nickname, you know."

"I'm Ellie."

"Is that a nickname too?" Benny asked.

"It is," Ellie smiled. "My full name is Eloise, but my mother called me Ellie. Because I love elephants. So, it stuck."

"I love elephants too!" he said, trying simultaneously to relay his excitement, and yet, keep his volume low to not upset his mother. He glanced at her again. "They're my favorite," he whispered.

"Me too," Ellie said.

"Mom has a nickname too," Benny said. "Everyone calls her Cece."

"Cecelia, actually," his mother interjected. "But yes, you can call me Cece." She tried to smile through the sorrow she hid from her children. "Everybody else does."

"Nice to meet you, Cece." Ellie turned and made eye contact with the boy. "Benny, how old are you?"

"Seven."

"And what's your sister's name?"

He peered at his sibling. "Nidra."

"That's pretty," Ellie said.

Benny scrunched his nose. "I guess."

"How old is she?"

"This many," Benny said, holding up three fingers.

"Did you see the box of toys near the couch there, when you came in?"

Benny shyly nodded, looking up at his mother. He tugged at her sleeve, and gazed into the living room. Ellie nodded at Cece, wordlessly asking for permission. Cece nodded back. Ellie helped the toddler onto the floor, then Benny. Nidra looked up at her in wonder.

Ellie knelt to Benny's level. "Can you do me a favor? Can you take your sister and go play? You can choose anything in that box. They're yours."

"Anything?" Benny asked, checking in with his mother again through eye contact.

"Anything," Ellie promised.

Benny held his little sister's hand and carefully led her towards the couch, sensitive to her awkward movements. He slowed his steps, so that his sister could keep up. Ellie watched the two little humans shuffle along the floor with a lump in her throat, wondering how anyone could hurt such innocence. She turned her attention to Cece. "You're very lucky to have those two," she said.

Cece tried at first to choke down her reaction, suppressing the guttural sounds in her throat, and holding a tissue to her cheeks. A torrent of warm tears fell from her eyes in a deluge. Still, she tried to squeeze her eyelids shut. Her hands began shaking. Ellie sat next to her, and held her hand tight.

Overcome, Cece finally released; once her children were out of view. She let her head fall onto Ellie's shoulder. She could feel Cece's muscles relax and the more they did, the harder she cried. The two women held each other, and embraced in the purging for as long as it took.

The two children hadn't noticed their mother weeping. They simply interacted with each other in their goodness, telling stories with their action figures, set in their colorful and imaginary worlds.

"Tell me," Ellie said.

Cece tenderly wiped her tears, especially careful around the bruising on her face. "What do want me to tell you?" she asked.

"Anything," Ellie said. "Everything. I want to hear your story."

Cece lowered her eyes. "He hit me again."

"We'll get to that," Ellie said. "But I want to hear about *you*. What were you like as a little girl?"

"Trouble," Cece laughed unexpectedly.

Ellie was glad to see her smile. She crossed her legs and leaned back in her chair. "I bet."

"I'm from Fiji, originally. We lived on a farm. There are fifteen of us."

Ellie's eyes widened. "You're kidding?"

"A family that size, is not uncommon over there."

"You all worked on the farm?"

"Yes," Cece said. "My mother used to tell me that she had us, just to work for her. 'Free labor', she'd say. In those days, there wasn't much do outside of school, and our closest neighbors were ten minutes away. I am the youngest of my siblings, and I'm as close to the oldest one, as I am to the others. They raised me."

"And your parents?" Ellie asked.

"My Dad worked on the farm with us," Cece answered. "When my mother wasn't cooking or cleaning, she was at the temple. After a while, she stopped the domestic work, because my brothers and sisters took it over, once they got old enough. She had more time to pray. And smoke. She smoked a pack of menthols each day, until the day she died. As each sibling married, the next one stepped in."

Ellie looked to the ceiling, imagining what that must have been like. "You go to temple with her?" she asked.

"Never missed day," Cece said. "No one did. She was very religious. Very strict. Missing temple, wasn't met with any understanding. *She* was religious, so *we* are religious."

Ellie listened intently to Cece's story. "Must have been hard on that farm."

"It was normal in those days," Cece said. "We were poor, but we had fun, my brothers and sisters. We had each other, at least. We laughed a lot. About all there was to do."

"Any of them here, in Vancouver? In North America?"

The momentary light in Cece's eyed faded. "They're all back home."

"You miss it?"

Cece burst into tears again, covering her face. This time, Benny noticed. He came running over and comforted his mother. Nidra looked on, little head propped against the armrest, eyes slowly fading into sleep.

Ellie held her chest, and stood. "I'm so sorry, Cece. I shouldn't have said that." She took a seat next to Cece on the bed. "I'm sorry," she repeated.

"Not your fault," Cece said. "I'm all over the place, you know?"

Ellie knew. It had been the same for her for so long, just for different reasons. The flux of emotions that came burying down like a landslide, entombing the world. She knew it all too well. Ellie rubbed the pain in her shoulder, not realizing it was there until that very moment.

Cece helped Benny lay on his side, not wanting to worry him. He rested his head on her lap. She softly ran her fingers through his hair, and he started falling asleep almost instantly.

"I met my husband in my early twenties," Cece said. "A long time ago. Being in your twenties and not married is a problem in our culture. By then you should have two kids, at least. There is a lot of pressure."

"How did you meet?"

"It was arranged. Well, that's a way of saying it," Cece said. "I did have some choice. It's a sort of matchmaking, facilitated by the parents. They bring by boys your age, and you meet. They try to match the families, not just each other. You talk awkwardly. You go out. But your clock is ticking; they never fail to remind you of that. Benny's Dad was handsome. Young. He was tall, and thin. Muscular even. He has curly hair. A strong jawline. He was quiet, and intelligent." She looked down at Benny. "And his son turned out smart like him, so I'm grateful about that."

"What kind of person was he?" Ellie asked.

"He seemed nice. He was studying engineering. So, I picked him. What was I supposed to do? And we got married. You just have to hope that love comes later."

"When did you come here?"

"Shortly after. It was bad, almost from the beginning. His college credentials weren't recognized here. He had to get a job. Anything. Our English wasn't very good. He got an entry-level job making cabinets, and eventually, I was hired at a commercial bakery. I'm still there. It's been almost fifteen years."

"When did it start?" Ellie asked, changing gears. "The abuse."

"Money was tight. We were trying to have kids, and couldn't," Cece said. "He started drinking a lot, and it went from yelling, to violence. It happened so fast, that I can't understand it. Even now." She hesitated for a moment, but found her strength again. "He's broken several of my bones," she said, clasping her jaw. "And there's too many bruises to count.

But I couldn't leave. Somehow, I tried to understand. His dreams of being an engineer, thrown in the garbage because he'd actually tried to pursue something in another country. To pursue a better life. And he was stuck, too smart for his own good. Working a menial job. Wife can't get pregnant. Poor."

"That's no excuse," Ellie said.

"I know," Cece agreed stoically. "But years go by, and you don't know where they go." She looked down at her sleeping son. "We had Benny, so all the more reason to hold the family together. But by then, he couldn't be reasoned with. The alcoholism changed him into another person. Into a monster. I've seen him arrested more times than I can count."

Ellie swallowed. "This happens in front of the kids?" she asked.

"He never goes quietly," Cece said. "They have to restrain him, choke him. Cuff him. They take him bare feet and without a shirt sometimes. Benny sees. The first time that I had the courage to call the police, they were caring. Sympathetic. They'd take him to jail for the night, and try to get me to press charges." Cece shook her head. "But I never did. Divorce isn't a thing in our culture. We're supposed to stick by our men. After dozens of times, the cops no longer had any sympathy. It became routine for them. My fault, for not leaving."

"Not your fault," Ellie encouraged.

Cece looked her in the eye. "It is," she said. "Benny's Dad would come home sober in the morning, and promise he'd never do it again. And I believed him."

"So, what changed?" Ellie asked.

Cece hissed her words, burning anger in her tone. She pointed her chin towards the ceiling, exposing a thin scar on her neck. "He held a knife to me. In front of Benny. That was it."

Ellie's heart stung. Appalled, she tried to let her anger come down. "I'm glad you're here now."

"Me too," Cece said.

"Thank you for sharing with me," Ellie said. "It's important. Part of your journey. And I know, you'll stay on course. We're here to help. The three of you. I'm not a counselor, but I can listen. Anything you need."

"Thank you," Cece said, glancing over at her toddler, fast asleep on the couch. "How long can we stay?"

Ellie stood. "As long as you need," she said. "For now, there are fresh sheets, towels, and essentials in the room. Food in the fridge. Tomorrow, we will get you fully checked in, and I can show you around. There is childcare, and there are resources. There is always someone in the office downstairs, twenty-four-seven. You're safe here."

"Thank you."

Ellie gently raised Cece's chin with her hand, and looked her in the eyes. "This is your new beginning, and you are *not* alone."

Cece nodded, her lips quivered.

Ellie placed a blanket on Nidra, and helped Cece take Benny's jacket off, while he slept. Together, they tucked him underneath the covers. She hugged Cece and excused herself, leaving her to settle in. Ellie turned when she reached the door. "Cece," she said. "I might be the least qualified person to give anyone advice, because my life's a mess too— and that's okay. That's the way it is. I'm here to listen and to help, that's my job here. But I need to tell you something. I hope that's okay?"

Cece nodded.

"You may not see it right now," Ellie said. "But you did the right thing. I can't imagine, and I know it must feel like rock-bottom. But you are not a failure, in case you needed to hear that. You're a fucking hero. That's what you are. And if I've learned anything about healing, is that it's gradual. You can't just cut out whatever is ailing you, and be done with it. It happens, one tiny cell at a time. You'll only see your progress, when you look back. I don't know much Cece, and I'm in it myself— just in a different way. But that much I do know."

Ellie closed the door behind her.

As she walked down the hall, she could hear the muffled sounds of crying coming from some of the other rooms. She picked up her step, and held her wrist to her mouth so that no one would see her breaking down.

Once she reached the sanctity of her vehicle, she wept uncontrollably.

Chapter Twenty-Three

Ellie reached for her basket of meds. She filled up a glass of water, and started meticulously lining up small bottles on the countertop. Some were glass, and others were plastic. Hannah watched worriedly at the sheer number of medications Ellie pulled out of the basket.

There were jars, bottles, and tinctures with little squeeze droppers. They varied in size and color: brown glass, transparent glass, and white plastic. Some were filled with powders, others with capsules and pills, and even more with liquids. Ellie consulted a sheet of lined paper with scribbled handwritten notes, and began systematically swallowing capsules, one handful after another; chasing each handful with a gulp of water.

"That's a lot of medicine," Hannah said, sipping her coffee with furrowed a brow.

Ellie measured a scoop of pure white granules and mixed it into a glass of orange juice. She scowled as she choked it down. "Yeah," she said, placing both hands on the countertop for balance.

"Doesn't look good," Hannah said.

"It's not."

Ellie swallowed again, and continued her regiment. She uncapped each tincture bottle and carefully squeezed counted droplets onto her tongue, following the dosage instructions on the sheet and using the reflection in the microwave door to count each drop. She logged each pill, scoopful, and drop onto the sheet with a blue ink pen. Her friend watched in astonishment. "How often?"

"All of this?" Ellie asked. "The basics, three times a day. Another few handful of pills twice more. And another round, once more before bed. I have to set alarms to keep up for Christ's sake."

Hannah asked a gentle question, "What does it all do?"

"Long story. But in general, they have me on a protocol to kill pathogens and detoxify at the same time."

"Is it helping?" Hannah asked.

Ellie shook her head. "Honestly Hannah," she said. "I don't know if it's killing me or helping me. It's a long game, it's always been. Bishop and I have been on this path before. You hope for the best. You go a few years of taking meds. After a few years, when you realize it's not working, you move on. You find another doctor that you think can help. And in between," she said, looking solemnly into her best friend's eyes. "You die a little more."

"This is it," Hannah said, reaching for Ellie's hand. "Stay on course."

Ellie's heart swelled, Hannah's encouragement reminding of her of Bishop. She smiled at her friend, and carefully put her basket of meds away. She turned to Hannah. "I've gotta go do this thing with Cece, but we're still on for dinner later?"

"Yeah," Hannah said. "You need some back up?"

Ellie smiled. "I think I've got it," she lied.

"They don't have someone at the shelter to go do that?"

"They do," Ellie said. "Me."

Hannah stood and gathered her belongings, and they walked towards the front door. "You know what I mean Ellie," she said. "Isn't it dangerous?"

"For him," Ellie winked, feigning confidence. Truth was, she was terrified, but she'd promised Cece.

Ellie placed a hand on Cece's shoulder, as she glanced silently through the car window. Ellie could feel Cece's pulse through her sweater. They were parked on a quiet street, save for the sound of gentle wind blowing through barren branches. Their seatbelts were still fastened.

"Take your time," Ellie said. "It's your call. We can leave and come back another day, when he's not there. But he's not going to hurt you; not anymore."

Cece took a deep breath and unlocked her car door. Ellie silently followed her to the house, placing a gentle hand on her back as they walked, to let her know she was supported. When Cece opened the front door, light flooded the dark home. Ellie followed her across the threshold. She could smell stale cigarette smoke. Instantly, a gravelly voice called out from the couch. "Who the fuck is this?"

Cece switched on a few lights, and opened a set of blinds. "A friend," she said.

The man squinted when the light penetrated his pupils. "Goddamn it Cece," he said.

Ellie glanced at the row of empty beer cans lined up on the coffee table, next to the ashtray, and a half-empty bottle of whiskey. She could smell the stale stench of booze and sweat emanating from his corner of the room. She remained silent, maintaining eye contact. He bared his teeth in a snarl. "Where are my kids?" he slurred.

"They're safe," Cece said, staring blankly at him. "We're just here to get some things, and then we're gone. The lawyer will be in touch."

"Lawyer?" he asked, casually rising from the couch. "Just that simple?"

Although his body swayed back and forth, Ellie could sense the control he still had over his drunken body, fueled by his seething anger. Before Cece could say anything, Ellie chimed in. She channeled her inner lioness, and spoke matter-of-factly. "Just that simple," she said.

He glared at her in surprise, obviously taken aback at being challenged by a stranger. A woman, no less; and in his own house. His steely gaze tried to penetrate her armor. Large veins formed on both sides of his temples, receding into his thick black hairline. He clenched his fists. Ellie raised her chin in defiance, never breaking the eye contact, and called to Cece over her shoulder. "Go get your things, Cece," she said. "Take your time."

He chuckled to himself and took a long drink of beer, until the can was emptied. He crushed the can into a crumpled ball, and let it fall to the floor; wiping his lips with his forearms, still sneering.

Cece shuffled into the bedroom.

He and Ellie stared each other down, as if preparing for a shootout in the old west. She could feel a lump in her throat, and her abdomen quivering. Still, she held steady.

Cece returned after a few moments, wheeling two suitcases. "Ready?" Ellie asked.

"Ready," Cece said. She looked around her home, closed her eyes, and sighed; saying to goodbye to everything she'd built. Ellie reached out and held Cece's hand for a moment, and took one of the pieces of luggage from her. Together, they headed for the front door. Ellie kept her eyes on him. He stared back for a moment, and unexpectedly looked to the floor.

Suddenly, his face softened. In an instant, his menacing expression transformed from raging anger to that of a concerned, needy man. Sensitive, even. He let his hands fall to his side. "Please," he pleaded after Cece. "Don't do this."

Ellie saw the noticeable change in him, and wondered how he'd altered so quickly from a werewolf, to a mortal being again. For a moment, she could see his kindness somewhere in there; past the alcoholism— past the disease. He was…handsome, even. "I'll change," he begged. "Please, sweetheart. You can't throw everything away."

"You won't change," she said. "You never do. You did this. This is on you. You did this to me; you did this to your kids."

Ellie watched his breathing increase, until he was gasping in short bursts; chest heaving rapidly. His jugular protruded from his neck. Still, they made for the door. He clenched both his fists until they were quaking, sinews twitching on his oaken forearms.

In a single fluid movement, he grasped the neck of the whiskey bottle and heaved it with all his might towards Cece, missing her head by only a few inches. The bottle crashed into the wall and exploded into tiny fragments; the liquor inside splashing over the framed family pictures she had fastened to the wall so many years ago. Cece barely flinched, as if she'd expected the violent outburst. He leaped over the couch and lunged at Cece like an apex predator pursuing its prey. Saliva leaped from his gnashing teeth. He moved, head-first and shoulders back— as if he were going to bash her head with his, in a final Kamikaze attack. The moment before his body reached hers, Ellie fiercely stepped in between them. Startled, he tried to recoil and stop himself. He slid on his heels and fell backwards; his skull hitting the hardwood planks like a sledgehammer, knocking the wind out of his lungs. He gasped in retreat, and his body turned into a flaccid jellyfish.

Ellie straddled her feet over his lying body, and leaned forward, bringing her eyes as close to his as she could stand. Her scarlet hair hung down over her face in long tendrils. As she spoke one final sentence, they danced over his flushed cheeks. "You won't change," she said. "But Cece has."

They left him lying helpless and defeated in a heap on the floor, and drove far away.

She could already feel her pain swelling the minute she'd dropped Cece off, as if on cue. The adrenaline may have kept her going for some time, but her disease always knew when to step in.

Ellie drove home, staring through the windshield in a state of utter disconnection. She gripped the steering wheel with force, white knuckles glowing on both hands. She occasionally let up her grip, but only when she'd realize what she was doing while practicing her anti-anxiety breathing exercises.

Regretfully, she had hit rush hour traffic. The lack of control and movement in the steadily diminishing light, created a claustrophobic coffin inside the cabin of her SUV.

Her vehicle was lined up amongst hundreds of cars in the dense traffic on the bridge; part of the congregation of poor souls commuting home from work. As far as she could see, there were a trail of red taillights curving into the horizon, inching along. Under normal circumstances, the drive home would have taken an hour. In the present moment, it was likely going to be almost double that.

The sky began to darken as the sun set, casting deep blues across the horizon. Ellie tilted her head and glanced upwards through the windshield at the drops of rain beginning to pour from the unseen clouds in the sky. She squinted through the reflection of bright city lights and vehicles on the highway, trying to control her impending migraine. Her wrists hurt. Her back ached. She felt a hollow chasm in her chest, and massaged the lump in her throat.

Ellie tried to focus on anything but her looming pain. The car behind her honked, snapping her back to reality. She glanced in the rear-view mirror, unable to see the driver through the rain. She clenched her jaw and inched the car forward a few feet in the evening traffic, before coming again to a complete stop. She tried to breathe, collectedly, through her diaphragm; channeling every method she'd learned over the years. She looked around, and considered fleeing on foot; if only her aching feet would take her.

Just before the world fully closed in, the traffic broke. Ellie drove in autopilot, floating in lost time; as if she'd been abducted by aliens. By the time Ellie made it home, it was already dark and the city was engulfed in a downpour.

She sat cross-legged on her office floor, trying to choke back the nausea. She swallowed watery spit, after spending most of the evening vomiting. She had tried to make a small dinner, but had found herself with the inability to swallow when it came time to eat. What little she had taken down, had ended up in the toilet. When these flare-ups came, they were relentless.

And they never came with a single symptom.

She squeezed her wrists, forcing blood into her aching extremities, balling and releasing her fingers as if they were doing squats. Nothing was helping.

Ellie pet Izzy's soft white fur, as she laid half-asleep in her pink dog bed. She had dragged it into the room with her teeth, and Ellie helped her pull it the rest of the way, so that she could be close. Izzy was her only saving grace at the moment.

Helplessly, Ellie tried to correlate the connection. She'd been doing so good. The medicine had been helping, she'd thought. But it was her fault. What was she doing? It was her own actions that had brought on the debilitating pressure headaches, and surge of neuropathy. She had known what the stress was going to do, and yet, she couldn't step away. She couldn't leave Cece, and those kids. It had been a victory; but at what cost?

Ellie's fingers tingled as she tried to exercise them. In her mind's eye, she used a Samurai sword to cut a path through the brain fog. She tried to find an opening. She willed her strength. Channeled her inner warrior. Searched for a beacon with which she could light her way.

Think Ellie!

She negotiated with the pain, begging for mercy like a recovering heroin addict.

I won't overexert myself. I'll manage my stress. I won't miss any medication. I'll sleep better, I promise.

Ellie laid her head down, left temple on the wool rug. Her brain sizzled inside her skull. She tried to focus on Izzy's large, brown eyes and little black nose. She looked like a miniature white, polar bear cub.

Ellie stretched her legs out on the floor, and stroked the top of Izzy's head, trying to redirect her focus. "Who rescued who?" Ellie whispered to her beloved pet.

Suddenly, Ellie's pain rose like a rogue wave, and her limbs straightened. Instead of resisting, she let herself be carried away into the depths. Tried to endure the swell until it passed. But she couldn't.

She let herself be swallowed into the black hole; let the matter of her being distort into singularity. The brain is a funny thing. It has safety mechanisms built in, to help usher its host to the other side.

Like when a person is being burned alive.

When the pain gets too intense, the mind will throw in the towel. Concede defeat. Shut itself down like a self-aware super computer, starving for electrical current. It knows what is about to come, so it prepares itself.

Ellie ground her teeth, and watched the room first blur, then blacken; before passing out.

Part IV
Metamorphosis

*One day you will tell your story
of how you overcame what you went through,
and it will be someone else's survival guide.*

– Brene Brown

Chapter Twenty-Four

Ellie instinctively squeezed her eyes shut, blocking the intense light from penetrating her pupils. She raised a hand, and covered her brow, immediately aware of the ocular pain in her right eye. When she pressed down, a current of electrical pain shot to the back of her neck. She winced.

Ellie sat up from the floor and leaned her back against the desk, trying to piece together the night before like a hungover drunk. Izzy was still fast asleep, and at some point in the night— it seemed Winston had made his way in. He had curled up his little body against Ellie's, bringing her his empathetic comfort, like he always tried to do. She recalled feeling his warm, soft fur against her skin, calming her nerves, even in sleep.

Ellie rose slowly, both hands on her knees, and performed a self-check along the way. She braced for the worst. Her back seared when her hips hinged with her legs, and she reminded herself to go slow. The muscles in her body shrieked in agony. Lactic acid coursed through her veins, settling in every sinew. She felt as though she'd spent twelve straight hours in the gym, without the benefits that come with it.

She staggered towards windows, and opened the drapes to look outside.

It was still pouring rain.

The streets were empty. The singular sound of pelting water on the rooftops, in contrast to the silence in the neighborhood, was soothing to her ears.

At least the house was warm.

Ellie turned and took inventory of the room, trying to piece together the scene like a forensics investigator. Books strewn about, pens and blue cards on the desktop. Bishop's belongings on the floor, unpacked from their boxes. Chair askew.

Then she remembered.

She had come into the office with the best of intentions, wanting to feel good. Willing herself to try and be positive. Optimistic, creative even. But the pain had come on strong, worse after dinnertime. The buzzing, low-grade aching she could always handle, but this had been something else.

Ellie was still reeling from her afternoon with Cece, and trying not to let it get to her. She needed to be helpful to others, but not let it past her own shield— because she too, had to protect herself.

That much she did know.

It was her job right now; work that she'd volunteered for— but she needed to create borders to be able to get through each day.

Bishop had always warned her about her natural sensitivity. She was an empath, and she knew it. But it came with a price. Compassion for others, often meant a breach for her own well-being. It was Bishop's belief, that her line of work had significantly contributed to her health concerns, over time. It was part of the reason he insisted she leave, so many years ago.

And now, her identity was inseparable between her former self, and what the government classified as a *person with disability*.

The night before, she tried to push through. Tried not to think about those women at the shelter, suffering so incredibly. She knew how it would affect her. Yet, she had opened up. It was her obligation to try and help. Those stories needed to be told, and needed to be heard. It was a part of the healing process, and she was honored to take on the responsibility. For them. It was the least she could do.

It was the power of hope. Of being human.

It was *love*.

Ellie had come into her home office with the intent, to start making up some plans. She no longer wanted to merely survive, or exist; but wanted something more. Something greater. She needed it. She had tried to push past the pain.

There was a time, when she couldn't shake the thought of ending her own life. The pain, the emotions— were insurmountable. Never more so, than when she had lost her husband. When she would've chosen rotting away in her bed. She had wondered once, how long it would take to starve to death.

Ellie had secretly held a blade to her own wrist, while her husband slept, on more than one occasion. She'd pulled out her own hair, attempting to exercise the demons from her brain. She had intentionally overdosed.

But not the night before.

Ellie had come in, with hope; despite the pain. She had wanted to plan… something else. She had wanted to execute… something else.

Ellie had come in, wanting to add to her *Intention Board*. She had wanted to choose one of her new poetry books to start reading. She had wanted to research cities she'd want to visit in the future, and courses she'd like to take. Exercises she could do, or recipes she could try.

All in an attempt to live a better life, and to envision the horizon.

But the phantom that lived inside her body would not let her. So, she fought it as best as she could, and woke up still sweating from the battle.

Winston stretched: downward facing dog. She looked at him with love. He returned the eye contact, pleading with his bushy eyebrows. "I know," she smiled. "I know you're hungry."

Her own stomach growled. She wiped her eyes.

Winston sauntered lazily into the living room, leaving Ellie in the silent office with sleeping Izzy. Ellie stretched, and began gathering up some of the books from the floor. She scanned each title, dusting off the covers with her palm.

Some were hers, and some were Bishop's. The ones piled on her desk were new: the ones she'd recently purchased from *The Last Chapter* bookstore. She set them aside, reserved for her to-do list.

Ellie made another pile, which were made up of ones from Bishop's collection. Those books were well-worn, but in decent condition. It was the mark of a man who loved to read, but who cherished and took care of the things he owned.

On the books that he connected with the most, he'd scribbled handwritten notes for reference, stuck little Post-Its on pages, and highlighted areas that he'd want to consult later on. His preference in books was vast:

philosophy, brain science, environmental, photography, and writing. The fiction he possessed ran the gamut; from award-winning classics, action and horror— to introspective literary. Peppered in, were some poetry pocket books: Robert Frost, Kahlil Gibran, and two different English translations of *The Divine Comedy*.

Ellie picked up a random novel from the pile.

The cover on this particular book, was tattered and several pages were dog-eared. It was obvious he'd read this one several times over, and may have even travelled with it. The cover's corner was curled in, with a small tear on the very edge. You could tell he'd tried to straighten it out.

She flipped through and searched for a page that he'd written in. It didn't take her long to find one. She focused on it, remembering Bishop from the handwriting that was uniquely his. Ghostly letters now; a mix of upper and lower case, some printed, and some cursive.

Ellie ran her fingers along the ink ledger he'd made, caressing the subtle etchings in the thin page, created by the heavy pen point. Ellie used her thumb to shuffle the pages like playing cards, half expecting them to reveal flipbook art characters.

Instead, flashes of yellow highlighted sentences sporadically appeared, as each sheet passed. She stopped on a random page, wondering which thought had won the lottery.

Ellie read the text that Bishop had highlighted:

He had learned that light came not in the form of a flood one day, but gathered itself over time.

Ellie smiled, basking in the thought. The idea, which she'd stumbled across at this moment in time, didn't feel like a coincidence. It felt like Bishop had sent a message from heaven.

Like a spark of lighting igniting a wildfire, an energy filled her soul.

She had work to do, and she would no longer let anything get in the way. Ellie took a seat at the computer, and opened up her word processor. She typed vigorously, so that she wouldn't lose any thoughts. It took her less than a minute to write several sentences. She hit the print button with vigor. Ellie waited with bated breath as her thoughts materialized on a sheet of crisp, white paper. She picked it up and read it over. Ellie tacked it onto her board, on the side that read: *Things to think about.*

She stepped back, and proudly read her words:

I **MUST** always be kind, especially to myself.

I **AM** confident, beautiful, & smart.

I **AM** loved, and I won't be afraid to love others.

I **DO NOT** have a terminal illness.

I **WILL** learn to manage this disease.

Some things are **OUT OF MY CONTROL.**

I **WILL** learn to be present in the moment.

I **DESERVE** happiness.

My mother's fate is **NOT** my own.

I will **PRACTICE** gratitude: Every. Single. Day.

There is **NOTHING** to be afraid of.

I'm **ALLOWED** to have bad days.

Light gathers itself **OVER TIME**.

Ellie continued, catching up from the lost time the night before. She moved in a frenzy. The clock felt like it was ticking in double time, as if she could sense herself aging; and she moved with urgency.
She wrote down list after list, in her notebook.
Things that needed fixing around the house. Ideas on how to redecorate.
She wrote down cities and countries on her travel list, and why she'd want to see those places:

Belgium for the architecture and landscape, which she could photograph. She'd finally be able to put the camera, that Bishop had bought for her, to good use.

France, for its prominence in fashion and interior design— and the romance, of course.

Germany, because they led the world in cutting-edge health treatments. Maybe someone there could help, maybe she could learn something in her own journey?

She Googled, and created a list of piano teachers in the area, and their corresponding rates, with her neighbor Sean's cousin at the top of the list.

Ellie spent over an hour reading about the Chronic Illness Women's Support Group that Liz had suggested, and jotted down some dates and times in her calendar that she'd like to attend.

Finally, the real task at hand.

It was time, but she was terrified.

She realized she'd been subconsciously avoiding it, and leaving it last.

Ellie looked down at her hands, and willed her fingers to stop shaking. She felt emptiness in her chest, adrenaline in her blood.

Jump in the water, she thought. *It will be okay. You can do this.*

She typed away furiously, and read for hours as the day went on; researching every ounce of information she could absorb. She'd dabbled in the past, and had a good starting point; but hadn't before considered it so seriously. Now, there was a renewed sense of focus.

Her heart was racing. She was afraid, but was exhilarated at the same time.

What if you're not smart enough? she thought.

Ellie heard her inner voice call back, *But what if you are?*

Her eyes dashed left to right, reading outlines, reviews, and course requirements. She read the program name with focused intent: *Body, Mind, & Spirit: Health & Wellness Coaching Certification.*

Ellie hoped she was doing the right thing. She had always instinctively known, that she should be pursing her passions; *following her bliss.*

In another life, she was a marathon runner. She was in healthcare and understood the world of allopathic medicine. Ellie loved the world of health and wellness, and everything about it; it just didn't seem to love her back.

All that she'd learned from her own path as a sick person, could perhaps help someone else. She was sure of it. She had learned so much from Ruth, although there was still so much work to do on overcoming traumas.

She had absorbed from Bishop, in observing how he tried to quiet his mind, and immerse himself in a meditative state. How he taught himself, and committed to learning new skills— to challenge himself in those pursuits. God knows, Ellie herself, had been to more than her fair share of naturopathic & traditional Chinese medicine doctors. Specialists of every kind. She had read more on the subject of chronic illness, than anyone she knew. She had devoted the last decade of her life, to finding the way.

All of this experience, had to have formed into a nexus in Ellie's center. Deep down she knew, to heal, one had to be mindful of the delicate balance amongst all body systems. Would this course be for *her*? Or to help others?

Maybe, a bit of both.

She stared at the button on the monitor: *Register Now*.

Her index finger quivered on her mouse. She delicately spun the wedding ring on her hand, over and over, and tucked her hair behind her ears with both hands. Ellie looked down at Izzy, who started wagging her tail the exact moment they made eye contact.

Bishop had always worried about her inability to draw a line between kindness and the resulting negative absorption, knowing how susceptible she was. As a being, Ellie had been fundamentally changed, taking care of her mother. Forever a different person, having gone through so many years of pain.

If Bishop had it his way, she'd be in a line of work where she'd never have to take care of anyone else. Something simple, where the discussion of poor health or sadness would never occur. A restaurant owner maybe, or a bookstore clerk. Selling trendy, high-end furniture to young couples.

Certainly not this.

This would be a complete pivot for her. She wondered if Bishop would have been disappointed; her intentionally walking back into a career where people may be at their worst. Drug addictions, terminal people. Those with chronic illnesses, suffering like Ellie herself. Or those who had lost every ounce of confidence and self-esteem because nothing had worked to get healthy, to lose that extra weight, or to quit smoking.

Coaching someone, helping someone; taking on someone else's anguish— could be the last straw. The thing that throws her into the final tailspin.

On the other hand, it could also bring hope. Purpose even. Sometimes Bishop couldn't see that. He was her protector, but the bigger picture was hard for him to see, sometimes.

The words beckoned to her: *Register Now.*

She hesitated for a split-second. A smile formed in the corner of her mouth. She stared at the words for another brief moment. Ellie closed her eyes, and listened to her heart.

After a few seconds, she clicked the button.

Ellie floated in her thoughts. She considered her own advice: *Be grateful.* More specifically: *What have you done to be grateful today?*

She stepped out onto the covered front porch, with her two dogs looking on from the warm threshold, watching the rain fall. Izzy's little white head peaked out through the doorway. She studied each end of the street, looking for friends to bark at, mouth agape in a smile, and tongue panting. Winston watched Ellie closely from the safety of the doormat, wondering what she was up to, determined to stay dry.

Ellie crouched and lit the end of an incense that she had found in one of Bishop's drawers. The box had said *Agarbatti*: a word that was entirely unfamiliar to her. When the flame ignited the end of the black stick, wisps of dark smoke danced in the air, swirling in reaction to the hovering dampness.

She blew out the flame to reveal a calming scent. A perfume of mystical aromas wafted into the air, and consumed Ellie's nostrils. It burned her sinuses initially, until she acclimated after a few seconds. The fragrance, so foreign to her, still somehow felt like home. Maybe because she'd remembered her husband burning it when he was having tough days. He'd come into the house with it still lingering on his clothes, but she never asked what he was up to. She just knew, that there was something he needed to take care of.

She took a deep breath and inhaled the scent, trying to decipher its enchanting origins, but couldn't quite place it. Might have been sandalwood, or patchouli. Frankincense maybe.

Ellie set the burning stick into a ceramic holder, and placed it on the patio floor, near the front door. This way, some of the purifying smoke could still enter and bless the house, without overwhelming the dogs— and some could float into the atmosphere, to carry her prayers.

Ellie knelt, and closed her eyes. She leaned back until her body was comfortable to hold itself up without her conscious direction. She placed her palms on her knees. She felt the wind. She heard the rain.

Ellie focused on seeing herself. Her face, and body. Her red hair; her every limb.

She slowed her breath, and dove deeper; focusing on every wrinkle, every pore.

Four breaths in, five out.

In her mind's eye, she imagined herself first, in a plain white room.

The more she breathed, the more those walls disintegrated, and the more her own body materialized in this magical place. Time began to dissolve like a vapor, until a second felt like an eon. She remained there, pushing on the outer the walls out of the white room, until there was only blank, colorless space around her.

Next, she pictured herself in her own back yard, with the dogs nearby. Close enough so that she could feel their security, and count their every breath. She knelt in the center of the grass, feeling its earthly connection. She could count each blade of luminescent green grass, as they combined together to tickle her bare feet. She conjured up a light, which emanated from the top of her head, and into the heavens.

From the sky, and through this celestial conduit, light and energy poured into her. It refilled her soul's vessel, providing nourishing vitality. In contrast, she imagined her own energy spreading through her rooted feet into the Earth, offering up her own sacrifice.

Moments later, she saw herself on a white-sand beach, and took a glimpse at her imagined future. There was no one around, as far as she could see. The sun was shining, and the sky was blue. She saw herself from outside her body.

Ellie was healthy, devoid of illness.

She could see it, and she could sense it.

It was overwhelming.

Her skin was radiant, and her thick, ruby hair exchanged a dance with the ocean breeze. Emerald waves crashed on the beach, and she could feel its wetness against her naked skin, baptizing her body in its cleansing elixir.

Her heart felt at peace. She registered no pain, and she experienced no sadness.

As she knelt on her front porch, dogs watching, she whispered to herself. "Thank you, for everything I am blessed to have."

Ellie opened her eyes.

The incense had barely burned, three-quarters of it was still left—but she was dumbfounded. It felt as if hours had passed.

Ellie sat on the top step, and called to her dogs. She hugged them both, thankful they were by her side. Her heart was full, as she reflected on the experience.

She had never before reached that deep state of meditative harmony, and her conscious mind tried to rationalize it. Even with Ruth's guidance, she had never before been able to isolate the focus. The helpless distraction of dizziness, soreness, or brain fog, always leapt in the way.

Even after her long and painful night, the evening before; even without a single step forward towards healing, in all this time. In all these years.

Why now?

Her symptoms felt as if they'd been getting worse, these last few weeks, in fact. She hadn't been sleeping again. There was never less hope than there was now. And yet, she felt as if she'd taken a step forward.

Free your mind, your ass will follow.

It was as close to praying as Ellie had done, since she'd been a little girl.

Immersed within that minute strand of a connection, as momentary as it was, existed an opportunity to say *thank you*— to whomever.

Whether that was Mother Nature, God, the universe; whomever cared to listen. But she took it.

And perhaps with it, came a single, infinitesimal atom of *acceptance*.

Chapter Twenty-Five

"It's been five years, Bishop," Ellie whispered. "Five years since you left this world."

The sun had just risen over the horizon, and the June sun cut through the blue sky. Its rays had already begun to warm up the day. The air was fresh in a way that only an early morning could bring.

Ellie sat on a rock outcropping at the beach, listening to the waves crash.

Bishop had introduced her to this special place, many years ago, so that she'd have a place to remember her beloved mother, Catherine. Ellie had returned every year since, to drop off flowers. White roses for mom, and red ones now, for Bishop— to be carried off by the sea.

The day of her visits never mattered, nor did the season.

No pressure, just whatever felt right. Sometimes she'd come on the calmest of summer days, and other times, when the winter waves crashed violently against the Earth. These last few years, Ellie had been coming during warm, quiet mornings in the summer. Mostly because Bishop loved the sun.

He had often described his happy place to her as sunrise on a tropical beach, with a book and an Americano. And so, she tried to honor that for him. It brought a pleasant thought to her soul.

She listened to the gulls, as they skimmed the water, looking for fish. There was no one else on the beach, except for a lone jogger whom she passed on her way down from the parking lot.

Ellie had carefully scaled their special place; a small, black-rock peninsula that jutted out from the beach. On some days, children climbed its surface, pretending that it was a deserted island. They'd chase each other with kelp, pretending to be sea monsters, while Ellie looked on from the beach.

It had become more than just a place of memorial to her, and she'd find herself driving down with a tea, to find some peace on hard days. Sometimes, she'd bring a blanket to lay on the sand, and give gratitude during one of her meditations. Over the years, one of the retired locals took it upon himself to donate, transport, and bolt two large wooden chairs at the small flattened peak, for his fellow beach-goers to enjoy.

Ellie sat in the red one, while the yellow chair remained empty, save for two bouquets.

She stared straight ahead, into the horizon.

The water was so blue that she could barely differentiate between the ocean and the sky. Ellie inhaled a chest full of sea air, and listened to the gentle surf.

"I miss you, Bishop," she said into the open air. "I've tried to live my life without you and mom, but it's been hard. But I have learned to release the both of you, so that you can go and do what you need to do, in the next world. I can't hold you back anymore. It's not good for either one of us. I needed that too, because it's helped my healing."

Ellie breathed deeply, collecting herself. "I realize that now. I've been holding trauma like a burden that weighs ten-thousand pounds, and I've been dragging it behind me most of my life. Then I only let myself add to it. I was never taught how to emancipate myself from it; it was something I had to learn on my own."

Ellie wiped tears from her eyes, and smiled with fondness. "I think about you every day, and I hope I made you proud. I'm still sick, Bishop— but it's better. It hasn't gotten worse. And I'm better able to cope. I've come to accept that I will have to manage this disease for the rest of my life, and that's okay. I've learned how, and learning more each day.

"You were right, it's the little things.

"It *is* the self-love; it *is* the gratitude. It is the allowance to fail if I need to, and the determination to get up again. Ruth helps me still, and I work at it every single day. I committed to it, finally. I was scared to, before.

"I have bad days, but I'll be okay. I know that now. I no longer live every moment in fear, nor do I dwell in the world of *'what if?'*

"I accept the pain, the discomfort, and the loneliness that comes with it. And I try to let it pass, because I'm sure it will. I collect my bruises, I covet my scars with pride, I dry my tears, I clean up the mess— and I shout back into void.

"Now, the darkness fears *me*."

Ellie peered into the horizon, knowing no one would be answering back.

She watched the water swirl and lap against the rocks, white foam collecting on the surface of the ocean.

From the street level, a man stood watch over Ellie.

Despite the expected heat, he wore a thin black wind breaker, zipped up to his chest. His dark hair fluttered in the wind, and he kept his emerald eyes locked on the woman on the rocks. After a few moments, he shouted over the wind. "Ellie!"

She turned her head, barely able to hear him over the surf. She cupped her hands over her mouth and bellowed back. "Yeah?"

"Do you want me to bring her down?"

Ellie's heart swelled. She smiled and nodded. "Of course!"

The man began walking down the embankment, gently helping a small child. Barely able to walk down the rocky decline, he held both of her hands in his, balancing them above her head. In her left hand, the child clutched a toy.

He tried crouching as he balanced her with his long arms, trying to minimize the towering distance between himself and the little girl. Step by step, they descended until they reached the beach. Ellie walked back from the rocky point to meet them in the middle. The closer Ellie approached, the wider the smile on the child's face became.

Finally, Ellie reached them and crouched at the child's eye level. She knelt on the sand, and straightened out the little girl's windblown brown hair. "Hi sweetheart."

The child laughed and held up her stuffed toy, in the shape of a soft gray elephant. "Hi mama."

Ellie gave her a kiss on the forehead. "Hi, baby."

Ellie took the child's hands from the man, and picked her up, nesting her small body against her chest. Ellie smiled at him, combing back her strawberry hair and squinting through the sunshine. "Thanks, Tom."

He kissed her on the lips, placing a gentle hand on her cheek. The child laughed. "Dada kissed mama!"

Tom laughed. "He did, and here's one for you too!"

He kissed his daughter on the forehead and turned to Ellie. "You okay?"

She nodded.

"Take your time. I'll be up there. Holler if you need me."

"Thanks Keanu," she winked. "I won't be long."

Ellie held the collar of his jacket. "Still not used to this weather?" she asked. "Too cold here, even in June?"

He smiled. "It's nice. I'm still figuring it out. It's no California, though."

She chuckled and gave him a gentle pinch on the cheek. She stopped for a moment to admire him, running her fingers through his dark beard. He held her for a moment, and gently kissed the back of her hand.

Ellie and the child waved, as Tom headed back to the parking lot.

She watched him reach the street level, before heading back to the wooden chairs on the rocks, with her little girl. Ellie sat her daughter on the chair and placed the bouquets in her lap. The child held onto them like a precious treasure.

Ellie scanned the sky, and surveyed the ocean surface. "This is my daughter."

"Who are you talking to, silly?" the girl asked.

"Well," Ellie said. "It's time you met some very important people."

The child looked forward, squinting into the sunlit horizon. "There's no one there."

"But there is," Ellie said. "I want you to meet your grandmother. Her name is Catherine."

"Catherine?" the little girl said. "Like me?"

"Like you, sweetheart. We named you after her."

Catherine looked at her mother in wonder, then back to the ocean.

Ellie held her daughter's hand with pride. "And someone very special to me, named Bishop. He was my husband, before Daddy."

"Oh."

Ellie laughed, and tucked Catherine's chestnut hair behind her ears. "I come here to visit sometimes."

"I don't see anyone," she said. "Where are they?"

"They're everywhere," Ellie said. "They're both in heaven now. But they are always here with us. With you, with me, and even with Daddy. Anywhere we go. I come here, to this special place, to drop off a gift. But I also come to think, and to relax. And to meditate. It makes me feel good, to connect with them. What about you? What do you think? Do you like this place?"

Catherine nodded enthusiastically. "It's beautiful."

"What about Zola?" Ellie asked.

Catherine looked down at her stuffed elephant, and back at her mother. "Zola likes it here too."

"Good," Ellie said.

She faced the water, her daughter's little hand placed tightly in hers. "Mom. Bishop," she said. "This is Catherine, my daughter. I haven't been ready to bring her here, but it's time. She's kind like you, mom. And she's funny like you, Bishop.

"I met her Dad, Tom, in California: where we had our honeymoon, Bishop. I was there for you; mourning you— and, life threw me a curveball. I left him there, never thinking I'd see him again. But, we connected again. I felt a lot of guilt at first. But he's good to me, Bishop.

"Like you were.

"He's patient, and he's understanding... of all that I come with. Sometimes, I think that you sent him to me.

"No.

"I'm certain of it.

"I miss you both so much, but I want you to know I'm okay. Things have changed for me, and I'm happy. It's a bumpy road, but I am. Truly. And I live my life every day, to honor you both as best as I can. And I thank God for your presence in my life, every day."

"You okay mommy?" Catherine asked.

Ellie wiped away her tears. "I'm okay, sweetheart."

"But you're crying."

"They're happy tears," Ellie said through the lump in her throat. "I promise."

"Okay," her daughter said with a smile.

"You ready?"

Catherine looked down at the flowers, and nodded her head. "They're pretty."

"Just like you."

Ellie and Catherine walked close to the water's edge, as safely as they could, and gently placed roses into the ocean, one-by-one. White ones for grandma, and red ones for Bishop. They sat together and watched the flowers gently float away with the current, until they disappeared.

A gift received.

Ellie piggybacked Catherine back up the beach to her waiting father.

"Thanks," Ellie said to Tom.

"For what?"

"For waiting. For giving me her. For everything, Tom. I know it's not easy for you. I know you left your home for me. And I know I come with a lot."

He hugged his wife and daughter as tightly as he could, never wanting to let them go. He valiantly fought back his own tears, but they came anyway. Tom kissed Ellie's forehead, and then his daughter's, without a word. He didn't have to say anything. Ellie just knew.

He grinned and moved aside so that Ellie and Catherine could see behind him. "Look who's here," Tom said.

A few cars over, stood Hannah and her daughter, leaning against their car; both smiling. Catherine ran over and hugged Hannah's daughter, Charlotte. Although they'd had a significant gap in age, they embraced and giggled like two old soulmates, reuniting after an eternity.

Ellie let the image of her best friend burn into her memory, and guided her thanks into the heavens. In an instant, she took a mental picture of the moment: the temperature, the smell of the ocean breeze. The way Hannah was dressed, and the way her blonde hair blew in the wind. Hannah's daughter, Charlotte, and the pretty way she smiled. The sounds around them. The waves. The sound of her own daughter's laughter.

Every. Single. Detail.

Hannah waved. "You ready?"

"I am," Ellie said. She opened the back hatch of their vehicle. There were two kennels stowed safely in the back.

Immediately, the dogs started whining.

Catherine came running over with Charlotte, and they both greeted the waiting dogs, who reciprocated with excited wagging and licks wherever they could sneak them in. The girls giggled as they pet the dogs.

Ellie leashed each one, and turned to Hannah. "Which one? Winston or Izzy?"

"I'll take Winston; he likes going fast. Even though he's old."

Ellie handed Hannah his blue leash, and started tightening her shoe laces with Izzy's leash wrapped around her wrist. Both dogs sniffed the ocean air, bodies wiggling in anticipation for the adventure. Tom opened the side doors, and turned to the children. "You girls ready?"

"Yeah!" the kids screamed in unison.

"Where we going, Dad?" Catherine said.

"Get in, it's a surprise."

The two children hugged their mothers goodbye. Tom strapped them into their car seats, and rounded the back. He peeked through the back windshield to make sure the girls weren't listening. "I'm taking them to the Planetarium. Should be good."

"They'll love it," Hannah said.

Ellie kissed Tom. "Thanks for doing this."

"I'll see you at home."

Hannah waved to Tom. "We'll see you in a bit. I have my cell on, in case."

He waved as the car sped off. Ellie noticed the silhouette of both girls playing with their toys in the back. She looked down at her wedding ring; the one from Tom, and gave it a rotation with her right hand. Then, she kissed the blue-sapphire dragonfly pendant around her neck. It had become a little ritual she had developed over time, to honor the two loves of her life.

Ellie took a deep breath, and began stretching her legs.

"You sure now?" Hannah smiled. "I mean, I'm ready. Winton's ready. Izzy's ready. But are *you* ready?"

Ellie chuckled. "Let's go."

They made their way back down to the sandy beach, towards the beginnings of a black asphalt trail. Ellie put on her sunglasses, and glanced down as far as she could see.

The pathway was lined with tall grass, rocks, and driftwood. It wound its way along the beach, up to street level, into forested parkland, and disappeared back along the beach again— until Ellie couldn't make it out any further. It seemed endless, and an apt place for her to be, in this very moment.

Splendidly unknown, and open to every possibility.

Ellie stood in the sand, feeling uneasy; hesitating to step onto the paved path.

Her pulse quickened.

Izzy the Bichon, looked on; patient, but curious to know which direction they'd be headed. Ellie looked forward at Hannah, who nodded back with loving encouragement.

Ellie took two deliberate steps and placed her running shoes onto the blacktop. She exhaled slowly. With Izzy keeping stride, she started to walk.

"We can go at whatever pace you want, Ellie," Hannah said.

"I know," she said. "Let's walk for now. I'd like to warm up."

Hannah paused. "How long has it been?"

"Since I ran?"

Hannah looked past Ellie, towards the ocean. "Yeah."

"About eight years," Ellie said. "And almost eleven since my last marathon."

"One step at a time, sweetheart," Hannah said. "We're doing this together. We walk today. Maybe get into a light jog. But it's going to take some time. So, allow that, okay? We aren't running any marathons today."

"I know," Ellie answered.

Winston walked along the path like a show dog, suppressing his hereditary Schnauzer inclination, in barking at every stranger; a surprise to Ellie. He looked up at Hannah as he walked, heeling alongside her steps and providing a little give on his leash, happily trotting along.

"He likes you," Ellie smiled.

"He does," Hannah said. "You pick a spot yet?"

Ellie turned and lowered her sunglasses. "For our girl's trip? It's a tie between Belgium, France, and Germany. I can't pick."

"No Italy?" Hannah said. "I'm still single over here. Italian men? You know."

Ellie's Albatross

Ellie laughed. "Yes, Italy too. I promise I'll make a decision soon. It'll be fun, the four of us. Charlotte and Catherine are going to love it."

"Congrats, by the way."

"On what?"

"On your first client yesterday," Hannah said, squeezing Ellie's shoulder. "That's a big deal. Did you celebrate? You should."

"Thank you," Ellie said timidly. "We're celebrating tonight. Going for a family dinner."

"What was she like?"

"My client? She was sweet. But she's terrified. She's young, and she's going through a lot of pain; so I can't blame her. That loneliness, I could see it in her eyes. She doesn't know what's going on. She feels lost."

Like I used to, Ellie thought.

"It was hard to get through to be honest," Ellie continued. "A lot of old feelings started conjuring up again. That will always be an anchor around my ankle. Something I'll probably always fear. But I'm going to help her. She needs to know it will get better. I was in her shoes, and I was honest about that. I'll share everything I've learned."

"You're doing a good thing," Hannah said.

"You know; I've been thinking about something since that meeting. I spent an hour journaling afterwards, remembering so many things I'd put aside. Things I'd compartmentalized in the little rooms in my brain. Doors, that I had locked. But I was thinking about you actually. And what you have overcome. Cancer. Rebuilding after your marriage ended. Raising Charlotte.

"I thought about Ruth and Ophelia, and the kindness they show me. Their ambitions and successes. Their instinct, and matriarchal wisdom.

"I thought about Cece, and so many other resilient women from the shelter I've met in all these years. I thought about my mother, and Bishop's too. Why they were the way they were— good and bad. What they had endured. You all find the courage to take leaps.

"And, somehow, you all made me who I am today. You are the reason I am better. You are the reason I am here. We are all woven together. And Ophelia was right.

"We women, are the heroines.

"And we need to tell our stories. We need to share them with each other; with our own children. All of you taught me to confront my own trauma, and free myself to move forward. So I want to say thank you, Hannah. For everything. For being here now."

Hannah, who Ellie rarely saw succumb to much emotion, dried her teary eyes. She held her friend's hand. And they cried together, in silence; finding cleansing freedom in the catharsis.

Feeling a little more confident, Ellie picked up the pace, with Hannah taking the queue. Izzy and Winston joined without hesitation. Ellie took a slow inhale through her nostrils and held it in her chest. She counted.

One. Two. Three. Four.

She exhaled through her mouth. And again, she counted, adding a digit.

Her feet moved a little bit faster, until both women were running at a slow jog. She repeated her mantra, until her breathing started to regulate naturally. She embraced the muscle memory, and relished in the rhythm of her lungs.

"I need you to do me a favor," Ellie said, between breaths.

"Anything."

"I need you to take Izzy and Winston. And I want you to run ahead. Don't look back."

Hannah glanced at her friend in surprise, but reached out to take Izzy's leash.

"I'm going to jog at my own pace. But no matter what. I will catch up to you. I promise. I need to do this part on my own."

Ellie watched Hannah disappear into the path in front of her. She was athletic, and in much better shape, so it didn't take her long to create a distance between them.

The veins in Ellie's temples pulsated as she ran. Sweat was streaming from every pore. Her every muscle burned in agony. Tom had cautioned her, but he'd been encouraging nevertheless.

She knew she'd be paying for this tomorrow. And probably for the next month. She prayed it wouldn't cause a flare-up. But knew it probably would.

Yet, she increased her pace; just a little more.

By her standards, by anyone's standards— she was barely past a jog. Running at beginner's level, slightly less so, even. Even though it felt like infinity, she'd probably end up running a very short distance today; a mere fraction of the hundreds of miles she'd logged as a marathoner.

But it was faster and farther than she'd ran in over a decade.

She remembered a time when there was no hope for her— when she couldn't imagine a future she wanted to be a part of. When she had laid on the floor, clutching her own hair. It would have taken but a split second to slide that blade. Or if the paramedics hadn't arrived when they did, she would have overdosed.

But now, she was running. Again.

And she did so, despite those scars and in defiance of those wounds.

She was both overjoyed and astounded at the same time. Ellie's expression wavered between an exhilarated smile and overwhelming emotion.

But there was no fear. Not the bad kind, anyway. The kind that destroys you. Fear is meant to keep you safe. To test you, and to prepare you. To keep you sharp.

Ellie sped up a little more.

She was certain around the next bend, there would be another.

The obscurity of the trees ahead, would eventually open up to the vastness of the open ocean. She knew the path in front of her, was boundless.

She also knew, that her friend was up there somewhere, so she wouldn't be alone. That she wouldn't be left behind. Ellie knew that she'd be in pain after it was all over, but she also knew that she'd heal again, no matter how long it took. And she knew she'd had a home to return to.

Adrenaline coursed through her veins.

Her feet moved faster.

She licked her lips, and adjusted her thick red ponytail from behind her hat. She wore it today, to keep the sun from her eyes while she ran— not to hide her once thinning hair.

Ellie reveled in the movement of her body, and celebrated the nature around her. The further she ran, the clearer her head became.

She remembered who she used to be, before the illness. And she thanked God that He had made her sick, because it had shaped who she'd become.

Who she was becoming.

Ellie embraced the metamorphosis, painful as it could be. She envisioned herself, bathed in blue and silver incandescent light. A cocoon, from which a phoenix would soon emerge. And she ran faster— nearly a full sprint now.

Ellie felt the cells in the soles of her feet, connecting to the terrain, like a bolt of electricity exploding to ground itself in the Earth.

She stopped.

Out of breath.

She hunched over, and composed herself, hands on her hips. It took a few minutes for her breathing to regulate, and her vision to clear. Her hands were vibrating. She tasted salty ocean air, and sweat.

She looked ahead, and saw Hannah far in the distance. She was sitting at a park bench with Izzy and Winston, gazing into the seascape. Ellie looked behind her, and could not see the place where she'd started.

She'd come so far, that the parking lot had vanished.

She was somewhere in between the two points, and felt only the choice of the space in between: the place she currently occupied.

Ellie conjured up the resiliency of those who came before her, and those that would come after her: her mother, and her child.

Strength, and *love*.

She turned forward, and began walking towards her friend, feeling her muscles still buzzing. Still out of breath. Barely able to walk. Yet she mustered forward; jaw clenched, but with a smile that still arose from the corners of her mouth.

As she walked along the path, she fondly recalled the words of her favorite poet, and whispered them to herself.

"Phenomenal woman," she said. "That's me."

THE END

Manufactured by Amazon.ca
Bolton, ON

30258170R00139